# ALL THINGS
## SEEN
### AND UNSEEN

# ALL THINGS SEEN AND UNSEEN

## RJ McDANIEL

This book is also available as a Global Certified Accessible™ (GCA) ebook. ECW Press's ebooks are screen reader friendly and are built to meet the needs of those who are unable to read standard print due to blindness, low vision, dyslexia, or a physical disability.

Purchase the print edition and receive the ebook free. For details, go to ecwpress.com / ebook.

Published by ECW Press
665 Gerrard Street East
Toronto, Ontario, Canada M4M 1Y2
416-694-3348 / info@ecwpress.com

Editor for the Press: Pia Singhal
Copy-editor: Jen Albert
Cover design: Michel Vrana
Author photo: Emily Ann Garcia

This is a work of fiction. Names, characters, places, and incidents either are the product of the author's imagination or are used fictitiously, and any resemblance to actual persons, living or dead, business establishments, events, or locales is entirely coincidental.

LIBRARY AND ARCHIVES CANADA CATALOGUING IN PUBLICATION

Title: All things seen and unseen / R.J. McDaniel.

Names: McDaniel, R. J., author.

Identifiers: Canadiana (print) 20230580084 | Canadiana (ebook) 20230580092

ISBN 978-1-77041-709-0 (softcover)
ISBN 978-1-77852-253-6 (PDF)
ISBN 978-1-77852-252-9 (ePub)

Subjects: LCGFT: Queer fiction. | LCGFT: Novels.

Classification: LCC PS8625.D36 A75 2024 | DDC C813/ .6—dc23

This book is funded in part by the Government of Canada. Ce livre est financé en partie par le gouvernement du Canada. We acknowledge the support of the Canada Council for the Arts. Nous remercions le Conseil des arts du Canada de son soutien. We acknowledge the funding support of the Ontario Arts Council (OAC), an agency of the Government of Ontario. We also acknowledge the support of the Government of Ontario through the Ontario Book Publishing Tax Credit, and through Ontario Creates.

Canada Council Conseil des arts
for the Arts du Canada

Canadä

PRINTED AND BOUND IN CANADA        PRINTING: MARQUIS    5   4   3   2   1

MIX
Paper from responsible sources
FSC
www.fsc.org        FSC® C103567

*For Taja:*
*without you,*
*I wouldn't have seen the birds*

# 1.

Alex watches as the nurse's eyes follow her. The two blue pills in her left hand, the right hand picking up the paper cup of water; the toss of her head back, pouring the water down her throat, where she holds it still; and then the left hand dropping the pills, clumsily, through her open mouth, into the water. A heavy swallow, and her eyes return to the nurse just quickly enough to see the disgust leave her face. She is a nurse Alex has never seen before, an older white woman whose thick, dark hair is flecked with grey.

"I've never seen anyone take pills like that," the nurse says.

Alex had learned the trick from another nurse. Back at the regional children's hospital, when she was seventeen and took all of this more seriously. It was her first time at inpatient, and the bitter-chemical taste of the pills made her cry. Everything made her cry, but this taste in particular was too much to bear. It lingered on her tongue, on her teeth, in her throat. Nothing she did could get rid of it. Not everyone tasted the sleeping pills, but Alex did, and it seemed, given everything else that was happening, like a curse.

"I'm cursed," she sobbed to one of the nurses, wailing on the floor of her tiny room. "I'm cursed."

The nurse — tall, blond, tattooed — assured her that she was not cursed, that the sleeping pills tasted bad to plenty of people, and that there was a way around it. You just had to drown them. Later, when Alex got back home, she thought about this nurse as she drowned six of the sleeping pills every morning, not to sleep, but so she could live in the daylight without remembering. He was a nice nurse, she thought, and she was a bad person.

"Sorry," she tells the nurse. "This is how I've always done it."

"Hmm." The nurse is already uninterested. Her back turned, she's busy writing notes in Alex's chart. "Well, goodnight then."

"Goodnight," Alex says.

She takes a step, waits to see if the nurse will watch her leave. But the nurse is already done with the chart and is rifling through a stack of magazines, ready to settle in for the night. Alex is always the last to go to sleep.

She lies awake in her room, eyes closed, timing her breathing with the ticks of the clock. Her latest roommate, a middle-aged woman with round spectacles who never offered a name, left this morning. Alex wonders why she was here, what her name was. She wonders who will be here tomorrow now that there's an open space.

*Maybe Adam will be here.*

The clock ticks twice, three times. She breathes out, stretching the breath over four ticks, trying to ignore the pounding of her heart. She had a thought. She had a thought that Adam would be here. But a thought is not reality. Focus on your breath. In, two, three, four. Out, two, three, four.

Even as she counts, the thoughts begin to appear again. How long has it been since she's seen Adam? Since she's talked to him? Since the first night she got here, when she could finally pick up a phone again after those weeks in the ICU, when it felt so hopeful even just to dial the familiar ten digits, to hear the ringtone: a reminder that there was a world outside the hospital — separated entirely from the horror she'd been trapped in — where other people lived normal lives, moving ever forward. And then to hear his voice, saying hello? Hello? She couldn't respond for a second; the words caught in her throat.

"Hello," she said, finally. "It's me, it's Alex." She coughed painfully. "I just — I just wanted to let you know that I'm okay. I mean, I'm alive."

There was a long nothing.

"Okay," Adam said flatly, and her throat closed even more.

"I just wanted to let you know."

Pathetic, the heat searing her face screamed, pathetic, but she pushed through. "And if you, you know, had some spare time, at any point. I know you're busy, but I — it would be great to see you."

"Okay," Adam said, and hung up.

Alex went to bed and tried to smother herself with a pillow.

In, two, three, four.

Out, two, three, four.

That wasn't the first time she'd tried to do that. She should have known better. The body is weak, but when it comes to staying alive, it will struggle as hard as it needs to.

In, two, three, four.

Out, two, three, four.

The tears are burning under her eyelids. She sits up, letting them run down her face, and reaches for her glasses. Through the foggy blur, the clock tells her that an hour has passed since she lay down. It has been long enough for her to get up and get water. She wipes her face as best she can, cleans her glasses on the edge of her pyjamas, and pads over to the nursing station. The nurse is reading *Vogue*, the only issue of *Vogue* that they have on the unit right now. Alex has read it dozens of times. At this point, Kendall Jenner is more of a friend than anyone Alex knows in real life.

"Excuse me?" She makes her voice lilt upward softly. "Excuse me?"

The nurse swivels in her chair, and when she sees Alex, she sighs. "I know what you're doing. It's in your chart."

"I'm sorry."

"You can't keep doing this, you know."

"I'm so sorry. I know."

"You're a nice girl. Everyone likes you. But you can't keep doing this."

"I know. It's just—"

"Yes, yes," the nurse says, and waves her hands. "Get your water."

This time Alex knows that the nurse is watching her walk away, that she is being observed as she turns the corner, hurrying toward the cafeteria. She passes through the TV room, then through the rows of long tables where they take meals, and finally to the little kitchen, the sink with an electric kettle and cupboards full of teabags and tiny packets of peanut butter. She takes a paper cup and fills it with water from the sink. The water here is never as cold as she wants it to be. She splashes some on her fingers and rubs it on her face.

Alex doesn't do this every night. If she tried to do this every night, they wouldn't let her do it anymore. She's been to inpatient enough to know how it works. Before, when she was new to this, she didn't do it the right way. She sat in her room and cried; she played music loudly over the ancient boombox and screamed along; she didn't eat when she wasn't hungry; and she didn't get out of bed when she felt tired. This, she had learned, was a surefire way to make all the staff hate you.

So now she gets out of bed when she's told. She brushes her hair. She doesn't cry. She goes to every group, does every activity, does not ask for more passes, does not complain. She is compliant, the nice girl everyone wants her to be, and in exchange for her compliance, every so often — once a week, maybe twice — she gets her reward: a moment, here in the cafeteria with a paper cup of water, to be completely alone.

One of the cafeteria's walls is made up of floor-to-ceiling windows facing a garden. The garden's dimensions are indiscernible from inside, and as far as Alex knows, no one on the unit has ever gone there. There's no door that she can see, never any sign of human life, only shadowy trees, evergreens and maples, and a path lit by small lanterns leading somewhere unknown.

She stands at the glass, staring out, and sees her reflection as though it is another person outside on the path, under the trees. It's almost creepy: the too-big beige pyjamas over her slight frame make it look like there's nothing filling the fabric, and her heavy hair falls over her face, far past her shoulders. It's been so long since she was able to get a haircut. There's an unfamiliarity to the way she looks, after spending so long in that ICU bed, not moving, not seeing herself. She takes a sip of water and imagines being that person, breathing in the night air, gazing up at the stars.

When she opens her eyes, she knows that she is being watched.

She whirls around, ready to plead her case with the nurse, but it is not the nurse who is watching her. There is no one standing behind her. There are only the empty tables, the ticking of another clock, the light from the hallway gleaming off the dull linoleum floor. No one is there.

The muscles in her chest begin to clench. She knows she has been standing here long enough, that at any second the nurse will come looking for her, and there is nothing she wants less than a confrontation. But she can't move. As long as she is being watched, as long as she doesn't know what is watching her, she can't move.

Something catches her eye, up in the far reaches of the ceiling. A glinting roundness. She takes a step forward. In the darkness, she can just make it out: the shape of a camera.

Of course — and it's not even sad to her, even though it should be. Of course the unobserved breaths that she's been chasing were, all along, a lie. It's actually funny, she tells herself, scraping her eyes with her knuckles — all the nurses who must have watched her doing this, writing their little notes about how crazy she is, crazy but harmless — standing in front of the empty glass with her stupid flimsy little cup of water. Or they're not, she reminds herself: that's what she's supposed to remember, that she is not constantly being surveilled by the hostile and unseen. But how could that not be the case? The whole point of this place is for people to observe her. They probably laugh at her, how oblivious she is. How desperate.

An urge rises to hit herself, but she can't. They are watching her. Alex needs them to see her as nothing, as flattened, smiling cardboard, and then she can go home. And then she can die, she realizes, with sudden, horrible clarity: then she can die, because after everything, after the ICU and the dialysis and the hallucinations, the weeks stuck in a bed and the weeks after stuck in these rooms, she is not better, not at all.

Through the bleariness, the camera shines, cold and black. And then it seems to fill with life, watchful and malicious and utterly empty.

Alex screws her eyes shut, watching only the throbbing red of her own eyelids. The camera isn't alive, she says to herself, you are. You're on drugs. You're seeing things — even though you've been on these drugs so many times before and never seen anything like this, never felt any fear like this. You're upset, and when you open your eyes and look at the camera again, it will be normal. It will be normal, and you will walk away, and you will lie in bed and go to sleep. Just breathe. Breathe, you fucking idiot. Open your fucking eyes.

She opens them. The darkness looks back at her, gleaming, darker than anything not alive could be.

Alex runs. Through the empty cafeteria, past the nursing station, she runs, seeing nothing, insensate with horror. She doesn't stop running until she is in her bed, the blankets pulled up, her pillow held tightly over her face. Not because she believes it will work this time, but because she can think of no other way to hide.

"So," the psychiatrist says, looking at her desktop. Beside her, the nervous med student clicks the end of his pen compulsively.

"Yes?" Alex says, pulling her hair away from her face. She straightens her spine, pulls her shoulders back, reminds the muscles in her face to smile. She tries not to hear the clicking.

The psychiatrist spins around abruptly. It is the afternoon, and she looks tired. Alex was supposed to meet with her at noon, but she was late. She is always late, at least when she shows up at all. In all her weeks here, Alex can only remember meeting her a handful of times. Clearly, Alex is not a matter of any great interest.

The med student scribbles some notes, glancing nervously at the psychiatrist. The psychiatrist only stares at Alex. The muscles in Alex's face, holding an expression she desperately hopes conveys ease, begin to ache. In the absence of the clicking, she becomes aware of the ticking of a clock somewhere she can't see. It takes all her focus not to start bouncing her leg — not to do something, anything, with her body.

Alex wonders whether the nurse saw her running last night, whether it made it into her chart. She wouldn't put it past the psychiatrist to simply ignore it, whether out of pure distraction or a desire to hurry her out. But if the nurse had seen her running, why would she not come to see if everything was okay? How would she have missed such an obvious aberrance happening right in front of her?

It is mostly the running that stays in Alex's memory. Through the fog of the sleeping pills, she remembers thinking about Adam, going to get her water, her unfamiliar reflection in the window. Everything beyond that fades except for the running. Her sock feet hitting the floor, the blood rushing in her ears. Then she woke up with her face directly on the mattress, a puddle of drool sliding up her cheek, her pillow cast down on the ground five feet away from her. The only evidence of what had happened were the telltale knives in her ankles. It has been so long since she ran. She thought she would never do it again. She promised herself she wouldn't try.

"Alex," the psychiatrist says, finally.

"Yes."

"How are you feeling?"

"I'm — I mean, I'm okay."

"Still tired?"

"Yes."

The psychiatrist flips through her papers. "And no side effects yet from the increased lithium?"

"No."

"Or the Seroquel?"

"No."

"Hmm." She spins back around. The med student, lost, begins clicking again.

"Well," the psychiatrist says, "it seems like you're about ready to go home, doesn't it."

It doesn't seem like a question, so Alex doesn't answer. She drums her fingers against her legs, beating out a rapid, haphazard rhythm. The med student's clicking intensifies.

The psychiatrist spins around again. "Doesn't it?"

"Oh! Um, I guess."

"You guess. Don't you want to go home?" The psychiatrist squints. "It says here you have a roommate."

"Oh." Alex's fingers clench as they dance. "She, uh—"

"Ah, yes, right, she moved out. Of course. Well, can you stay with your parents for a while?"

"I, uh—"

"Or your friends? Surely you must have some friends who can keep you company."

"I'm so sorry," the med student blurts out. "I'm so sorry, but can you please stop drumming your fingers? It's making me anxious."

"Oh." Alex balls her hand into a white-knuckled fist. "Sorry."

"Thank you," the med student says, and resumes clicking.

"It says here," the psychiatrist notes, "that you're in school. How are you doing with that?"

"Well, I haven't really—"

"What do you study?"

"Kinesiology," Alex says slowly, the syllables sounding like nonsense.

"Huh. And what do you find interesting about that?"

"I've always been interested in, um—" She struggles to find the right words. "I guess, movement, and why people do it, and what makes it important to people."

"Lots of athletes in that program."

"Yeah."

"Or, rather, what I meant is that there aren't a lot of non-athletes. You must find it lonely."

*I am an athlete*, Alex wants to say. But she isn't. The psychiatrist is right. She isn't an athlete, not anymore. And it is lonely. Even before everything, she was beginning to wonder why she was still in school at all.

"Or maybe not! What do I know. As long as you're doing what you're interested in."

The psychiatrist turns in her chair, slowly this time. She holds Alex's gaze. The clicking now feels like it's pulsing underneath Alex's skin. She is gripping her legs so hard it hurts.

"Are you anxious, Alex? About leaving?"

She shakes her head. "No."

"You have no desire to hurt yourself anymore? No plan?"

She shakes her head again, again says, "No."

"And you have someone who can stay with you, or someone you can stay with? Friends, family?"

"Yes." She's almost out now. This is almost over. "Yes, I'll stay with my dad."

"And — I'm sorry, but I just want to check. No more paranoia?"

"No." She shakes her head a third time, a little too vigorously, the thrill of lying spiking her energy. "No."

"And you've been well-equipped to recognize any thoughts like that, I'm sure."

"Yes. I feel grounded," she adds, just for good measure.

"Great." The psychiatrist stands. The med student nearly topples his chair. "Well, it was nice talking to you, Alex. You're a bright young woman with a great future ahead of you."

"Nice talking to you, too," Alex says, but they are already gone, and she can hear the footsteps of the nurse approaching to lead her back onto the unit. When she releases her grip, pain shoots up her arm. Even when she stretches her fingers out, the memory of their previous tension holds within them.

She's not going to stay with her dad, of course. And she's not going to stay with her friends. After this long, her friends probably don't even remember her. She didn't even bother telling them she was in the hospital. They wouldn't care. And the only person who would have cared— the only person who would have cared now wouldn't give a shit if she was dead. There was no one outside this place: nothing but an empty future, waiting to consume her whole.

━━.

Two days later, they let Alex out of the hospital. The nurses wish her well as she shoves her few clothing items in a backpack and retrieves her phone. Then she walks out. It seems so easy, crossing this forbidden threshold. Why had it seemed so impossible before?

━━

The day is grey and chilly, and the air bites Alex's face as she begins to walk back to her apartment. On her phone, there are dozens of unread texts and emails: classmates needing her input to complete group projects, worried professors, her manager at the store. This is why, when given the opportunity, Alex had not taken a look at her phone during her time on the unit. She is only a little guilty at letting everyone worry about her. They should know by now what kind of person they're dealing with.

She begins with the worst: her manager. The most recent message informs her that he is going to fill her position, and that he's very disappointed in her; he thought that they had a better relationship than this. She doesn't need to scroll up and read the rest. She knows what it'll be like: increasingly hostile questions about why she's missed her shifts. Secondhand reproaches from coworkers who never liked her in the first place. More reproaches from her manager: how she didn't appreciate how much he went out of his way for her, how he let her sit on that barstool sometimes (a fireable offence under anyone else's supervision). She deletes the thread, blocks the number. The messages from group project partners, bemoaning their supposedly jeopardized final grades, don't even need to be looked at. All of them equally unreadable, impossible to engage with. From Adam, nothing.

"I don't care," she says out loud. The students hurrying down the sidewalk cast her bewildered looks.

"I don't care." Her voice sounds wobbly, weak. So, she says it again, hard and cold, her mouth moving on its own. *I am not weak. I am hard and cold and sharp.* A business student on an e-scooter slows down and stares at her. She covers her face with her hair. "I don't care," she says, and he speeds away.

There's a voicemail from two days ago. She opens it, plugs in the passcode and the horrible robotic voice berates her, and is instead greeted by the aural assault of her dad's burry phone-yell. Where is she, why won't she respond. She promised him 200 dollars and he came all the way from the big city and went to the place and stood there like a goddamn idiot, a goddamn stupid idiot, his own daughter standing him up, making him look like a fool. He tried to get into the apartment and got thrown out of the building, some nice girl opened the door for him, but her ugly little roommate called campus security — why didn't she just let him copy a key; he told her so many times he needed it.

"Hope you're enjoying yourself," he crows, before a noise like rocks in a blender consumes him. The call cuts off.

It's actually funny. She keys herself through the dull glass doors of the student residence, taking the turn into the dank grey stairwell. The fact that he didn't bother calling until two days ago. The day she was supposed to meet him to hand over the money would have been the day after she ended up in the hospital. He waited weeks to do this, weeks and weeks. Maybe he was holding out for her to call him, which he knew she wouldn't do, building up grounds for a grievance. The longer he waited, the more anger he could release, the more rage tumbling from him. That's how he'd always done it: the weeks of thick, heavy air, the prickling static charge of brewing disaster, before the storm finally came and tore everything down. She'd thought, a long time ago, that coming here, a drive and a ferry and another drive away from him, would move her out of his climate. She changed her body, she changed her name, her whole life transformed into something unrecognizable to him. But she couldn't get away. She didn't do enough.

I wish I was with mom, she thinks, and the grief opens wide and unbidden like a wound.

She can feel her breath in her ankles, throbbing through every bruised bone. She sees it, there it is, just up there, the door with the crooked, chipping plastic 6 on it, closer with every slow step. Six flights of stairs and she's destroyed. She pictures her old trail-running friends watching her, Samuel and Evan and James and all of those guys, as she struggles to turn the handle, to pull the heavy door open just enough to slide her body through. What happened to her? Samuel says. I don't know, says Evan. It looks like she died. James bounces lightly in the toes of his Sauconys. Yeah, he says, it's pretty grim. I heard—

The door slams. The hallway is silent, the thick carpet and plastered walls muffling every sound. Alex inhales, exhales, and the air drags through her lungs. It takes a few attempts for her to find the right key, a few more to get it into the lock and turn it. Finally, she wrenches the door open.

Behind it, a woman is screaming at her. She stands behind the open door, her phone held outward like an unconvincing shield.

Alex stands completely still, retreating away from her body, her mind smoothed down into a small hollow pebble, suspended in nothingness. Okay, she tells herself. Okay. Aisling is going to get me locked up again. Okay. It's okay.

Aisling grabs her hand. The pebble shatters. Alex flinches away so hard that she slams into the wall of the narrow hallway. The door has been closed behind her; Aisling is no longer screaming. She is just talking, talking, talking. "And you look so different. Your hair is so long, and you're so thin. And some crazy guy was here," she says, breathless, "he was yelling and yelling for you, banging on the door. Like, using your name and everything, this huge white man. It was so scary, I don't even know how he got in here. I thought, and I'm so sorry to say this, that you'd been murdered. Are you okay?"

"Um," Alex says, trying to remember how to speak. "Yes."

"Where were you?" Aisling's back is already turned. She is walking to the couch. This, apparently, is time for a Roommate Meeting. As Alex slowly follows, her shoulder throbbing, she curses herself for not having prepared for Aisling to be here. Of course things with Nathan — fucking Nathan! — wouldn't work out for more than a few months. Hadn't she thought, the day Aisling moved out, that she'd be back before the end of the school year? Alex perches on the edge of the couch, conscious of the size of her limbs compared to Aisling's, how much space she takes up even while doing her best to shrink.

Aisling scoots closer. "Hello? Alex, where the hell have you been, girl?"

*Girl.* She knows Aisling has good intentions, but it still has the effect of a fingernail in the eye. Alex blinks away her discomfort. "I was in the hospital," she says. She lets her hair fall over her face.

"Hey!" Aisling says. "Don't hide from me. Do you even know how much I've missed you? I was so fucking worried, Alex. I didn't text because I know you hate texting, but I wanted to so badly! And I am so, so, so, so sorry you had to be in the hospital. And even though I could never understand what someone like you has to go through, I'm here for you. Every day! Even when, you know, I'm not physically here. You're safe with me."

Aisling is expecting something in return for this generous statement. "Thanks," Alex says. As soon as the word leaves her mouth, it is obvious that this was not what Aisling wanted. As if to lead Alex by example, she tucks a few errant strands of yellow-gold hair neatly behind her ear.

"Yeah, like, thank you," Alex says again, and she cringes at her own voice. There is a wrongness to it, an obvious, innate insincerity.

"You are so welcome." Aisling lays a hand on Alex's leg, just above her knee. "I am so grateful to have you back here, safe and healthy. Wait, no!" She draws the hand back to her face. "I'm sorry, was that insensitive? I guess I just don't know, you know, the whole situation."

When Aisling's hand once again rests on her leg, Alex realizes what is being demanded of her.

"It's okay," Alex says, and it's easy for her to talk. The tremor in her body recedes. "I had appendicitis."

"Oh," says Aisling. "But doesn't that—"

"No, yeah," says Alex, "I went full Madeline."

"Is that a medical term?"

"No, you know, like the little old house all covered with vines, and there were twelve little girls, and the smallest one was Madeline."

"What?"

"Never mind. Basically, my appendix burst, it was horrible, the recovery process was brutal." The words pour out of her, effortless and unthinking. "I went to stay with my parents, just learning how to be a human again, healing from such an invasive procedure—"

"I totally understand. Oh my god."

"—I didn't have a chance to call you, or text you, to tell you what was going on. And that was wrong of me, and I'm sorry."

"Please don't apologize," Aisling says, wobbly.

"But I am sorry. Especially after everything with Nathan."

Fucking Nathan.

"He actually just texted me again today. Some 'can we talk this through' bullshit. It's so much, I don't know how I've been able to deal with it all, honestly."

She leans over, ready to drape her body over Alex's, but Alex is prepared this time. She rises abruptly. "I'm so sorry. It's just, you know." She gestures vaguely to her abdomen. "The scar is still healing."

"Oh my god, I—"

"No, no, don't worry about it. But I think I need to rest." She is walking away, the silent door of her bedroom beckoning. "We'll talk again soon, okay?"

She doesn't wait for an answer before she shuts the door. She collapses on the bed, face down, her boots on, her body trembling.

━━

When Alex wakes up, it is unclear how much time has passed. The blinds are pulled down over her small window, blocking all evidence of existence beyond these walls. Only a haze leaks in, the way the sun shines through the smoke when the fires are raging: thick, reddish, smouldering. It used to be a catastrophe, but now it's every year. This, though, is only May. And the window is sealed. Alex breathes in as much air as she can, a way of testing its quality. She has no chance to exhale before a pounding sound from the hallway knocks the air out of her by force. Maybe it's one of the guys down the hall. Breathe. Her heart is already racing. It's okay. Just because something is happening doesn't mean it's happening to you.

But then she hears the voice, calling her name, and she knows her fear is justified. She leaps up, rubs the spit from her mouth, adjusts her glasses — feels the red indentations on her face from sleeping on the frames — digs through her bag for her wallet.

"WHERE ARE YOU," the voice booms through the wall, "ALEX I KNOW YOU'RE IN THERE," and as she hurries to the door she is already rehearsing her lines: I am so sorry, I was in the hospital, here's ten dollars and my debit card, you can take whatever's in there, just leave me alone, please stop yelling at me, please stop yelling, please just let me go back to sleep. The door handle shakes so much that it's hard to turn it, and she's afraid that when she pulls it open it might come off the hinges and topple over onto her.

The person waiting in the hall isn't her dad. He isn't even standing near the door. Where Alex had expected to see her dad's large form, his slumped shoulders and huge clenched fists, there is only a slender young man in a hoodie and jeans, his hair light blond, his eyes downcast. His foot taps out a silent rhythm on the ground, and his hands are shoved in his pockets.

"Adam?" Alex says, the name strange in her mouth, a form that no longer fits. He turns and looks at her. He looks tired. He is disappointed.

"I was waiting for you," he says.

"I know," she says, and it seems true even though it isn't. "I'm sorry. I just—"

"After you hear it enough, sorry starts sounding like an excuse," he says, in the same dead, flat voice he had on the phone.

"I know. I know. I won't do it again." She sounds panicky. He hates it when she sounds panicky. She can hear the reproach, the one at the root of so many of their arguments: *Whenever I get angry with you, even if I'm just a little frustrated, you act like I'm this terrible person. Like I'm some kind of scary monster. Like I'm going to hurt you.*

There is a part of her that wants to try to explain the way his anger makes her disappear. How she can't move her body, can't find any words; how her only need, in these moments, the only thing animating her, is for it to stop, to run away, to find a quiet place where she can slowly return to herself. But this time, he isn't saying anything. The argument is happening only in her memory.

So she says something different. "Shall we go?"

Without a word, Adam turns. He opens the door and disappears into the stairwell. The door closes behind him.

——

Outside, it is nighttime. But the haze that seemed to fill Alex's room when she awoke is everywhere, swallowing the light from the stars and the moon and dispersing it as an eerie, omnipresent glow. Adam walks quickly, and Alex follows a few yards behind. She can't see his face; she can't read anything from his body language other than the steady rhythm of his footsteps. The streets are silent and unfamiliar.

Alex wonders, as her breathing grows laboured, where they are, where they are going. Her fault for never exploring this vast campus all these years, for only walking the main paths to the quad and back. She wants to ask Adam how he knows this place so well. She wants to ask him what he's been doing, how he's been doing. She wants him to know that she never told anyone. That she doesn't blame him. That she's sorry. That she wants him to be okay. That she wants to be okay along with him.

Instead, she walks behind him, trying to understand what, if anything, his shoulders are telling her. Without warning, they are no longer on the blank campus streets; they are at the beach, at the bottom of the cliff, and Adam is walking toward the waves. Alex has been here before, once, years ago. It was the first few months they were together, and they went down here because this is where everyone came to do drugs at night, even though there were whispers of how dangerous it was, especially for a woman, especially after sunset: people had been assaulted; people had died. Walking down the steep winding stairs with Adam, the wood slick from the seawater air, she could see nothing. But everything was so vivid to her, the bend of the steps under her feet and the moss on the railing coming apart in her fingers. The beat of Adam's pulse in his hand as it clutched hers, pulling her downward. She felt safe, completely safe. They fucked on the beach, the tide coming and coming and coming, and with Adam inside her, his fingers in her mouth, the waves lapping up against the edge of their blanket, Alex thought she understood how it felt to be the ocean.

She had forgotten that. She looks at the moon casting its soft glow on the water, the same waning crescent sliver that hung over them back then. The memory had been swallowed up by the fight they had the next day. They had both sobered up, and every noise was a slap to the side of the head. Adam broke her glasses in half. He slammed the door behind him. That was the only thing that reverberated into the present, the cruelty of the sound of wood on wood, metal on metal; the way that the sound was the only thing there with her in the empty room; the way it seemed to fill every corner, plugging her ears, creeping from there into her brain, until there was nothing left but the pain. Now, the waves lap up against her feet again, and she remembers. She is barefoot — how did she not notice she was barefoot until now? There is no soreness, only the soft, warm sand massaging her blisters and the cool, gentle fingers of the water.

"It doesn't hurt," she says. "Why doesn't it hurt?"

Adam doesn't look at her. He is standing in the water, ankle-deep. He stares straight out over the horizon. In the absence of pain, the fear rushes in, clamping down on Alex's lungs. The light from the moon, distorted by the haze, starts to blink and flare. "Adam," she pleads, the world beginning to bend around her, "why did you bring me here again?"

He steps forward, huge, heavy steps, walking deeper and deeper. Alex tries to chase after him, but when she lifts her foot, all the pain comes rushing back. The sand, so soft only a moment

ago, burns against her skin. The cool of the water stabs like net-
tles. She cries out, losing her footing, and then her cry is choked
by saltwater, her ribs slamming into the ground with a thud.
Relentless, the waves knock her back again, then again, and when
she at last sinks her fingers into the shifting ground, pushing herself upright, all she can see through her spattered, foggy glasses is
Adam in the distance, Adam against the horizon, Adam a severed
head on a neck that is fast disappearing. She screams his name,
hoarse and terrible, her throat tearing open.

He turns, and even though he is so far, even though it is night
and she can barely see, his face is as clear as if he were on top of
her. There is no gold left in his eyes: only pupils, gaping and bot-
tomless, utterly empty.

"This is your fault," he says. When he disappears, the sky
goes black.

—

When Alex wakes up again, the first thing she notices is the pain.
The left side of her body, her feet, her legs, her hands: all of it
is one pulsing mass of hurt. Her pillow is on the ground in the
corner of the room. Her glasses are so stained that, for a moment,
she worries she has lost her vision.

Slowly, gingerly, she sits up, wipes her glasses off. She slides her
feet out from under her. They are bruised and swollen, blisters forming on her heels. Her nails are dirty, and she feels strangely chilly.
Like she's been visited by a ghost. That's what her mom would say.

From behind the door, she can hear the sizzling of bacon. It is
Saturday morning, the day Aisling always cooks bacon and eggs.
Or, rather, the day she always *used* to cook bacon and eggs before
she left to cook them for Nathan. The smell of the salt makes Alex
woozy. Her mouth is dry, and the faint taste of the sleeping pills
sticks in her throat. She rises, each step effortful, making her way
to the dining room.

"Hey, girl!" Aisling sings.

"Hey." Alex sits down heavily, and something in the way she says it makes Aisling take a second look at her. One thing Alex appreciates about Aisling is that she makes no attempt to hide her stares. There is no guile behind her love of Alex's spectacle. She watches Alex, spatula dangling over the crackling pan, her other hand on her aproned waist.

"Alex, no offence," she says. "I know you just got out of the hospital yesterday. But you look like shit."

"I know."

"No, but I mean, you look, like, concerningly terrible. Do you think you need to go back to the ER? You can borrow my e-bike if you want."

"It's okay. Just, like, don't talk to me until I've had my coffee, you know?" She hopes Aisling recognizes, in how bad this joke is, a genuine plea.

Aisling wordlessly opens the coffee jar and begins spooning grounds into the French press. Sometimes Alex feels like she could be talked into living with Aisling forever.

"Seriously, though," Aisling says as she puts water in the kettle. "I'm a little worried. Also, you did sleep for like twenty-five hours."

"Yeah. I guess my body is still exhausted from everything." She watches as Aisling turns off the stove, slides the bacon from the pan to a plate, and places the plate on the table, a series of motions so fluid that they seem to be a single action, perfectly choreographed. Then she flicks the stove on again, takes an egg from where it waits on the counter, cracks it perfectly into the pan. Just one egg, for her, because she knows Alex won't eat them. She knows Alex won't eat a lot of things. She knows Alex doesn't cook. When Aisling moved out to live with Nathan, Alex didn't use the stove at all. The only thing she did in the kitchen was make coffee. She ate the same thing every single day: one protein bar in the morning, one protein bar in the afternoon, and two chicken salad wraps from the campus McDonald's for dinner. Aisling would occasionally bring her a Tupperware of some delicious meal: a creamy pasta, a salmon roasted with garlic and dill. She would watch Alex eat, making sure she at least came close to finishing it, trying and always failing to hold back a reproach about her eating habits. She didn't understand.

"Well, you better eat then." Aisling brings the French press over, then Alex's special mug, the round earthenware with the thick blue-green glaze and a curved lip. Then her own plate with the lone, perfect egg, sunny side up. She puts two slices of bacon on her plate with a fork, then pushes the rest toward Alex. "Bet they didn't serve you bacon in the hospital."

Alex almost laughs. "Oh, you would have gone insane if you saw it. Tapioca pudding for breakfast, pea soup for lunch, soggy macaroni for dinner."

"Stop, you'll make me vomit."

"Maybe some peaches from, like, a twenty-five-year-old can."

"No."

"The slimier the better."

Aisling pretends to cough up her egg. In spite of herself, Alex had actually missed her.

"So," Aisling says, as Alex nibbles on the dauntingly large pieces of bacon on her plate. "What are you going to do now?"

"What do you mean?"

"Well, did you like—" Aisling looks upward, thinking. She pushes a strand of hair behind her ear. "Did you talk to — I don't even know who you would talk to after missing the last two months of the semester. Academic advising? Because you can't stay here if you're not a student. Did you enrol in summer classes?"

*No,* Alex wants to say, *I didn't enrol in summer classes. When registration for summer classes opened, I was strapped to a bed with tubes sticking out of me.* Instead, she pushes the plunger down on the French press, slow and hard, until it squeaks to a stop. She pours coffee into her mug.

"No," she says. "But I'll figure it out."

"Are you sure?"

"I'll figure it out," Alex repeats, and the cold edge in her words surprises her. Aisling stares at her again.

"Okay," she says after a pause. She returns to her egg.

Alex nurses her coffee. They weren't allowed coffee in the psych ward. During one stay when she was younger, a nurse had smuggled her some, a fistful of individually wrapped instant coffee packets. Alex made them last the whole month. But that was only once. She cradles the mug in her hands and takes a tiny sip.

"How is everything with Nathan?" she asks.

Aisling seems to inflate, then deflate, with a sigh so dramatic that it almost comes off comical. "I'm going to see him tonight."

"Good, then? Or, I guess, better?"

She sighs again. "I know you're going to think I'm just, like, this dumb, delusional straight white girl—"

"That's not what I think about you."

"—no, no, I totally get it, because I'm literally doing exactly what a dumb, delusional straight white girl would do, which is believe this stupid guy when he comes to me crying and says that if I move back in with him everything will be different this time, and that he's going to change for us. Like, I can't believe I even responded to his text. It's such bullshit, honestly." She doesn't look at Alex as she talks, only at her empty plate.

Alex should never have told her how fucking dumb Nathan is. She should have let her be happy.

"Well," Alex says, imbuing her voice with a hopeful, chipper tone, "maybe the fact that you set firm boundaries by leaving actually did make him reevaluate. Maybe he's telling the truth." She takes another sip of coffee.

"You think so?" Aisling says to the plate.

In three years of knowing him, Nathan has never failed to convince Alex that he is incapable of change. He has never said a single word that didn't bore her to death. His habitual mode is on the couch, his arm clutching Aisling to his torso, his eyes always somewhere else.

"Yes," Alex says. "I really do."

And for some reason, seized by impulse, she reaches across the table and puts her bruised, puffy hand on Aisling's slender pale one. Aisling is startled. She looks first at her hand, and then at Alex. Her expression is alive with something complicated. She turns her hand over and laces her fingers through Alex's, softly, without squeezing.

For all the years that they've been roommates, every time Aisling has touched Alex — so many times, never asking if it was okay — Alex has found some reason to squirm away. In their dynamic, Alex was always an object of fascination, an oddity of flesh to be prodded at, observed, never fully engaged with. And so Alex had never thought to touch her back. But she has spent the last months of her life being prodded, poked, observed, with needles and bright lights and tubes and cameras, by dozens of pairs of unknown and unseen hands, and there is a charge running between Aisling's fingertips and hers. It has been so long since anyone touched her who cared.

Aisling reaches out with her other hand. Her fingers graze Alex's tangled hair. Slowly, she guides it back. Alex has seen her do this to her own hair so many times. She's seen the longing in Aisling, scanning her own thick, dark, unkempt tangles: if only Alex would give in for a second, if only she would go soft, then Aisling could fix her. Until now, she resented it. But she lets it happen this time. The curve of a finger tucking the heavy strands behind her ear, grazing the top of her ear; she moves her own index finger slowly, softly, against the hand that is in hers. Her mouth opens, and as Aisling draws her hand back from her hair, the ghost of a thumb brushes against her lips, so close she can almost taste it.

It crashes into her, then, the memory that had resurfaced, as if it was all happening again in one bursting moment. That night on the beach, and Adam's fingers reaching down her throat, and the slamming door, and his head in the ocean. His empty eyes. The taste of salt. *This is your fault*, he said, and she was screaming. *This is your fault.*

Alex jerks her hand away. She stands up, trying to stop her chest from heaving. Aisling, flushed and confused, stands up, too. "What's going on?" she says, and now it is the fear that has taken over. "Did I do something—"

"No, no, no, no," Alex sputters. "No. You're fine. I just—" She looks for a way to escape, but she is at the end of the table, and the only way out is to squeeze past Aisling. So she does, her bruised side shooting pain through her ribs as it bumps against Aisling's elbow.

"Are you okay?" Aisling says. She sounds incredibly small.

Alex can't look at her. She can only move forward, lurching on her failing feet. "I'm fine," she says. "I just — I'm going to lie down. I have to."

"Sorry." Her voice is almost imperceptible.

"Sorry." Alex closes the bedroom door behind her.

On the bed, facing the ceiling, she counts her breaths. In, two, three, four. Out, two, three, four. From the kitchen, the sounds of running water, the clanking of plates. In, two, three, four. Out, two, three, four. After a few minutes, the door to the hallway, opening and closing, the lock clicking.

In, two, three, four.

Out, two, three, four.

———

A knocking on Alex's bedroom door: tentative, almost inaudible. The walls are reddish with afternoon light. Alex has been asleep again. She tries to convince herself that she still is, but the knocking doesn't believe her.

"Alex? Are you awake?"

Alex rolls over onto her stomach, her face buried in her pillow. "Yes."

"Sorry?"

"Yes," she says louder.

"Oh, good." A pause. "Can I come in?"

With effort, Alex pulls herself upright. "Yeah."

Aisling looks nervous. Her hands are in the pockets of her jeans, and she sways slightly as she stands beside the bed. She knows better than to ask if she can sit down. Alex coughs into her elbow, the silence dragging the sound out of her.

"How are you?"

"Eh." Alex shrugs.

"I'm sorry if—"

"No, I'm sorry."

"I—"

"Let's just drop it." The words sound much harsher than Alex intends. She wishes there was a way to muffle her voice, to make it permanently softened and muted. "Thank you for making breakfast."

"Oh, you're welcome. It's been so long. I'm happy to do it."

"It means a lot. And maybe," Alex says, talking herself into envisioning a future beyond here, beyond now, "maybe — I mean, I don't know if I ever told you how much I liked that. Our little Saturday morning tradition. Because I did. I do. And maybe we could bring it back? Now that you've moved back in. Maybe I could do something for you sometime. Try my hand at cooking."

Aisling digs her hands in her pockets.

"It might be fun," Alex offers, her resolve fading.

"I talked to Nathan on the phone," Aisling says, "while you were asleep. He actually called me rather than texting, so I knew it had to be serious."

"Oh."

"We talked for, like, two hours. And I was thinking about what you said at breakfast. About change. And committing to change. And I think he does want to be better."

Why had she said that?

"And," Aisling says, "I do think he needs me to help him. I can do it. I think."

Alex doesn't know what to say.

"So," Aisling continues, "I'm going to move back in with him. And I know you just came back, and I'm so sorry, but I think it has to be now, or else I might lose him. I just don't want — I'm sorry. I know you probably don't get it, because it sounds stupid. But that's what I'm feeling in my gut. It has to be now."

Alex does understand. She doesn't say anything.

"Do you hate me?"

"No, of course not. You have to do what you have to do."

"And you'll be okay? We could try to find a roommate—"

"No, I'm fine."

"Okay." Aisling finally looks at Alex. "As long as you'll be fine."

"Don't worry about me."

"Okay. Thanks." Aisling turns to leave, then stops. "I think I'm going to try to be out on Monday."

"Okay." Alex rolls back over. "Good luck."

She can hear that Aisling is still standing there, thinking, perhaps, of some final words to say. They don't come to her. Soft steps walking away, then the creak of the door, the click of the latch, and Alex is alone again.

———

It is only when she hears Aisling leave the apartment that Alex gets up. On her way to the bathroom, she sees on the kitchen table the half-full French press, her special mug sitting where she left it. The coffee is stale and cold, a film coalescing across its inky surface. She picks it up and drinks it all.

———

Alex spends Sunday in her room. She does not open the blinds; she does not look at her phone. On a brief sojourn to the kitchen, she finds an old container of vegan protein powder, abandoned or forgotten by Aisling in some fitness-conscious past. She stirs it into tap water like sugar in tea, and then she downs the tepid, chunky liquid, dry patches of powder lingering on the edges of the glass and the surface of the greyish-brown water. It's terrible, but it's not the worst. At least she can survive on this, and that word — *survive* — ignites some small, persistent pain in her mind, like a finger-embedded sliver that, once forgotten, can be agitated again by a touch. The word follows her all day, every time she takes a sip of water, every time she makes another terrible shake. Survival. This is what it is, isn't it, this relentless, airless nothing, this eternal suspension in lukewarm fluid. This is what she'd spent so long avoiding.

In bed, lying on her side on top of the duvet, Alex watches a two-hour-long makeup influencer drama video. The matte woman cries, yet stays matte; her watering eyes, her cheeks, her lips hold their glitter. Her hair is so smooth that you would never believe she'd been so betrayed. Sometimes her mood changes, and she becomes a righteous crusader, unstoppable, her ring light igniting flames in her pupils. Alex has missed out on so much, has done so little: not like this woman, who has been through thousands of drugstore mascara applications and lived to tell the tale. And yet she is perfect, or at least able to fabricate perfection. Alex can't even move when the video ends, can't stop the auto-play pushing her toward yet another, even longer makeup drama video. At some point, she falls asleep, and when she wakes up, she is parched, and someone who has been called a predator is calling someone else a predator. After so many months sharing her space with dozens of people, the silence behind her bedroom door, the knowledge of Aisling's absence, is terrifying. An emptiness beckoning the unknown, an invitation to be filled.

So she keeps the door closed, even though she is thirsty, greasy, and in need of a shower. The blinds stay shut. She tries to masturbate, but her fingers grate like sandpaper. And she doesn't want to come, anyway. She would vomit if she came. She doesn't want to think about it. What really happened and what didn't. Both possibilities make her bed lurch sickeningly beneath her. She shouldn't have scared Aisling away, shouldn't have let the craziness show. It was so easy to leave her body when she didn't want to. Why was it impossible when she did?

Outside the door, the emptiness grows thicker. Alex covers her face with a pillow.

"There is nothing here," she breathes into it. "There is nothing here." Somehow, this thought brings her no comfort.

━━━

The phone buzzes, rattling against Alex's jaw. Her mouth has fallen slightly open in her dead, dreamless sleep, and she snaps it shut, the joint cracking and grinding, her teeth slamming against each other like pile-drivers. Squinting at the screen, she sees who's calling: enrolment services. Declined. It is past noon. Aisling must already have come and gone. All of it, just gone, gone like it was never there: her fancy pans and her clothes and the soft throw on the couch, her shelf of skincare and makeup in the bathroom. The bedroom she always invited Alex in — Alex always felt weird about it, always said no — never an object out of place, all the clothes neatly tucked out of sight in the closet, the only decorations a few strings of lights and Etsy-core floral art prints. Aisling had left before, and then she came back. But when she left before, she didn't take everything. The throw and the lights and the shelf, everything that had been in the exact same place for years: all of it remained, even when it was just Alex rotting in her room, alive and waiting. Now there is nothing, the apartment holding nothing but dead air, and every minute that passes in it unfilled makes it deader. Aisling will never come back to this place. And without Aisling, Alex doesn't belong here.

The phone buzzes again. The same number. Declined. It was always a struggle to get the healthcare side of the university to communicate with other departments when it came to getting accommodations, proving you were sick, demonstrating that you did need that extension. But as soon as they could punish you, all units worked as one, fast and decisive.

Part of Alex wants to get up and look at the dead places where evidence of her shared life with Aisling used to be. Instead, she stares at a cobweb, thick and heavy with dust, hanging in the far corner of her ceiling. It moves slowly in the air, pushed and pulled by some unseen draft.

I could just stay, she thinks, listening to the *thud-thud-thud* in her ears that the buzzing phone set off. Aisling's still paying her rent, at least until the end of the summer. They wouldn't know I'm in here. When they come in to find me, I'll hide. I know where to hide. They would never find me in that weird extended space under the sink, and it's so gross down there they wouldn't look long even if they thought to. I'll buy a new phone and duck their calls. I can just stay. I can just stay here. And she sees herself like a ghost in a children's story, the blur in the corner of the eye of the new roommate, the misplaced items and disappearing food. That might be a good life for her: as a non-person, fearful and dissipate. To let the hostile space consume her. But it's a stupid fantasy, because already they are onto her, already they are calling her and not stopping, and she knows what's going to happen. There is nothing to be done except deal with it or die, and she already tried dying. Look where that's gotten her.

She gets up. Without changing her clothes, without looking up from the floor, she walks into the hallway and straight out the door.

The campus is largely empty of students, the sidewalks shimmering in the heat. Perched on the end of a peninsula, the university towers over the whitecapped ocean that surrounds it on all sides, the wind the school's one consistent feature: a punishment in the winter, but in the summer a blessing, keeping the skies clear of city smog, the pristine blue free even of passing clouds. Even now, with the solstice fast approaching, a breeze buffets Alex's face, sends strands of hair flying. There is noise everywhere she walks, flags and banners and tarps flapping against the winds, the ever-present hammer-buzz-screech-yell of campus construction. They are building high-rises, glassy-new and imposing, and to go along with the high-rises, there are boutique coffee shops, organic grocery stores, artisan pizzas; on every block, the flapping banners advertise LUXURY LIVING AT THE HEART OF CAMPUS. Each unit will go for hundreds of thousands of dollars, some of them for millions, and the happy people will move in — some of them already have: there they are, carrying fresh flowers from the organic grocery store, talking on the phone through wireless earphones, their clothes fresh and new like the air — and they will be glad to live in such a beautiful place.

By the time Alex reaches the enrolment services building, her feet are throbbing, every step sending pain dancing up from her ankle bones into her shins. The blisters, not yet healed, start to tear open anew. She begins to miss the hospital, the way all she had to do was sit, and then resents herself for missing it. Everyone hurts, but not everyone complains about it, and she knows what people think about complainers. Her mom was not a complainer. She strides harder, into the scraping and sparking of each step, willing herself to inhabit everything possible in the pain.

The building that houses enrolment services is one of the oldest on campus. It reminds Alex more than anything of the hospital: the sterility and dullness, all ageless linoleum and flat carpet and broad sheets of fluorescent light. And the people, too: blank-faced, nervous, either sitting or standing, suspended in desperate waiting for an appointment they do not want to have. Those who are here right now, well after the winter term has ended, are even more purgatorial than usual. Expressionless, they sit, and they stand, and they pace, maybe, a few steps here and there, a sigh betraying their nervousness, before returning inevitably to the spot where they began, where they wait to find out what decision has been made about their continued academic existence.

Alex checks in at the computer. She is sixth in line. There are no seats, but the idea of standing in this large empty space, becoming one of these spectral figures, disturbs her. So she wanders, even as her feet beg for pause, around the edges of the room, past the corner, into a narrow, dimly lit hallway. Closed door after closed door, none of them labelled except for their room number, none with even a tiny window to see inside. At the end of the hallway is the building's lone gender-neutral washroom.

When the door locks behind her, Alex finds herself in a lightless cage. It is utterly dark, not even a line of faint hallway fluorescence coming in from under the door. There is no sign of the lights turning on, no light switch on the walls when she runs her hands over them. When she manages to grip the invisible door handle again, it doesn't budge. She shoves it downward, pulls it up, rattles it. Nothing but the sounds of metal, echoing off unseen surfaces. Panic.

She opens her mouth to yell, then closes it. What a stupid thing this would be to yell about, what a waste of everyone's time, and what a terrible person she would be, to make people afraid for her safety when she's just an idiot who locked herself in the gender-neutral washroom. The energy from the aborted yell jolts through her, so she kicks the door, hard, because it feels like the only thing to do, and the lightning-bolt pain of impact almost makes her yell anyway. She falls backward, her hands clawing for something to hold onto and finding nothing before she lands flat on her ass.

At almost the exact second Alex hits the floor, the lights begin to turn on. Slowly at first, a candle-flame flicker and the buzz of electricity, and the room is flooded. The washroom, though its fixtures are obviously old, is so spotless that it appears never to have been entered, and everything is bright and shiny, the harsh white ceramic and cold steel gleaming. No wonder the lights took so long to start working. A tiny gender-neutral washroom, the farthest washroom from the waiting room by far, at the end of the worst hallway in the worst building on campus — Alex would be surprised if anyone else has used it this year.

She rises carefully, testing the weight on her ankle. When she rests on it, her leg nearly buckles. She stands, using the sink as a grip. The mirror above the sink is, for some reason, decrepit. It seems to be hanging loosely from the wall; the coating on the edges is chipping, and the surface is warped. Random scratches cover it, lines that might have once formed words, and in its centre, right above Alex's face, is a phrase written in letters so huge and bold that no amount of later scratching has been able to cover it: I AM GAY.

In the warped mirror, Alex's bespectacled eyes look massive, and the top of her head looks tiny. Her mouth seems to bend upward and left. Her hair seems to expand ever outward. I AM GAY, reads the crown on top of the distorted image.

Alex finds this hilarious. She swells with goodwill toward whoever was responsible for fucking up the mirror this badly. She smiles at herself, and in the mirror, her smile curves horrifically, her teeth huge and off-coloured.

It was worth getting trapped, worth the redoubled pain in her ankle, for this idiotic little joy.

As she makes to leave, still admiring her distorted, gay face, she notices a disturbance in the background, somewhere behind her. A flash of something. A mark on the mirror she didn't notice? Because she saw the entire room from the floor as the lights came up, and the entire room was white, white, white, unmistakably white. She turns back to inspect the mirror more closely, and she sees it, out of the corner of her eye, on the wall behind the mirror. A chip in the white paint. How did she not notice that before? It is not a small chip, either, some fingernail-scrape accident, but a chip that looks intentional, that seems almost to expose depth beneath the thin white surface.

Dread creeps up her spine. She doesn't want to look at it. She wants to leave, to return to lobby limbo, the familiar stale smells and the waiting. And her phone is buzzing, too, the automated system letting her know that her place in line has come up. She declines the call, but it keeps ringing like a broken alarm clock, the vibrations so loud in this shiny room that the entire building might be able to hear them, and she remembers, as she turns the door handle once more, a small, locked room, a weight pinning her down — a place and time that she is unable to leave.

Now she really yells, shaking the door handle with all her strength, unable to avoid putting weight on her fucked-up ankle. Why does she know this fear, why does it know her, why won't the fucking door open — until it does, flying backward, almost knocking her over again, and though she can't run anymore she does, phone still vibrating in her shaking hands, every step landing like a brick in flesh, until she is back in the lobby and they are calling her name.

"Is Alex Nguyen here? Alex Nguyen?"

Scan the row of cubicles, scan the faces behind the computers. Find the person who's saying her name, who for once is pronouncing it correctly. There she is, on the left, the young Asian woman looking confused. Try not to limp too much. Try not to breathe too hard. Try to smile.

"Hi!" Alex says, pulling her voice up into her teeth. "Hi, I'm Alex. Sorry to keep you waiting."

"Oh no," the enrolment adviser says, "don't apologize. It was only a few seconds." Her nametag says LINDA in big text, she / her in small, and she glances down at Alex's foot with concern. "Did you hurt yourself? You were limping."

Alex laughs unconvincingly. "I just tripped on the stairs coming up here. They're kind of—"

"God, we have been trying to get them to repair those stairs for ages." There is genuine consternation in Linda's voice. "It's such a hazard. This building should be the *most* accessible on campus, not the least." She scribbles on a sticky note, then looks up. "I'm so sorry you had to deal with that."

And when she looks at Alex, even though she's the enrolment adviser and her job is to ruin Alex's life, Alex almost believes that she really is sorry. "Thank you," Alex says. "I appreciate it."

"As soon as you and I are done," Linda says, putting the sticky note on the screen of her monitor, "I'm going to put in another complaint about those stairs. That's a promise."

"Thank you."

"And so," Linda says, "Alex Nguyen. What can I do for you today?"

Alex shrugs. "You guys were calling me all morning, so." She adds another laugh. "You tell me, I guess."

"Huh." Linda returns to her screen. "Well, don't worry, we'll get to the bottom of whatever the issue is. Let me just pull up your file. Do you have your student card?"

Alex slides it over the desk. Linda does a little double-take when she sees the photo. But she returns, quickly, to her screen, her fingers tapping in mechanical rhythm across the keyboard. "Can I ask you something, Alex?" she says.

"Go ahead."

"Were you surprised to hear your name being pronounced correctly?"

"Yes," Alex says. A pause, and then she can't help herself: "Why do you ask?"

"They don't let us put last names on these name tags," Linda says, returning briefly to her typing. "I think only having a first name is supposed to make us seem more approachable." She slides the student card back to Alex. "It'll just be a minute while your information loads. Our system is super slow."

"Oh," Alex says. "Okay."

"I've been trying," Linda continues, "to push for IT to incorporate phonetic pronunciations into student profiles. So many students come here for help, they're super stressed, and the first thing they hear is their name being butchered. How is that supposed to make them feel like their concerns are taken seriously? But, of course, it's always too time-consuming. The school has always bigger priorities financially. Like letting kids trip on broken staircases, you know?"

"Yeah," Alex says. "I know." And hope starts to flicker within her.

Linda looks at Alex and then says something in Vietnamese: a long, earnest thought, ending in a question.

The flicker sputters out. "I'm sorry," Alex says, "but my—"

*My mom never taught me,* she almost says, before stopping herself. She can't just leave her sentence half-finished, but she doesn't know what else to say. "I'm sorry," she repeats lamely.

The disappointment is, for a split second, obvious on Linda's face, before professionalism takes over. She shakes her head a little, as though to cast off some invisible gathered dust. "No, no, don't apologize. I'm sorry. I shouldn't have assumed." Her eyes drift back to the monitor. "Ah, finally. Your file is up. So it looks like . . ."

She scrolls wordlessly, then sighs.

"So it looks like, Alex, unfortunately there's a lot of stuff we're going to have to deal with." By *we*, of course, she meant Alex, Alex alone. "You didn't complete any of your courses this term."

"I think I was supposed to be able to do late withdrawals. For medical reasons."

"Yes, I see that. And I'm so sorry to hear — I hope you're doing okay."

"Yeah, I'm fine now," Alex says quickly.

"Oh, good. Your medical reasons did allow you late withdrawal from all three courses you were in. But, unfortunately, your lack of completion means that the student loan funding you received this term, you'll have to start repaying that this year, unfortunately."

"Oh."

"And that includes the low-income and disability grants."

"Okay."

"And until you do that, your ability to secure future student loan funding will be jeopardized."

"Okay."

"And as far as things go with the school, financially, you know, you paid your tuition for last semester, so even though you were withdrawn from all your courses, as far as the school's concerned, you're square. But academically, because you didn't actually complete any courses, you're now on academic probation. It's really vital that you get registered and back to school full-time this coming term, because you're still eighteen credits short of your degree requirement."

"I can't," Alex says, and her voice sounds like it's coming from somewhere far away.

Linda finally takes her eyes off the screen. "Yes, you can! Aside from this year, your grades are fine. I'm sure—"

"I can't afford it," Alex says flatly.

"Alex," Linda says, "because you're on academic probation, you can't go on academic leave. Unfortunately — unfortunately, if you don't register for courses by the fall, you'll have to withdraw."

"Okay."

"Alex." She is pleading, leaning forward in her ergonomic chair. "If you're having financial problems, even if student loans aren't accessible to you anymore, there are other avenues we can pursue. You don't have to give up on yourself and all the hard work you've done to get this far. You can apply for—"

"I'm okay," Alex says, not making eye contact. "It's fine. I'll figure it out."

"Are you sure? Because if you're not registered for classes, you'll also have to vacate your student housing unit by the end of the month."

"Yeah," Alex says. "I know."

"Alex—"

But Alex is already limping away. "Thank you," she says to the empty air in front of her. Behind her, she can hear Linda saying she's sorry, saying it was so great to meet her, to please come back if she needs anything. As if she wasn't already humiliated enough. The poor sick girl with the fucked-up leg. The poor girl who can't even speak her own language.

She replays their interaction in her head. Why had it made her feel so doomed? Maybe if she had acted a little nicer, or if she'd been able to speak Vietnamese? But the real problem is that she doesn't want this kind of help anymore. There's no point in getting back to school. Even before she ended up in the hospital, she was barely hanging on, sleeping through classes, missing assignments, too deep in failure to reach out. To try to fix her life through the opaque paper-workings of the university and the government would be absurd. There's no future for her here.

And yet she had been momentarily convinced that Linda might actually be the one to help her. She wants to let Linda know that: that she had given her a little bit of hope, even if it came to nothing in the end.

When she opens her mouth to say it, she can already hear herself stumbling, the tones flat and wrong in her ugly droning voice. Just like the people butchering students' names, the people who won't do anything to change. She leaves without looking back.

—

Alex tries, for as long as she can, to hide. She burrows under the blankets. She brings the protein powder and a jug of water into her room. She turns off the phone, blocks all social media on her laptop. But the emptiness outside the door keeps expanding, extending its long fingers under the door, leaving its touch on the doorknobs.

When she finally leaves, standing under the yellowing streetlights outside the student residence towers, she ponders contacting

Tingting, maybe, or Em. Surely Em's queer collective house had experience taking in the disenfranchised. Or maybe one of the exes from before, the ones who wouldn't recognize her: maybe it would be worth the awkwardness to try talking to them again. But as she stares at her contact list, it gives her nothing but dread. Why would they want to hear from her after all these years, only for her to beg for a place to live? It would come off as unbearably manipulative. Even if, for some reason, they let her into their lives again, they would resent her, adding constantly to a ledger of things to hold against her if she ever did something unforgivable. Tingting would want to have fun, and Alex is no longer sure she's capable of fun. And Em and their queer collective house, if they even still lived there anymore, would have questions. It wouldn't be enough for her to just accept their kindness silently. They would want her to process and share, to trust and commit; they would act like they knew her, that they needed to know her, even though they didn't. Aisling is with Nathan, and Alex is sure she would rather be left alone. The only other option is her dad, and if she wants to live, that isn't an option at all.

That first night, shivering in her thin hoodie, Alex stays awake. She takes the bus to the twenty-four-hour café, the best place to study near campus. During the winter terms, it's always busy. Now, though, near midnight in the summer, it is quiet. The employees lean against the wall, chatting idly; the only patrons are an elderly man flipping through a newspaper and a girl crying on FaceTime.

As she stands in line for her coffee and donut, leaning lopsided on her left leg and slouched under the weight of her backpack, Alex notices a printed-out sign taped to the register: JOIN OUR TEAM! Hiring now for part-time and full-time roles. The words are accompanied by clip art of confetti and coffee cups, the coloured ink fading.

"Are you still hiring?" she asks the barista as she enters her tip into the card reader.

"Oh, yeah." The barista, short with dyed hair and a septum piercing, looks her up and down. "Do you have barista experience? Or, like, baking experience? Cause that's mainly what we're looking for."

"Yeah. Both, actually. I can—"

"Also you'd have to take night shifts."

"That's fine."

The barista seems satisfied with this. "Cool, hold on a second." They turn around. "Hey, Marcus!"

"What?" a deep, unseen voice responds.

"Someone wants a job. They've got experience."

Out from the kitchen appears, presumably, Marcus. He has long, dark hair and a small moustache; he looks exhausted. Wiping his hands on his apron, he, too, looks Alex up and down. "Is this the person?"

"Yeah."

"I'm Alex," Alex offers, hoping to approximate friendliness.

"Sorry," Marcus says, already turning back to the kitchen.

"What?" The barista is incredulous. "What's wrong with them?"

"You have to be able to stand for eight hours." He disappears.

Alex, conscious of her distorted frame, straightens up. She pulls her shoulders back, shifts her weight painfully over to her right foot, holding back a grimace. "I can stand for eight hours. Seriously. This is just, like, a temporary, super mild injury."

"Sorry."

"And I'm actually an athlete," Alex adds before she can stop herself.

"No, no, I believe you. But he's not going to change his mind. We've been through this before. And this is why we're so *fucking* understaffed!" This is directed at Marcus, who remains nonetheless silent and invisible. "Do you need a receipt?"

"Uh, no." $6.53 for a coffee and a donut, with tip. $158.74 left until she hits her credit limit. And she can't stand for eight hours.

"Thank you," she says, and shuffles over to the saddest corner of the café, where she sits doing crosswords until the morning, trying not to read anything into getting theythem'ed by the barista. $158.74: twenty more coffees and donuts, if she keeps tipping.

———

For the rest of the week, she spends her days at the public library, napping intermittently, moving from floor to floor to avoid arousing the suspicion of security guards. When the library closes, she gets one extra-large coffee from McDonald's. Then, every night, she returns, as though pulled by some unseen force, to the beach.

Like a penitent pilgrim, she carries her heavy backpack in the cold, and a driftwood walking stick she found on the beach the first night she went there — smooth and light, yet sturdy, some kind of pale wood she can't identify. Finding it had felt like a sign — she makes her slow way down the winding stairs. The tide is high at night this week, so she perches on the big logs and rocks washed up at the bottom of the slope, wearing three layers of sweaters but still cold, the waves coming close enough to spray her feet. She torrented some movies while at the library, horror classics she'd always wanted to watch, but taking out her laptop so close to the water seems risky.

And besides, it's beautiful. She doesn't want to look anywhere other than the horizon. There are mosquitoes everywhere, and little biting flies, but watching the undulation, the sparkling of the stars on the waves, the gradual lightening of the sky as the sun rises on the other side of the world before the fog comes again — it makes Alex feel achingly close to peace. Her breath settles up against the rhythm of the waves.

She has yet to see anyone in the nights she's passed in silence here. There is no moon tonight, and for the last week, it has been constantly and unseasonably cold. A fog has hung over campus, thick and unmoving, its damp chill seeping into everything. It obscures all light even as it traps it. Only in the dead of night does the fog lift, rolling back out over the ocean; the real cold exposed, the sharpness of dewy green and grey, the endless water unwarmed by the sun. And then, sometime before dawn, it comes back in again, coalescing slow and secret, like some movement spotted in the corner of one's eye, unnoticed until it has already arrived.

She has come to the conclusion that she did not, in fact, come here the night she returned from the hospital: that it had to have been a dream, that the bruises and the pain were unrelated. Her body, after all, had long proved itself full of unpleasant surprises. She isn't afraid anymore. She doesn't wish she had asked Aisling about it, or that she had done anything differently. Sitting here under the moonless sky, shivering and delirious with fatigue, she is simply grateful. Before, she had only remembered the fight; now, she remembered what came before. It was almost enough to make up for the terror behind her, the terror that certainly lies ahead. She won't last much longer out here on her own. Soon she will have to go to her dad's, and that might finally be the end of her.

More than anything, it makes her want to call Adam, to tell him about everything. Do you remember? Did you dream it, too? It had to have meant something. And for the first time since the phone call from the hospital, since she heard his terrible dead voice, she wants to talk to him. She picks up the phone, and when she feels like crying again, it doesn't make her hate herself. She believes, sitting here, that something good is possible.

There is a new message. It hangs suspended on the phone's cracked screen, the bit of preview text barely visible. It's from Ella, whose pool Alex swam in at class parties in elementary school; Ella, who was both rich and nice to degrees that seemed fake. They had stayed in touch, even though Ella went to the private college up the hill for high school. Every winter they went for coffee, delicate lattes from one of the award-winning cafés downtown. They would sit there for hours every time: Ella talking about her exciting life in New York, Alex offering less-exciting accounts of running, school, the people she met. And every time, Alex was surprised anew by how good of a listener Ella actually was, how genuine and unprying.

Ella went away for college, to New York or Connecticut or one of those places. Alex stayed, and then Adam happened. The annual coffee meetings turned into annual texts; eventually, they faded into nothing. It had been years since Alex had even considered what Ella might be up to.

*Hey* ☺ the message reads. *Thinking of you tonight!* ☺

It is almost time; already, the sky grows shallower. The message gleams white in the cold. It is May 31st. Alex has not been in the dead apartment in four days. In two hours, she can never go back.

She types a reply to Ella. She hits send.

———

Fifteen minutes before Ella is scheduled to arrive at the brand-new French café she suggested for their meeting — *a cute little coffee date (w/cocktails??? ☺)*" was how she described it — Alex is crammed into a bathroom stall, her backpack hung on the coat hook, rifling through her severely limited supply of clothing. She hadn't bothered changing while she was drifting from the library to the beach and back; there didn't seem to be any good reason to. Now she finds herself in a predicament. All her T-shirts are unwearably rumpled. She has only one top that isn't a T-shirt, but it's tight black nylon with mesh panels and pleather sleeves. The Ella she knew back in high school wouldn't have minded, but she doesn't know about eastern seaboard Ella. She texts the same way, but she might not be the same person at all. And it is critical for Alex to make a good impression. This is her one chance, and this is a fancy French café.

Fuck it. Mesh shirt it is.

She hasn't worn the mesh shirt for years. She kept it around more as a memento of her party days than anything else. When she slides it over her head, it is looser than she thought it would be. Where the pleather once hugged her arms tightly, it hangs loose; the mesh hem sags around her hips. Her top surgery scars are slightly visible; she can only pray that Ella is too polite to say anything.

Imperfect as the look is, it'll have to do. The only other option is to look like a crumpled piece of paper. She emerges from the bathroom stall, and the person that faces her in the mirror looks bizarre. She quickly runs the brush through her hair, but the brush can only go a few inches before it catches painfully, and there is no time for the kind of detangling operation that would be necessary. Her eyes are bloodshot with lack of sleep, and her permanent dark circles are so deep that they are starting to carve space out of her cheekbones. No concealer, but she does have silver eyeliner. She hastily runs a thin, winged line over each eye, a dab at the tear duct, and rushes out, hoping for the best.

It doesn't take long for her to spot Ella, because she looks almost exactly the same. The only difference is that she appears to have been run through an Instagram filter. Everything about her glitters. Her dark hair, falling in perfect, shiny waves; her lip gloss; the bejewelled watch on her wrist; the diamond pendant around her neck; the bright white blazer she wears; and the tasteful enamel on her fingers. When she looks up from the menu and sees Alex, her eyes sparkle.

"I am in shock!" she exclaims, after the hug. "Where did all this hair come from?"

"I grew it myself," Alex says. "Steroid-free."

"It's incredible. And this top. This is just vintage Alex." She fingers a cuff. "Pleather?"

"Only the finest."

"Amazing. I love it." She folds her hands under her chin and smiles. Alex grins back. She made the right choice after all.

"So I look hot," Alex says. "We knew that."

"Of course."

"But you look *amazing*. How much did this fucking blazer cost, like, eight thousand dollars?"

Ella grimaces. "Do you really want to know?"

"Yes. Hurt me, please."

"Two thousand."

Nine more coffees until Alex hits her credit limit. "Oh, so you're buying cheap shit now."

"You've always got jokes," Ella says. "Even after everything. I was just thinking after I texted you the other night: I don't know anyone who's really funny anymore."

"Yeah, because the people you know own yachts. You have to be kind of pathetic to be funny."

"You're not pathetic."

"I'm also not funny."

"Sure." She waves the menu in Alex's face. "So what are we getting? Listen to this, this sounds amazing. Tito's vodka, spiced pear liqueur, cherry juice, splash of lime. Mmm."

Alex scans the menu. The drinks do sound delicious. They are also expensive, and even though Ella does seem to be the same as she always was, she can't be sure that she isn't expected to pay for herself. "I think I might just stick with water."

"You can't be serious."

Alex holds steady.

"No way, you're serious? Alex." She leans forward. "Alex, I will buy you twenty drinks. I'll buy you the glassware they come in. Just tell me."

"Okay. Well. In that case, I'll have one of those spiced pear things."

"That's more like it."

"And, like, uh, one of these mushroom burgers. With the truffle fries. Is that French? That doesn't seem French."

"Where is the waiter?" Ella cranes her neck. "Excusez-moi?" she says, her studious French accent pitching her voice up half an octave. "Excusez-moi?"

This was what Alex always found so incredible about Ella. She'd never had any reason to believe that she was unwanted. Doted upon her whole life, she moved through the world entirely without fear. She was openly ridiculous, and it didn't matter.

When the drinks and food have been ordered, Ella turns her focus back to Alex. "So," she says. "Tell me everything."

"Everything about what?"

"About life." She gestures vaguely. "You have, like, fourteen more inches of hair than you did the last time I saw you, and you look like you've lost twenty pounds. Are you still in school? Are you still with that, uh, I forget her name—"

"No," Alex replies quickly, not waiting for Ella to clarify which girl she's talking about. The waiter reappears, depositing a bevy of drinks and snacks on the table.

"Too bad."

"No, I actually—" She takes several inelegant gulps of her drink. It is unbelievably good, and on her empty stomach, the alcohol hits fast and hard. "I actually ended up in a serious relationship with a, uh, with a guy."

Ella looks genuinely surprised.

"Yeah, it surprised me, too." Why did she bring this up? She doesn't want to talk about it, but for some reason she barrels on, like her speech is being compelled. "And there was this person, Em, who I met at a club night who I actually was with for, god, over a year? Around the same time. They were really cool. They *are* really cool, they're not dead or anything. But yeah, me and Adam—" She stops. Her body is board-stiff, and her breaths are shallow.

Alex blinks. She pauses to grab some truffle fries. "Sorry," she says, her mouth full. "Oh my god, these are good. I know this is a lot, but I just — I haven't, like—"

I haven't talked to anyone, she wants to say. I haven't talked to anyone about him. Not ever. I couldn't. But that would sound pathetic. "I'm just really excited to see you," she says instead. "And it's been so long."

"No, please go on." Ella munches on a fried olive. "Truly. I am mesmerized."

"Okay." Alex takes a deep breath, steadies herself with a hand on the table. Her momentum has been broken.

"Yeah," she says, hesitant. "I don't know, actually. I kind of hit the end of the story there."

"Wow. Dramatic."

"It *was* dramatic."

"I mean," says Ella, "nothing I've done has been nearly as interesting as all that."

"That can't possibly be true."

"I guess I did do some things I set out to do a long time ago." She shrugs, seems hesitant to elaborate, waiting for Alex to either change the subject or dig deeper.

Alex decides to dig. Anything to turn the conversation away from herself. "What happened?"

Ella sighs. "I mean. It was my dream."

"Sorry, which dream?"

"You know. Fashion stuff. Remember when we were teenagers?"

"Yeah. You were always talking about wanting to do design. Or have your own label."

"Yeah. I made it happen. And then it launched, and everything went really well. Not setting the world on fire or anything, but that was never my goal. It just went well. People liked the products, and they bought them."

"It sounds like you did amazing."

"No," Ella says. The fried olives are gone, and she taps the empty dish with a toothpick absently. "I didn't do amazing. It was just a bunch of nothing. I felt nothing. And I was sitting there thinking, like, not just 'where do I go from here,' but about the fact that this was ever my 'dream' in the first place. How I spent so much of my life thinking about it. Would I have wanted this if my parents didn't do what they do? I definitely wouldn't have been able to achieve it if they didn't. I had all these resources at my disposal, and what I chose to do with them was a stupid vanity project."

Alex sips her drink in silence. Her impulse is to comfort Ella, to tell her it wasn't all nothing, that it wasn't a vanity project. But she's right. The only comfort Alex can think to offer is that poor people are self-centred, too, and it seems unlikely Ella would appreciate that.

"Anyway," Ella says. "That's why I'm here. I closed up shop. I holed up at my parents' for a while, reconsidering my entire life." She smiles. "And then I thought about you."

"Yeah, I mean, when you think 'existential crisis,' I understand why I would be the first person to come to mind."

"Okay, wait. I'm not saying you're a cautionary tale or anything—"

"No, you can say it. It's true."

"No, not at all!" Her eyes blaze. "You have so much — you have such a depth of understanding. I think you would even if you hadn't gone through what you've gone through. And that's why I want to—"

Ella is in a heightened state that Alex has never seen before. Her cheeks are flushed, even though she's barely touched her drink; the words seem to tumble out of her mouth end-over-end. She takes a deep breath. "Alex," she says. "I have a proposal for you."

"Yes," Alex says immediately.

"Okay—" She laughs. "Okay, but seriously, listen. I'm going off the grid. Have you ever heard of El Camino de Santiago?"

Alex recalls a sleepy afternoon in tenth-grade Spanish class, a videocassette accompanied by the drone of the uninterested sub-stitute teacher. Trees and cliffs and blue sky, streams of people in dusty hiking boots, the ocean shining below. "It's that thing in Spain, right? That huge pilgrimage hike."

"Exactly. That's what I'm going to do this summer." She laughs again. "Can you imagine? No fucking cop-out guided tours or pre-booked B&Bs or any of that. No cell phone. Just me and my boots and my camera and my paper map." She reaches out and touches Alex's hand, softly, her energy focused. "And you."

The two of them under the huge, starry sky. Laughing in a little tent. On the trails winding through the mountains, one foot in front of the other on impossibly narrow paths, high on the thin air, running just for the thrill of it, just because they're alive.

"For real," Ella says. "Almost as soon as I thought about doing this, I knew I wanted to have a buddy. And when I thought about you, it was like — of course. They would be the perfect person."

Alex is about to cry.

"I can't," she says.

"No, Alex, I've got everything covered. You won't have to—"

"It's not that," she says, and she can already hear the sobbing in her voice, even as she presses it down. "I can't. Like, physically. I can't."

"But you're the most athletic person I know." Ella is confused. "You did all those insane trail races back in high school."

"There's something wrong with me." It comes out as a whisper, even after all this time. Like a shameful secret, even though everyone who looks at her standing can see it.

"Did you get injured?"

"That's what's so fucking frustrating." She wipes her eyes angrily. "I didn't even get injured. Now I can't even stand for fifteen minutes. You should see it. My joints swell up like balloons. And nobody — nobody will tell me what's wrong with me. Because the first thing they think is just, like, oh, you're crazy. You've got mental illnesses. You have low pain tolerance. You're too stressed out. And I can't—"

She is vaguely aware of how loud her voice has gotten, how it's rising over the subtle café din, but Ella's hand is still resting on hers, and it is so clarifying, so refreshing, to allow herself this anger.

"I can't do anything that used to make me feel good," she says. "And now I can't do this with you. Even though I want to."

Ella rises from her seat. She slips into the booth beside Alex, drapes an arm around her waist, leans her head against Alex's shoulder. The touch is enough to make the floodgates burst. Alex covers her face.

"What do you need?" Ella says, her voice low and steady.

"I can't go back to school. I don't have any money. I don't even have anywhere to live." Her knuckles press red and white into her eyelids. "And it's my fucking stupid fault."

"No. It's not."

"You don't know what happened."

"It doesn't matter what happened."

Alex's sobs turn into laughs. It's actually funny, she reminds herself. It's actually funny.

Ella isn't laughing. She holds Alex tighter. "I'll stay with you, then."

"No," Alex says immediately.

"Yes."

Alex looks up. Ella's face is right next to hers.

"Ella," Alex says, "I'm not going to stop you from living your life. That would make me feel worse. You understand, right? Like, not only taking your charity, but wasting your time. I would be guilty forever."

Ella doesn't understand. "I have the perfect idea, though," she insists. "We can stay at my parents' place on the island. The summer house. They just had it built maybe a year ago? We've barely even been there."

The island: an hour and a half on the bus, and then almost an hour on the ferry. Alex went there once on a school field trip when she was very young. They hiked up to where the fish spawned, and watched, in the cool September rain, as the red-backed salmon packed together, struggling up the creek, desperate to return to the place where their life began, the place where they would die.

"I'm not going to let you just sit doing nothing with me," she says, her voice regaining strength.

"Well, I'm not going to let you just rot alone. I want to help you, Alex."

"I guess we're at an impasse, then."

They sit, both staring at the empty booth in front of them, arms still around each other. Alex can't see her, but she knows the gears are turning in Ella's mind.

"What if," Ella starts to say, then stops. She turns to face Alex again. "What if it was a job? Like, my parents are so paranoid. They're always talking about how they think the house is going to get vandalized, or that people are trespassing on their property. What if they hired you to look after the house for the summer?"

"I don't know how to garden or anything like that."

"No gardening. It's got a cliff on one side facing the open ocean, and total thick forest on the other. The only other living things I've seen when we've been there have been deer and seals and killer whales. Literally all you would have to do is hang out there and make sure there's no one suspicious around. Which there won't be, because, like I said, it's in the middle of nowhere."

"Why would your parents hire me, though? I have zero relevant experience. I don't think I'm a very good crime-stopper, either."

"Because they love me." Ella grins. "And when I tell them it's Alex who used to do cannonballs in our pool every summer, there's no way they would say no. They were always so charmed by you."

Alex doesn't remember ever seeing Ella's parents, let alone talking to them. "I don't know."

"And I could join you."

"I told you, I don't want you to—"

"After I do El Camino, if that's what you want."

Alex remembers the island: the gleaming, the smell of fresh death in the water. The way the trees seemed greener than anywhere else.

"Well?" Ella's grin grows wider. "What do you think?"

"I've always wanted to see a whale," Alex says. She is smiling, too.

# 2.

Alex watches as Ella's blue Tesla speeds away. She turns and looks behind her. This early in the morning, the ferry terminal is empty. The sky is pale, and so is the ocean. The forested cliffs loom on either side of the bay, and Alex can just barely make out a pair of eagles, circling slow and even above the trees. If it weren't for the cries of the seagulls, it would be nearly silent. For the first time in weeks, she is really, truly alone. She takes a deep breath, in and out, and the smell of saltwater is miraculous.

She had been trawling through nature guides and Instagram location tags the entire time she was staying with Ella, distracting herself from being an interloper, an ill-fitting installation in Ella's velvet-trimmed spare room, sometimes tagging along on Ella's various social excursions, but mostly there in the apartment, becoming one with the furniture. Everything she has seen of the island has made her more convinced that she is going to a place where she will be happy. There are hiking trails all over, loops around lakes populated by bright migrating birds; quiet beaches with docks to jump off; green swamps full of ferns and wet earth and chirping frogs. On certain shores, sea lions lounge on the rocks, their fur growing bright in the sun, and every so often there will be pods of transient orcas coming through to chase the sea lions, the seals, the salmon. Last summer, people saw a humpback whale, swimming lazily through the glittering schools of herring, right off the very shore upon which Ella's parents' summer home is perched.

Ella gave Alex a detailed list of things she would need to know about the house. The pages of printer paper are tucked into an envelope, folded into her backpack, along with all the hiking clothes she and Emma bought together. They tell her how to access the security cameras, the codes to the locks, and the backup codes to the locks; which rooms are off-limits; how to find the laundry room, because it really does seem to be hard to find, deep in the basement whose floor plan Alex can't make sense of at all. Ella warned her, too, about how the house is inaccessible by road. You have to hike in on a barely-there dirt path through the forest from an abandoned parking lot. The buses are unreliable, when they run at all. Alex will have to get comfortable on an e-bike in order to get food. There is only one restaurant, and no delivery. It's expensive and time-consuming to go back and forth to the city; there's no urgent care, no hospital, the doctor only there a day or two a week.

But Alex can't see herself worrying about any of this. Not on this island, which seems to be more beautiful than she even remembered, and not when the house is what it is. Alex has never had more than a tiny room to herself in her entire life, and most of the time, it was hers in name only. There was always someone who felt entitled to her space. Now she is going to have a beautiful custom-built mansion, its huge glass windows facing a private beach, a lighthouse, the western horizon dotted with islands, and all of it is entirely hers, with a whole forest for her to explore. Alone. Not holding anyone back, not having to keep up with anyone's pace. If she wants to rest, she can rest. And she is getting paid to do it, to keep the house clean and safe. She's not accepting charity. She can pay the government back. She can even start school again, once everything is said and done, if she wants to. It's hard to get used to that idea: that she can want something and choose to do it.

Alex has still had no contact with Ella's parents. They were supposed to all meet to finalize the arrangement, but their plans fell through. This remains a little concerning, but as she thinks more about it, she talks herself around the anxiety. It's a sign of incredible trust, really, in Ella and in her, to sign off on letting her stay on their property. And Alex, for once, doesn't feel like she is being patronized. This is something even she will be able to do.

There are twenty minutes left until it's time for the ferry to board. Alex buys her ticket from the kiosk: twelve dollars closer to her credit limit, but it doesn't matter anymore. She buys a coffee from the only place that's open; it's burnt, but she enjoys it anyway. Inching down a set of sea-worn concrete steps, her driftwood walking stick in hand, she makes her way to the little rocky crescent of beach that lies between the ferry terminal and the marina.

Despite the presence of the marina, the many yachts and skiffs crammed aside the narrow floating docks, the water is sea-glass clear, green and deep. A family of geese floats along the surface near the shore, the fuzzy grey-yellow goslings peeping and splashing, the parents occasionally honking with concern. Through the fog, anything that moves seems ominous, like a vision, or a ghost.

Her mom believed in ghosts. Alex doesn't remember much about her life back when her mom was alive, but for some reason, she remembers that: how attuned she was to the possibilities of spirits, the conversations she had with Alex about what might be visiting her in her dreams. The dead world was firmly present in hers. Now she was the one who was dead, gone for more of Alex's life than she'd been around for. Back when she had just left, Alex wished often that she'd explained what kind of ghost she would become, what kind of signs she would leave behind for Alex to find. There was no doubt in her mind that the signs would be there. It seemed impossible that someone so attuned to the world of spirits would seemingly vanish without a trace. But then, she hadn't planned on dying. Maybe she just hadn't had enough time to prepare.

That was when Alex started looking for signs. Once she started seeking them out, she saw them everywhere: in her environment, in her dreams. And yet none of them seemed like her mom, or even like anything that cared about her. The signs added up to something worse than what they were. Their meanings were obfuscated by each other. There was only confusion and a sense of hostility: a deficiency within her, a language she'd heard enough to recognize but not to understand.

Her dad, of course, thought it was all bullshit, "Vietnamese bullshit," so she never talked about it, and as she got older she tried to convince herself that he was right: that there was no secret logic, no currents running unseen just beneath the surface of the world. It was all surface, even if the surface seemed to ripple when she stared at it too long. There was nothing to anything except what it was.

Farther out, the shiny heads of floating logs bob in the waves, pulled into the bay by the ferries' churn and the roiling currents. One of the shiny heads seems to turn and look at her. She does a double-take — is it alive? Is she seeing things? — and then laughs. It is, indeed, alive, but it's no log: it's a seal, lounging upright in the water, peering at her. She waves.

The seal points his snout up toward the sky before fading backward into the water, the picture of leisure. Alex wonders where the seal will be swimming off to, how far they might travel. Perhaps they'll see each other again on the other side. She hopes so; she believes, for no real reason, that she'll be able to recognize them.

The sky lightens around her. It is chilly, still not quite bright, but it seems almost like she should have her sunglasses on. The peeps of the goslings, the guttural honks of their parents, grow more urgent; above her, the seagulls are flying in raucous chaos, screaming and diving. An eagle raid, perhaps, or the prospect of one. She squints into the sky above her head. Far, far up, a shape with black, ragged wings — a figure that seems to have no head — soars ominously, not flapping or changing direction.

When she looks back to the water, the ferry is approaching the terminal. It is time to go.

Alex is one of only a few foot passengers boarding the ferry. Since there are so few of them, they are herded into the dingy car boarding area, all pavement and dust and exhaust fumes. There is a man in black sunglasses and a baseball hat, a kerchief pulled over his face, carrying a huge backpack; a pair of serious-looking cyclists with fancy bikes; a girl, crying on FaceTime. When she hears footsteps coming up behind her, heavy and fast, she looks back and sees the security guard, heading her direction with a bulletproof vest and a sniffer dog.

She is gripped by panic. Does she have any drugs in her bag? Does she have any drugs that a sniffer dog could sniff out? There's only the sleeping pills. No more anti-psychotics, no more SSRIs. She decided, as soon as she rolled into Ella's, that she didn't want to take them anymore. She didn't need to. She was going to be fine — on the island, she was going to be fine, and the pills had never helped her before, only ever made her feel sicker, and besides, where would she pick up her prescription?

The sleeping pills are controlled, not illegal. But does she have an illegal amount? Will they believe her if she says she has a prescription? Now she's tensed up. Animals can sense fear, she knows, and if the security guard sees her nervous face, he'll immediately identify her as a criminal. She should have put the sunglasses on; she should have shaved her legs. The beginning of the rest of her life will end before it even starts, and she has no one but herself to blame.

She stares at the ground. The security guard and the sniffer dog pass her by. As the ferry docks, the hull squeaking against the metal buffers, the security guard yawns. The dog yawns with him.

This is a flaw she'll fix, she thinks as the boarding ramp lowers, while she's on the island. She's going to become less paranoid.

The ferry elevator doesn't work. The button is jammed. Alex slams it once, twice. Nothing. She waits at the bottom of the narrow stairs for the other passengers to make their way up. Then, slowly, she scales the stairs, step by step. Her bag — she packed light; she figures if she needs more clothes, she'll be able to buy them once she starts getting paid — starts dragging her backward. By the time she gets to the top of the stairs, she is bent over, heaving. It takes the full force of her shoulder to shove open the heavy door to the outside.

Once she does, it is heavenly. The wind is cool, not too strong; from here, the swallows dipping and diving mid-air, catching flies in their tiny beaks, are at eye level. The family of geese is far below her, and the seal is nowhere in sight. She leans against the railing, catching her breath, getting a good look back at the ferry termi-nal. If everything goes according to plan, she won't be seeing this shore for another three months.

Then the rumble of the ferry's engine grows more intense, and she walks along the railing to the front deck. There, she sits on a bench, stretches her feet out. In front of her is a row of flags, flapping lightly in the wind, and among them, hilariously, a rainbow flag. It is June, after all. She wanders up to the flag, holds her fingers up in a V in front of her extended tongue, and snaps a picture. She considers sending it to Em, just to let them know she's alive, but she doesn't.

Behind the flag, the ocean stretches huge and green in front of her. The summer glacier runoff has given it a jewelled tone, almost the colour of turquoise, and the peaks of island chains layer over each other into the horizon. To the northwest, she can just barely make out the point of the island to which she is headed, extending out into the ocean. There could be anything out there. Anything. There could be whales, dozens of whales, just underneath the sur-face. There are, she knows for a fact, thousands of fish, so many different kinds of fish: rockfish, bobbing lazily near the surface just off the island's shore; the salmon powering through deep water, snatching up the tiny baitfish swimming along; huge halibut and lingcod; flounders goggle-eyed on the sandy seafloor. This whole world underneath her, alive. Ella said that the house had kayaks, lifejackets, wetsuits, snorkels. Alex has lived near the water for all of her twenty-four years, and she's never even gone under the surface. But now she will. There won't be anything stopping her, nothing more to regret. The ferry begins to move underneath her. She closes her eyes, taking in the motion.

Without warning, an ear-splitting blast shakes the boat, so loud that it is physically painful. Alex yells, involuntarily, and covers her ears. It ends after a second or two, but within Alex's skull, the sound keeps on ringing.

To distract herself from the pain, she wanders over to the railing, and for a while she leans out, experiencing herself as part of the wind, watching as the ocean spreads underneath the ferry, the looming shape of the island growing clearer. With every passing minute, she can make out more concrete details in the distance: houses on shores and nestled within trees, the shape of a power line cut into the top of a mountain. Bright dots on the water's surface show themselves to be early-morning kayakers, or jet skis tethered to buoys. Occasionally, she turns and looks behind her, at the receding bay in the distance. It doesn't take long before it disappears entirely.

As the boat begins to enter the cove where it will dock, the sound of a message playing over the speakers cuts into Alex's reverie. Out here on the deck, she can't make out the words. Presumably, it's almost time for people to get off the ferry. She peers over at the dock. There is no ferry building, let alone a passenger deck walkway. She'll have to go back down among the cars again.

For one last time, she leans out over the edge of the railing, as far as her body will let her. A deer stands on the rocky shore, its slender legs stepping carefully on the rocks, nibbling on seaweed. It stops, looks up, and Alex could swear that it's staring right at her — straight into her. She smiles.

The deer jumps straight into the water. It does not resurface.

Alex looks back to where the deer jumped in. There is nothing, just the quiet spray of water against the rocks, the waves growing progressively bigger as the boat's churn hits the shore. Can deer swim underwater? Was this just a deer behaviour she didn't know about? She pulls out her phone to search for an answer, but there's no reception, and now she can no longer even see the place where the deer was, and the ferry is about to dock. She turns around to pick her backpack up off the bench just in time to see the deck door slam shut.

It takes a few seconds, as she grabs her backpack and walks toward the door, for Alex to process what has happened. Her mind is overtaken by the vision of the deer: its huge, shiny black eyes boring straight into hers, and then disappearing into the water. But when she touches the door handle, it is wet: just slightly wet, and slightly warm, as though someone with damp hands had just grabbed it. She was alone out here on the deck. She had walked up here alone, had been alone the last time she looked behind her. Why, then, had the door been opened and closed? Perhaps a misguided foot passenger, thinking that offloading would happen up here before realizing their mistake. But that didn't explain the outside door handle being warm and wet, the way it felt like it had been just now held in someone's hand. She opens the door hastily, begins her careful, steep descent as quickly as she can. She can't shake the fear crawling up her spine. As she was watching the deer — and maybe even before that, when she had had her eyes closed, when she had felt herself so at peace — someone had been out on the deck, watching her.

Huffing and puffing, she comes up behind the scant group of foot passengers just as the gate to the boarding ramp is opened. The sunglasses man has pulled his kerchief nearly over his face. The FaceTime crying girl is still on FaceTime, crying. And up ahead of them, walking incredibly fast, a figure already rushes onto the road, hands in pockets, hood pulled over their head.

That must be them. That's the person who was watching her.

The person she didn't see boarding. But no, it could have been anyone; could have been one of the people in the cars, come out for some fresh air. That's what she's supposed to keep reinforcing in her brain, every time one of the paranoid thoughts comes up: re-rooting herself in the ground of reality, allowing her thoughts to rotate around something solid.

But she doesn't believe it. She hurries as much as she can up the boarding ramp, careful not to trip on the bumpy metal plating, the end of her walking stick hitting it with increasingly urgent *clangs*.

By the time she reaches the end of the ramp, the person in the hoodie is already gone.

———

True to what Ella told her, the bus does not come when promised. It is scheduled to come with every other ferry; she took the ferry she did specifically to line up with the bus. Alex sits at the bus stop for twenty minutes before she gives up. She walks up the street to the lone structure in view, a shingled little building nestled in the trees against the long, empty, winding road.

Despite how early it is, the tables outside the café are well-populated with people: mostly women with women and men with men, the men hardy but polished late-middle-aged white types, the kind who are retired from owning successful contracting companies or law firms, or otherwise serious cyclists or hikers. The women are mostly blond in athleisure, ready to go on their morning walks by the sea or bike rides up the cliffs; otherwise, a few corner tables are crowded with elderly women, knitting and chatting with equal vigour. Living on campus, and before that in the city, it has been a long time since Alex has been somewhere with mostly white people, and she is aware again of the state of her hair, her unshaved legs, her narrow, haggard eyes. I am not paranoid anymore, she tells herself, as she walks around the café to the door. These people are not staring at me in order to wish ill on me. They are just looking because I am new. If I were them, I would be looking, too. She thinks of the deer, the door closing behind her, and before that, the locked bathroom door and the darkness, somehow familiar. She shakes her head, as though the motion will shake the thoughts out. *I am not paranoid. These are nice people.*

It takes a while for the woman at the counter to notice her. Alex, when she was working, always felt extremely harassed by customers who called for her when she was obviously distracted. So she stands, silent, holding her face in a friendly position as she peruses the menu. Considering the homey, small-time vibe that the place seems to be trying to cultivate, she is disturbed by the prices. As she debates whether she's hungry enough for a eighteen-dollar sandwich, the woman at the counter turns to her.

"Are you waiting for someone?" she says suspiciously.

"Oh, no, I just—"

"Well then." The woman sighs. "How can I help you."

"Uh, could I get an iced coffee? Large and black?"

"No."

Alex is unsure how to respond to this. "No?" she repeats stupidly.

"We don't do iced coffee. Did you read the menu?"

"Yes, but I thought—"

"So you want an iced americano then."

"Yes please. I mean, if that's possible—"

"ICED AMERICANO," the woman yells into the kitchen, then turns back to Alex. "Name?"

"Alex."

"$4.95."

As Alex enters the tip into the machine, the woman stares at her. "Here for a hike, Alex?" the woman says.

"No," Alex says. "I'm actually going to be living here." She hopes the woman can hear a faint exclamation point at the end of that sentence, that her newness will be seen as endearing rather than threatening.

"Oh," the woman says, and some kind of understanding seems to dawn on her. "You going to be up at the Cathedral?"

"I, uh. No, I'm sorry, I don't know what that is."

The woman doesn't seem to believe this.

"I'm house-sitting," Alex offers as the transaction goes through.

"Really. For who?"

"The Smiths?" She doesn't know why she phrased this as a question.

The woman slides her a tiny receipt and turns away. "Never heard of them."

"Oh, I don't need a receipt," Alex says, but the woman is already busy doing something else.

She picks up the receipt, immediately crumpling it in her pocket. The layout of the café makes it unclear where she should be standing to wait for her coffee. The hostile energy radiating from the woman at the register makes loitering in place seem like the wrong answer, but there's no space at the other side of the bar, and a small line is already beginning to form. Alex hustles back outside; the woman did get her name, she reasons, and if they can't find her, they can certainly call for her.

Outside the café, finding herself with nowhere to sit, Alex mills around, searching for something to look at. Eventually she fixes her sights on a small wooden kiosk nestled in a hedge. The kiosk is disintegrating, obviously poorly maintained, and when she gets closer, Alex sees that it is housing some kind of community bulletin board behind the glass. The latch is rusted shut; when Alex tries to move it, the entire kiosk lurches. The notices look years old. A picture of two lost tabby cats, dated five years ago, is partially covered by an advertisement for tarot readings from three years ago. Many of the pieces of paper pinned on the board, Alex discovers, fall into these two categories: missing pets and advertisements for spiritual services. One particularly large piece of paper, its garish colours bleeding with moisture, invites those interested in "mental, physical, spiritual, relational, and sensual healing" to meet on Sunday at noon. Which exact Sunday is unclear, as is the location of the meeting, which seems to have long ago run off the page. The same goes for the face of the healer, whose greyscale face has come to resemble a pale orb with huge, black eyes, no hair, and no mouth.

Alex busies herself trying to memorize the names and faces of all the lost pets. Maisie Lou, a golden retriever, last seen on the beach in December four years ago. The tabbies, whose names she can no longer read. A six-month-old Australian shepherd, stolen from outside the cafe three years ago. The name is smudged, but Alex can just make it out: Ella. "Our sweet Ella," the drooping letters say. Ella loves everyone; Ella will go with anyone. Ella's sweetness was probably the reason she got stolen.

What an odd coincidence: that this creature whose absence is welcoming her to the island shares a name with the friend whose absence has allowed for her to be here in the first place. It must have some meaning, a significance she'll be able to parse out as she spends more time here, and in her mind a vision blossoms of her encountering Ella the dog in the woods, maybe somewhere near the house where she'll be staying. She can picture it so clearly, even though she's never been in these woods or met this dog. She doesn't even particularly like dogs. Not even picturing the scene, but feeling it, like something that has already happened. A blurry shape in the forest, the faint sound of a ringing bell. It gives her thoughts a comforting stillness.

But it's fake, a stupid coincidence, devoid of any meaning whatsoever, and the stillness is replaced by the prickle of self-resentment. She told herself, not two hours ago, that she was going to be less paranoid, stop drawing connections between unconnected incidents. It means nothing. It's a missing dog poster. She's being an idiot.

Out of the corner of her eye, as she looks again at Ella's smiling doggy face, she notices a posting, nearly buried under the other ones, that looks bright white, crisp. It is up near the top of the bulletin board, and Alex has to crane her neck to see it. Just under half of the sheet is visible, but as she gets a better look at it, its newness becomes obvious. The mostly covered text is bold, each letter distinct; the edges show no signs of wear. Why, if someone went to the effort to pin a new message up on this long-abandoned bulletin board, would they bury it under years of old postings?

It is weird enough that Alex needs to get a closer look. She uses her backpack as a step stool. The text is what she can make out first. Four numbers: the last four digits of a phone number, the rest of which remains covered. *Home.* And then, above it, the corner of a photo: a shoulder, maybe, in a blue plaid shirt. A dark brown background. The edge of a half-smile.

"Adam?" she says out loud.

"Hello?" yells the woman from the register. She is standing in the doorway. "Iced americano for Alex? Is something going on over there?"

4736. Those are the numbers. Alex repeats them to herself as she rushes to get her coffee from the disgruntled woman. 4736. 4736. All the patrons of the café are actually staring at her now; she can't stop her mouth from moving, willing the digits to stay in her memory. Numbers are so hard for her, always evaporating as soon as she stops focusing on them. She snatches the coffee from the woman, more roughly than she intends to, and opens her mouth to ask her when the last time someone put a poster up on the bulletin board was, who had posted it, if she could open it up and see for herself.

"Four," she says, and immediately wants to die.

"Excuse me?"

"I'm so sorry," Alex says. "I just wanted to ask—"

"There's a line," the woman says.

Over her shoulder, Alex can hear the telltale rumble of a bus engine. The next bus wasn't supposed to come for another two hours. She can't have missed it. She can't.

"Shit!" she blurts. "Oh my god, I'm so sorry. I have to—"

She stumbles over to her bag, slings it over her shoulder, takes one last glance at the poster. 4736. There, sure enough, is the tiny bus, already trundling up the hill. She turns her walking stick parallel to the ground and runs, the bones grinding in her ankles, waving her arms and yelling. "Hey!" she screams, and it's all she can think to say. "Hey!"

At first, it seems like the bus isn't going to stop. But gradually, gradually, it slows to a standstill. Alex catches up, almost trips on the steps. "Thank you," she gasps, "thank you so much."

The bus driver is a bearded man in a green baseball cap. Instead of a uniform, he wears a T-shirt with a very dramatic eagle on it. PROUD TO BE AN AMERICAN, the shirt proclaims.

As Alex tumbles into a seat, the bus driver calls back to her. "Where you headed?" he asks.

Alex can no longer remember the street address of the house.

"I, uh," she says, buying some time as she fumbles with her phone. She knew this would happen, her shitty fucking evaporating memory. That's why she texted the address to herself before she left.

"709 Cliff Drive," she announces, relieved.

The bus driver doesn't react. After a minute, country radio begins to play over the bus speakers. There is no one else on board.

The cove disappears in the rear window of the bus. Alex no longer has any idea what the four digits were. The only numbers she can think of are 709. No matter how hard she tries, nothing else appears, not for the entire long journey across the island.

———

The bus pulls up, eventually, at a dirt parking lot so small that it's hardly worthy of the name. Trees tower above it on either side; an impossibly large number of potholes are crammed into the tiny space. Alex barely notices where they are, anyway; she is thinking of that corner of a half-smile, of the numbers she can no longer remember.

"Here you are," says the bus driver.

Alex thanks him again, stumbles out of the bus. It's getting later in the morning, and back at home, it would probably be starting to heat up. This part of the island, though, faces west, and surrounded by trees, it is only tickled by a few rays, as though it was still early. Only the patch of bright blue sky burning above betrays the truth. As Alex looks up, a shadow passes over the blue: a pair of ragged wings, faceless and slow. In front of her is only a small sign that says NO TRESPASSING, one of many such identical signs that dotted the side of the road at random, distant intervals. There are openings on all sides of the little no-parking lot that could very well be trails.

She pulls out her packet of instructions. It wouldn't bode well to be lost in the forest before she even sets eyes on the house. Flipping through the pages, she eventually finds the one that seems to depict the parking lot, the trails winding around it. But the little map only shows two trailheads. She sees four. The one she's supposed to take, the one Ella highlighted in green on the map, heads west.

In the absence of any concrete information, Alex briefly considers simply picking a path based on vibes. The one closest to the NO TRESPASSING sign seems to have a good energy, despite the warning. Maybe she could just follow it for a while: she figures, this close to the ocean, that she'll have to find her way to shore eventually, even if she is otherwise lost. As she slides the packet of papers back into her backpack, though, a sharp edge pokes her from one of the backpack's side pockets. A compass. Ella had made her buy one, even though she'd scoffed at the idea of needing it. If she'd remembered this was in the bag, she wouldn't have stepped on it.

The compass is intact. Alex quickly calibrates it. Sure enough, the NO TRESPASSING trail is the one she needs to take. It's only a light walk, according to Ella, ten minutes on soft, flat ground, and Alex hopes this is true. She has been on her feet too long today, and her ankles are beginning to burn. The winged creature loops back around before disappearing into the trees.

———

The trail is overgrown, obviously long unused. Alex can barely see where she's stepping. The salal, its leaves crisp and waxy, reaches around her legs; the yellow-orange buds of nascent salmonberries, their leaves with their peach-fuzz bristles, brush against her face, sometimes catching in her hair. Another thing she'll have to remember: to put her hair in a ponytail when she goes into the forest. As a kid, she once read a very frightening article about Lyme disease, and as she walks, praying that there are no unseen roots underfoot waiting to trip her, visions of ticks in her hair and ticks latching onto her mostly bare legs haunt her.

Ten minutes pass, and where Ella had promised a clearing beginning to emerge, Alex sees only the forest continuing onward. She stops to have a drink of water and listen for the ocean. The occasional chirps of unidentified birds, the rustling of leaves in the wind — but there, she can just barely hear it, the low murmur underpinning it all, off to her right. She's on the right track, though. She has to be on the right track. There's no reason to worry about something that isn't happening.

She continues onward, branches crackling beneath her and around her. Slowly, the green world begins to grow brighter; the sliver of blue sky above her widens, and then widens more, extending down in front of her as the trees and brush part. The ocean's voice grows clear. Here she is, and her tired feet pick up the pace despite themselves.

And there it is, right in front of her — manifesting itself whole and all at once — the place that was going to house her, protect her, in exchange for her protecting it: 709 Cliff Drive, though it had a street and an address in concept only. On the right, a sudden cliff before the sparkling ocean, the sun now fully apparent above the crest of trees, and on the left, separated from the cliff only by a narrow patch of thin, yellowing grass, is 709, massive and imposing, a cacophony of incongruous shapes smashed together. The front of the house is all glass, a series of transparent cubes interlocking, with wood-panelled sides that look like the folds of an accordion; a glass cylinder encloses a narrow corkscrew of a staircase. The glass that forms the upper floor is opaque, and in the sun, it looks like onyx. Above it all, a silvery fin, asymmetrical and nearly doubling the height of the house, cuts into the sky.

Alex had expected to be taken aback by 709. She didn't expect to find it overwhelmingly ugly. She feels guilty as soon as she has the thought: this structure shouldn't be here; it doesn't belong here. This is, after all, the place she is supposed to take care of.

But it is ugly, it is, in a way that the pictures that Ella showed her didn't at all capture. Maybe it's the way the forest just stops, artificially, right behind it, the way the shrubs are trying to reach over to the places where they once were, where their roots were pulled up to make room for the concrete foundations; maybe it's the colours, the obvious artificiality of it against the blues and greens around it. Maybe it's the way that everywhere the house is, the cliff is dead. Dead grass, exposed concrete, crumbling rock; there are not even bugs flying around it. Or maybe it's just the fin. What is the fin for? Is it a home movie theatre, a silver screen on the inside? What could possibly justify its size, its bizarre, sloping shape, the way it gestures only to itself?

The house was designed by some award-winning European architect, who then won another award for it. It was controversial, Alex remembers Ella telling her; her parents were only able to build it after a long, protracted fight with a citizens' group. The fact that this land was even available for sale was a matter of bitter public dispute, and most people on the island thought that it should have been bought and kept as part of a nature preserve, if it had to be bought at all. But Ella's parents won out in the end: they, after all, had the money, and the municipality ultimately needed the money more than anything else. The cape was mostly inaccessible anyway, they reasoned; it wasn't like the coves, or the lakes, or the mountain lookouts, or the galleries, all places that tourists came to be part of nature that they fancied undisturbed. In those places, the naturalness needed to be maintained, the image kept, even as the shrubs around the trail were always conveniently pruned, the view from the lookout kept clear of any interrupting tree branches, the winding roads down to the sandstone shores paved and pothole-free. But the cape was simply nature left alone, genuinely untouched, and if a few trees fell in the forest, if they were replaced by 709 — if all of that made any sound, there was no one there to hear it but the ocean and the trees, and they spoke only in whispers.

Up to this point, Alex had been nursing a secret fantasy: that 709 would become her home. That she would do so well this summer, make everyone so proud of her, that Ella's parents would hire her on to stay there full-time. She would pass the seasons here, see how summer faded into autumn, pick apples from the little orchard before the winter chill, bake fresh bread and pastries for Ella in the cold of December; and then, in spring, she would learn to plant and grow, have her own little patch of soil spread with bursting seeds. A wild cherry tree for the birds to pluck when they returned from their long journeys north. And then, in the summer, as the birds raised their young, she would be back out at sea again, floating in a kayak as the sunset world turned pink-orange-red around her, the cool ocean water liquid gold. Ella would be there, too, when she wanted to be, and when she saw what Alex was doing with the place, how lush and beautiful it was, how at ease Alex had become (letting her hair grow all the way down her back; letting her skin tan in the sun; the coarse little hairs on her face left unshaved), she would want to be there more and more. That would be her life, Alex had thought; all of this was possible for her.

It still was, perhaps. But in her fantasy, 709 would become Alex's home. And this, Alex knows as she stands under 709's shadow, will never be home.

———

The to-do list is clear. First: enter the front door (the code is 5648). Take off your shoes, your bag. Shoes go in the closet in the column, as does any outerwear. Check for ticks: this was a last-minute addition Alex made to the list. And from there, it is straight to the security room to double-check the camera footage, to ensure that the locks are secure, that she wasn't followed, that there was no suspicious activity accompanying her arrival. And once that's done, "whatever you want!! ☺" Ella wrote in her sloping script at the bottom of the page. The smiley face was most certainly meant to leave her with a sense of ease, but in combination with the many injunctions about surveillance, it seems almost sinister. Alex tries to shake her concern: surely, with a house like this, there were good reasons for Ella's parents to be so concerned with security. But why would anyone bother following Alex to the house? What was so important about this place that would make it the likely subject of hostile interference? And why, then, if they were so worried, would they leave all this responsibility to Alex, who had no experience in ensuring the security of anyone or anything? The instructions, when it came to this subject matter, seem almost targeted, like they somehow know exactly what to say to make the paranoia flare again in the back of Alex's mind. It can't be, though; this must be normal. It is Alex who is strange, Alex who always reads too much into things. There is no real reason to be afraid.

Still, fear jolts through her as she enters the door code, checking over her shoulders for any movement behind her. She's been having such a terrible time with doors lately, and it seems like a logical progression of events for her misadventures to be leading up to this one catastrophic door failure. But the keypad beeps green, and on the little screen, the anxiety washes off Alex's pixelated face. The door, even though it is glass, is easy to open, as though it is being powered by some invisible motor, or guided by a strong, unseen hand.

The main floor of the house is one massive room, everything out in the open. In this case, though, "everything" means almost nothing. There is a grey couch facing an empty fireplace on the left; on the right is the kitchen, its appliances shining chrome, also entirely empty. A lone palm plant of some kind, deep green with spiky leaves, stands in the corner. Alex can't tell, from this distance, whether it's real or fake. Beside it is an extremely large telescope. Directly in front of her, bisecting the massive space, is a thick white column. That's where the closet is, the second task. With no doormat here, Alex's boots have already tracked dirt and pine needles into the entryway. Add that to the list: she has to sweep later, or at least figure out how to set the robot vacuum up.

She puts her shoes in the empty closet, confirms that no ticks or other creepy-crawlies have hitched a ride in on her body, and then turns to admire the view. It is dimmer in here than Alex would have thought. Perhaps things are different when the sun is setting, facing the windows directly, but right now, it almost looks like nighttime. The glass is tinted, and the light reflecting off the water doesn't seem to penetrate the barrier.

All the same, it is an incredible scene. From here, the dead cliff grass is barely visible, and it seems like the house is floating above the infinite water. Off to the south, the lighthouse stands on an outcropping projecting into the ocean. In the distance, more islands dot the horizon. There's a ferry, too, that she can just make out, heading off to some other island destination. The sky, unmarked by clouds, goes on and on. Her mind turns to the promise of kayaks. First, she has to find the security room.

Ella said that the easiest way to the security room is to take the elevator, which is embedded in the column. The elevator has its own code for security reasons: enter that, and you can descend to the labyrinthine basement. ("Literally no one goes there," Ella said, "except to go to the security room. Whenever we've been there, we've just sent the housekeeper down with the laundry, and even she hates it.") The security room is the closest room to the elevator. There's no need to go any farther into the depths.

So Alex enters the code — this time, 7007. The elevator doors slide open. It is an unnecessarily large elevator, the inside all mirrors. When Alex steps in, she is surrounded by herself. There are three buttons on the panel, and only one of them is green. This is, Ella said, the default setting, and one that was not to be changed: the only place the elevator was to be taken was to the security room and back up to the main floor. Where the elevator went upstairs was firmly off-limits; with no stairs other than the spiral up to the bedrooms, anywhere else was entirely inaccessible.

Alex presses the button. Silently, the elevator begins to move. She tries not to stare at the many selves reflected back at her from all sides: their sunburned cheeks, their hips wide after two weeks of eating out with Ella, the redness and swelling in their ankles visible above their socks. The elevator stops so smoothly that it is dizzying. The doors slide open, and she steps into the darkness.

The hallway is narrow, long, dimly lit, lined with closed door after closed door. At the end, it splits off in two directions. Looking at it gives her an eerie feeling of familiarity, and she has a strong urge to walk the hallway's length, to look down the splitting paths, but she must stick to the task list. The closest door has another keypad over the handle, another four-digit code. 9854. Alex wonders how the housekeeper could possibly keep track of all this. She imagines a ring of index cards clipped to her belt buckle, laminated, all of them with their own codes.

The lights in the security room turn on when the door opens. Alex lets the door fall closed behind her. In front of her, nearly covering the wall, is a series of screens. One of them, its image framed in green, shows the front door, where Alex just came in.

One screen, facing the forest, seems to be the back door. There is a screen that shows the main room, just outside the elevator, and there is one that shows the hallway Alex was just in. There is one outside a completely separate building: the garage, presumably. And there is one that seems to be showing a view from atop the fin, or at least somewhere close to it: the roof of the house, the edge of the cliff, a wall of the garage just in frame.

Beneath the screens sits a desk with a mouse and a keyboard and an ergonomic chair. Alex sits down. When she hits the right arrow key on the keyboard, the green highlight switches screens; when she moves the mouse, a scrollbar appears on the screen with the green highlight. She clicks the dot at the end of the scrollbar and moves it back. As she does, she watches as the scene of the back door unfolds in reverse, the light slowly growing dimmer before it fades into nighttime, bugs buzzing around the camera. She switches screens and does the same thing. The same result: the light disappearing into itself, bugs the only life on the screen.

Finally, she comes back around to the front door. She scrolls it back, and this time there is something novel: herself, first appearing outside the door, then backing away from it into the forest. While she is at the door, the screen splits, showing the footage of her face that she saw while she was entering the code. When she reverses away, the image disappears.

Watching the tiny, grainy figure of herself advance and retreat — her obvious anxiety and focus as she entered the code into the door — strikes Alex as hilarious. She moves the mouse back and forth, back and forth, watching her little avatar approach and retreat, approach and retreat. She is a very stupid, very power-less god, and she amuses herself for a few minutes this way until her stomach lets out a menacing growl. She has completed the tasks on the list. The only thing that remains is to do whatever she wants.

As she slides the scrollbar back to the present, something catches her eye. In the moments after she disappears inside the door, there is a movement. Not a full figure like her own, moving slow and predictable back and forth, back and forth. Just a flash. She scrolls slowly, pinpointing the exact frame when it appeared onscreen.

It is about thirty seconds after she entered the house. Standing in the doorway like a waiting guest, a shadow, slightly slouched, with no hands, no hair, no visible features. No face appears in split-screen. There is nothing there but a hint of a shape of a person. And then, a second later, it is gone.

"I am not paranoid anymore," Alex explains to her shaking hands. She wants to be anywhere other than this tiny, gloomy room, deep in the concrete belly of this house. She gets up quickly, grabs her bag. "I am not paranoid," she says, opening the door, letting it fall shut behind her as she looks up the elevator code again — 7007, she has to fucking remember at least one of these idiot codes, let it be this one, 7007 — and punches it into the keypad, her hands visibly shaking. "Cameras do fucked-up stuff all the time. That's why people get ghost hoaxed so easily. It's just a weird shadow. Maybe it's even my shadow." She looks at one of her selves in the elevator's mirrored walls as she speaks, trying to convince them that what she's saying is true. She presses the green button. "It's probably just me. No reason to be afraid." Her stomach lurches. "There's nothing to be afraid of."

She smiles, and in the mirrors, the many selves smile back at her, their eyes betraying their fear.

———

By the time Alex reaches the top of the spiral staircase, she is nauseous and extraordinarily hungry. Over her two weeks with Ella, her body must have realized its previous state of deprivation and gotten reacquainted with eating a human amount of food; now it demands it angrily, and her guts are constantly tying and untying themselves. And the journey up a glass-enclosed corkscrew, steep and suspended in air, hasn't helped her queasiness. Ella had been apologetic about the inaccessibility of the bedrooms, evasive about why the elevator didn't go there, but nothing in her description had prepared Alex for this ascending hell. It takes her what feels like an hour to get up the stairs. She keeps having to stop, perching dangerously on the tiny rectangles, to sit and catch her breath. When she reaches the top, she is on the verge of collapse.

But there are still a few steps to go. According to Ella, she can sleep in whichever of the four bedroom suites she wants to. They all have adjoining bathrooms, all have little living areas with couches and chairs for guests, all face the ocean, and apparently one of them has a library of sorts. "The library room is the best one, in my opinion," Ella said. "But it's up to you. There's no accounting for taste."

Alex opens the hallway's first door to a bright white room. The bed is the size of a boat and the texture of a cloud, draped in a bulbous white down duvet and stacked with dozens of plumped pillows. There are no books to be seen, but there is a TV mounted on the wall, and a hard sectional couch facing it. On a shiny black coffee table rests a stack of architecture magazines.

The second door opens to a room exploding with colour. Floral shapes dance across the walls — ovals of pink, yellow, red, purple with veins of green — and the small bed, low to the ground, is covered with several different fleece throws. A trio of plush armchairs surround a round glass table. It is, on the whole, garish. Alex can't imagine how anyone would be able to sleep in this room, with these colours shining so relentlessly.

Beginning to feel a bit like Goldilocks, Alex opens the door to the third room. Immediately, she knows she has found the library room. It's not just the oak bookshelves, crammed to bursting, that line the walls. It's the way the room is homey, warm and safe, even though Alex has never stepped in a room like it in her life. She walks in, runs her fingers over the quilt on the bed, an extraordinary patchwork of tiny triangles depicting a lighthouse in a storm, a boat crashing over the rocks. There is only one chair in here, but it is tall, sturdy, with the texture of crushed velvet, and beside it is a hefty slab of cedar that has been fashioned into a table. The window that faces the ocean, Alex notices, is split into sections, unlike in the other rooms. When she gets closer to it, she notices that there's a door to the outside. When she slides it open, she discovers a small balcony, invisible from outside the house, where a red blanket has been left draped on the glass rail. She doesn't even need to go back to the hallway. The pull of the forest, her dreams of the sea, even the fear, the forgotten four digits, the corner of a smile: all of them fade, and Alex can see herself staying in just this room, not going anywhere, for the rest of the summer.

Slowly, luxuriating in every detail, she hangs her clothes in the walk-in closet, scans the spines of the books, feels the cool marble floor of the bathroom against her hot, throbbing feet as she goes to run a bath. The bathtub is round, deep, with seats and jets at the feet and the back. Alex almost shivers envisioning the baths she'll be able to take here, every single day the tension her body has held for so long unravelling in the hot water. In the cupboard under the sink, she finds an unopened package of Epsom salts and a sea sponge. Folded neatly on the side of the tub are fresh towels and a bathrobe. Alex unravels the bathrobe with delight, and to her great surprise and amusement, finds the initial *A.* monogrammed on the breast pocket. Maybe Ella ordered this for her, had it delivered because she knew she would love it. She can't wait to put it on after her bath and lounge in bed, maybe with one of the books from the bookshelf. She can't remember the last time she read a book that wasn't for school.

She picks up her phone and almost texts Ella to tell her that she was right, that the entire house might as well not exist except for the library room, but she remembers that by now Ella will be on her long flight, will have given her phone to her parents, who, in turn, are on their way to Tenerife. Besides, the reception doesn't seem to be good in here. In certain spots in the room, the bars go full, but some — the bed, the chair, the bathroom — are total dead zones. Even the Wi-Fi doesn't seem to work. The quirks, Alex supposes, of a structure that exists for its form rather than its function.

Alex scarfs down two protein bars from the box in her bag. Then, pouring water into the well of her throat, she drops four of the sleeping pills into her mouth, lets them sink, swallows. She hasn't taken any since she left the dead campus apartment, but she kept refilling her prescription, telling the psychiatrist on their occasional phone check-ins that she was taking everything as normal. The sleepless nights, the sweats and shaking of withdrawal, were worth it for this: the ability to disappear whenever she wants to.

The steam from the bath starts to waft out of the bathroom. Alex is already starting to melt into her skin. She lowers herself into the bath. The jets drum gently against her spine and her feet like a second heartbeat. The hot water holds her as she drifts off into nowhere. Warm, at first, and hazy — then growing colder, the light diminishing.

—

Alex is drowning. She jolts up out of the tub, coughing, arms flailing. She had been in the dark: what happened to the dark? She is cold, but there is a burning around her wrist, as though someone had recently grabbed and twisted it.

This has happened before, hasn't it?

She tastes the pills in the back of her throat, remembering where she is. She is at 709. She is not paranoid anymore. She is safe; she hasn't spoken to Adam in months; she doesn't know where he is, but it is certainly not here. That was a dream, she tells herself, rubbing her pruny fingers, even though whatever the dream contained is already slipping away from her. That was just a dream.

Though the bath does seem to have helped her ankles, she has been asleep for god knows how long in a bizarre position, her back sliding out from under her, her neck bent over sideways. The water has gone completely cold. When she stands, pain shoots up from the base of her spine; when she turns her head to look at herself in the mirror, the same pain explodes in her neck. She should have known better than to take four pills just to relax; her tolerance after two weeks without had to be as low as it had been in years. Now she'd deprived herself of the benefits of her bath and given herself new aches on top of the existing ones.

She clambers out of the tub, drapes the robe over her body, closing it tight around the front. She is shivering slightly, a result of having been asleep in the cold water. Carefully, trying not to disturb her back and her neck, she walks back into the library room, where the red evening light is beginning to spill into the western sky. It is a magnificent view. Maybe she could get the telescope from the main floor up here, somehow, up the stairs in separate pieces, or as an exception to the no-elevator rule.

But for the moment, she is so achy and tired, and she needs to lie down, to actually lie down, in a bed, and get some actual rest, even just for a little while. She buries herself under the covers and closes her eyes, and it seems like only moments pass before she bolts up again, unrested, like someone had shaken her awake. Her phone tells her that it's 7:36. The brief instant she was asleep was, it seems, the entire night.

She wishes she felt rejuvenated, but at least she can get an early start. Today will be her first day really living on the island, and as such — even though it falls under the purview of Ella's directive to do whatever she wants — there's a steep learning curve ahead of her. The most pressing need is food. There is nothing in the house, she's been told, except for an unknown amount of indeterminate game meat, delivered by a local hunter and frozen months ago in a freezer room somewhere in the basement. The idea of going into the basement again is daunting enough, but thinking about attempting to cook deer or rabbit or whatever creature is in that freezer is enough to make Alex never want to eat meat again. In order to get food, she will have to find an e-bike in the garage, figure out how to ride it, and then figure out how to get across the island to the village and back without getting lost or hit by a car. And Alex, who has always preferred to have her feet on the ground, is not at all a confident cyclist.

She gets dressed quickly. Pants and long sleeves this time, now that she knows she'll have to bushwhack. She slams back one of the meal replacement drinks she brought with her from the city, runs her hand through the pocket of the robe. Sure enough, she finds a hair elastic and pulls her hair back tight. When she looks in the mirror, she sees almost a completely different person than the one who came in yesterday, haggard and cargo-shorted, bent under the weight of the backpack, the many copies of that person who surrounded her in the elevator, their mouths smiling and their eyes stricken. The person who looks back at her now is still tired, a little weathered, but ready to face the world. With her ponytail positioned behind her neck and the pants hugging her long legs, it's like she's stepped back in time: like she's seeing herself four years ago, up at seven for a sunrise run around the seawall, believing even then that everything would turn out alright.

She takes off her glasses, puts on her aviators. Out over the ocean, the colours grow brighter. Alex steels herself, readies her bottle of Aleve, sets aside her driftwood walking stick — if she's going to be riding a bike, there's no reason to be carrying it around. It's time to go down the stairs.

———

The staircase is no more forgiving in descent than it was going up. As she inches down the stairs, every shuffling step hurting her more, Alex wonders why she couldn't have just brought the stick for the stairs and left it in the main room. She wonders, too, why the architect would create a staircase this narrow and winding and steep without any railing, and why he chose to encase it in a tube of glass, like the people within were some kind of experiment to be observed. She uses the glass to steady herself, but the squeaking of her skin against its smooth surface makes her queasy. Eventually, she sits down and lowers herself painstakingly from stair to stair on her butt. Will she have to do this every time she needs to leave the library room? Will she have to adapt, convert the barren, cavernous main floor into her living space? But she wouldn't be able to do that, not with the windows surrounding her, the cold vastness of this space, and not when she knows that the library room exists. No, she'll have to figure out some way to deal with it.

It is surprisingly cold outside, and even colder as Alex walks around the back of 709 to what Ella called "the gear shed." It's not much of a shed. It looks like a small house, and, apart from the lack of windows, would certainly be nicer to live in than many of the places Alex has lived in her life. Alex wrote the door codes she'll need on her phone before she left the library room, saving her from toting the papers around with her. This door code is 8122. The door is heavy, reinforced, and it takes Alex some effort to shove it open.

True to the name, the gear shed is packed to bursting with gear. There are kayaks, e-bikes, paddleboards on one wall, power tools and other scary-looking maintenance equipment on the other. At the end of the shed are closets where all the little accoutrements are held, the helmets and air pumps and oars. Alex marvels at the size of everything. She picks herself out a shiny black helmet from the closet and peruses the selection of bikes. Most of them are the same model, a modest, chunky, matte-black affair, but tucked into the middle of the row is a bike that is clearly special. The frame is light and sleek, even as it bears the electric motor. The paint, which Alex figures must be custom, is an iridescent silver.

This bike obviously belongs to someone specific. But as she scans the rest of the bikes — all plain and clunky — it seems to Alex that this is the only one she could possibly ride, the only one she'd be comfortable with. She could never commandeer the other bikes, not with how heavy they were. It's probably Ella's bike, anyway, she reasons, as she unlocks it, wheels it out, grips the thick handles. If it's Ella's bike, then she'd want Alex to use it. And there's no way Alex will crash hard enough to actually damage it. She might not be a good cyclist, but she's not hopeless. The seat, wide and cushion-soft, is already right at Alex's hip. Ella's height. She needs no other sign.

She pedals cautiously at first, doing small circles around the dry grass until it feels natural, steering well clear of the cliff. Then she turns up the motor boost. She wasn't pedalling hard before, but it has somehow gotten easier. Another notch, and her legs are encountering barely any resistance at all, like they're suspended in thin air. Too much for her, too fast. She turns the resistance down another notch and sets off down the trail to the parking lot. She enters the trees at a slow, steady pace, but as the brush grows thicker, she figures that being careful is hindering her, not helping her; at this speed, every bump in the ground is a roadblock. So she picks up her feet, leaning into the handles, ducking under the salmonberry branches flying at her with increasing speed. Almost without noticing, she is going faster than she ever has on a bike in her life, and just as she notices that, she emerges into the parking lot, out beside the NO TRESPASSING sign.

Alex brakes. She looks behind her in disbelief. It seemed impossible that that was the same trail she'd struggled through the day before. It was like nothing, like a passing breeze. She's barely even sweating.

Energy floods through her body. It really is like four years ago. She hops back into the saddle and hits the pedals hard, dust kicking up from behind her. Four years ago was the first time she actually tried to kill herself. She'd had the half-hearted gestures toward it before, back in high school, that got her nowhere: brief hospital stays and overmedication and counsellors who didn't follow up. This time, though, for real: in the hospital for three months, bored and lonely and sad, every day in tiny rooms taking long tests, picking plastic buttons out of a tin to represent her relationships with other people as the elderly psychologist silently took notes. The psychiatrist kept forcing her into family therapy with her dad, even though it always ended up with him yelling at her. Staring at the ceiling, praying that if she fell asleep, she would fall asleep forever. And then she got out: in the worst shape of her life after months of rotting on failed medication after failed medication. And she started running again, even though she thought, at first, that there would be no point.

But it was better than ever. The struggle made her clean. After a few months of morning runs, it was personal bests on every trail. She started thinking about training for races again, real races, full days on the mountain. She went to parties. She bought clothes she liked, for the first time in her life. She was confident. When she was sad — and she still got sad, crushingly sad, so bad that she couldn't move some days — there were people who said they wanted to help her, and she really believed that they were telling the truth. She didn't talk to her dad, didn't return his increasingly rage-filled calls.

And then one night, a few years down the line on the way to a party downtown, she sat across from a weird guy on the bus. He was fidgeting with what looked like a roll of thread. They stared at each other for five stops. At the sixth, he got up and sat beside her.

"What's your name?" she said, even though she never talked to strangers like that. She was grinning like an idiot.

He smiled: a half-smile, amused but trying not to show it, the corner of his mouth turning up just a little bit. He adjusted his glasses. "I'm Adam," he said, extending his hand, and Alex grabbed it.

"Alex," she said, and they shook. His hand was a little sweaty. His grip matched hers exactly. Some part of her must have known what that handshake was agreeing to.

But none of it matters now. Everything bad has already happened to her. It's already happened to her multiple times over. Here she is, though. Here she still is, flying, unstoppable.

Up and down the winding island road she sails, no cars in sight, pedalling hard and fast but not off-balance, not so much that it hurts, like the wind itself is carrying her forward. She can't believe she ever tried to ride a normal bike. She can't believe no one told her this was possible. The odometer ticks upward, the kilometres building up behind her with unbelievable speed.

A big climb appears ahead of her, the one she had been afraid of while plotting her route. The elevation change is huge. But Alex is unfazed. She turns the boost up to maximum, then turns it down a level. Then another.

I can do this.

*I can do this.*

And she stands on the pedals, tensing the muscles in her legs, fingers white against the handles. She digs. It gets harder, but she knew it would: she let it get harder because she knew she could do it anyway. Halfway up, her thighs are burning, and her breath comes in gasps — no longer easy, in through the nose and out through the mouth, but taking all the air in that she can get, any way she can get it. She visualizes the oxygen all around pouring into her, running red through her veins, powering every molecule in her body. *I'm almost there* — her pedalling slows, she sits back on the seat — almost at a crawl, unable to form a thought, the sweat dripping down her forehead — and then her eyes open, and she leans over, rests her foot on the ground.

Below her, spread out like a tapestry, is the entire world. The rolling green hills of the island, dotted with rooftops, tumbling down to the shore, where the ocean is blue gold. The waves, from up here, look like wrinkles. There, the other islands, tall shapes emerging from the deep. Ferries off in the distance. The horizon, going on forever. Alex stands there at the top of it all, drinking the view in like water.

"Made it," she pants, and her face hurts from smiling.

It isn't until she is almost down to the village that Alex starts to encounter cars. Just a few of them, at first, mostly pickup trucks hauling gardening material, plants, or planks of wood, slowly making their way down the steep descent of the main road. Those are easy to hear coming, easy to pull off to the shoulder for, and even when Alex doesn't have time to pull over, it's easy enough for them to gently swerve around her. Soon, though, the frequency of cars increases, their speeds faster and their movements more erratic. Alex doesn't want to get off her bike here; on this hill, and with limited space at the side of the road, it would certainly be more dangerous. But she proceeds slowly, braking almost constantly, her senses activated like a prey animal. It doesn't help that her neck remains nearly immobile. She worries, now reaching the beginning of the line of idling cars waiting for the ferry, their fumes surrounding her, about what might happen if a car moves behind her too fast for her to react to. She slows down even more. Not far now from the grocery store: the turn into the parking lot is up ahead, blessedly on her right, and she readies herself to pull in.

Just as she does, a car comes up fast and loud behind her like a sudden wave. She swerves hard, off the shoulder, barely managing to brake in time to avoid slamming her body into an embankment. The car screeches to a near-halt, and the smell of burning rubber and fuel surrounds her. The passenger-side window rolls down, and a young man in a baseball cap and sunglasses leans out. He flicks the end of a cigarette.

He yells, and even though she can't hear it over the din of the road and her blood pumping, the sharpness of it hits her in the chest, the spit in each consonant. The window rolls up, and the car speeds away, weaving through the ferry line, its engine revving. Alex can't hear it, but she knows that whoever is in the car is laughing.

On the dry ground, the cigarette continues to burn. Alex has a horrible vision: flames leaping up, catching the line of hot, idling cars. The smell of gasoline. She hops off the bike and stomps frantically on the cigarette, then pours what little is left in her water bottle on it for good measure. The result is no fire, an end to the smoke, but a crushed-up, soggy cigarette on the ground, too disintegrated for Alex to pick up and dispose of. If she hadn't been biking there, if she hadn't been biking so slowly, then maybe this piece of toxic waste wouldn't be lying around for some poor creature to eat.

Here on the east side of the island, the pavement getting the full power of the sun from the time it rose, the heat is bearing down on her. She walks her bike the short remaining distance into the parking lot of the little shopping square. There's knick-knack shops, a bookstore, a pet store, the post office. She spies the grocery store over at the far corner. Alex locks her bike outside, takes off her helmet, and subtly checks how she looks in the mirror. Stray hairs are frizzing up from her scalp, escaping her ponytail. She is visibly sweaty, and her cheeks are flushed with exercise. She does not look sexy. But, she figures, with her helmet in hand, at least it's clear what she's been doing. A cyclist on the island who can say that they're there for a purpose.

The grocery store is less stressful than the grocery stores back in the city. It doesn't have the peeling linoleum, the bright, buzzing lights, the obnoxious music blasting from the speakers; the few people milling around the store don't have the same frenzied energy as the overloaded cart-pushers Alex is used to. But it also doesn't feature many of the recognizable cooking-minimal items she normally gravitates toward, the good instant ramen and the frozen pizzas. Alex wanders around, trying to identify ingredients to make burgers; they seem like an appropriate food for the season. She throws in a big bag of rice, too, even though she's never made rice without a rice cooker. The bill is more than she was anticipating for the quantity of food she's bought, enough to nearly max out her credit card, but she pushes away the instinctual fear. She no longer has to worry about where her next dollars will be coming from.

The grocery journey having been, despite the cost, far less of an ordeal than she expected, Alex decides to take this opportunity to explore the amenities that the island has to offer. She pokes around the knick-knack stores, which mostly seem to be catering to tourists. One of the stores does have a range of bird-themed merchandise. Alex takes a picture of a shirt with a portrait of a turkey vulture on it. She'll have to come back and get it once she gets paid. The tiny bookstore is far more fruitful, with one of its three displays composed entirely of self-published island-specific nature guides. Those go on future Alex's shopping list, too. She considers going to the post office to set up a P.O. box, but it would be more hassle than she's willing to deal with today.

Down the road to the cove, the ferry line has grown oppressive. Cars are packed together, and those who are this far up the line are beginning to realize that they're not going to be making it on the next ferry sailing. Some stay seated inside with the windows rolled down, clinging to the hope that they'll be able to squeeze on. Other people are leaning on their cars tragically, and still others seem to be lost, wandering off aimlessly across the road to nowhere.

Alex's thought, as she drifts lazily down the street, is to turn right and coast down to the end of the road, to the ferry dock, and turn around there. That way she can avoid having to take a hard left through the ferry line and run the risk of being surprised by an oncoming car.

As she rolls down the slope, though, she passes the café, and another thought stops her in her tracks. She hops off, jumps up to the sidewalk. Now that she is not in a frenzy, she can actually take a look at those four digits she failed to remember yesterday, and stare, again, at that familiar corner of a photo, the edge of a half-smile. She hurries up to the kiosk that houses the bulletin board.

It is empty. The rusted-shut latch no longer exists. There are no papers pinned to the board; there is, in fact, not even a board at all. There is just a space where something used to be. Alex swings it open, just to make sure all the posters haven't been moved into some secret hidden compartment within the kiosk. But there is nothing.

The café is extremely busy, the tourists stuck in the ferry line all walking down to get some sustenance while they hang in limbo. The woman from yesterday is not at the register. Instead, it's a teen — a boy who is, absurdly in this heat, wearing a black beanie and a textured wool cardigan. He is rushing around placating disgruntled customers, correcting orders, being politer than polite, occasionally running back into the kitchen to relay some change in directions to his colleagues making the food. By the time Alex gets to the front of the line, the teen is wiping sweat from his brow with the sleeve of his sweater. He looks up, and when he realizes that Alex saw him run his arm across his forehead, he looks a little sheepish.

"Hi there!" he says, pitching his voice up brightly. "What can I do for you!"

"Could I get an iced americano to go? Large and black?"

"Sure thing!" He punches numbers into the register vigorously, single-fingered, like he's popping bubbles. "Anything else I can do for you!"

"Yeah," Alex begins to say, and then hesitates; she doesn't want to make this kid's life more difficult when he's clearly busy. But if she comes back later and that woman is at the register again, she'll have zero chance of getting any answers about the poster that was on the bulletin board.

"Yeah," she says, "actually, I was wondering about the bulletin board. You know, the one outside? There was a poster that I was interested in. I saw it yesterday, but I didn't get a chance to write down the information on it, and now it's gone."

"Oh, yeah," the kid says. "My boss — the woman who owns this place — she actually cleared it out yesterday." He looks apologetic. "I'm sorry. She said that no one had used it in a long time, and that it was just attracting 'weird people.'"

"That's too bad."

"But," the kid says, "if you come back some other time, like later in the week, I can ask her if she put the posters away somewhere and tell you what I find out."

"Wow!" Alex is surprised. "Uh, thank you. Yes, I will do that."

"Great!" The kid beams at her. "And so, is there anything else I can do for you today?"

"Nope, that's it."

"Great!" he says again and rushes away before she even finishes paying.

When he delivers her iced americano five minutes later, he presents it to her with a little flourish. "For you," he says.

Alex laughs. "Thank you."

"When you come back," the kid calls to her, already hurrying away, "if you don't see me, ask if Leo is around. I usually am."

"Thanks, Leo."

"No problem, Alex!" he says. And before Alex can ask him how he knows her name, he is gone.

———

Alex gets back to 709 just in time for the hottest part of the afternoon, sweaty and tired and sunburned. She didn't make any effort to push hard on the return trip, content after her earlier triumph to just set the bike to maximum boost and let it do the work for her. Every summer the sun seems to get closer to her skin, and at this hour, she just wants to be inside: ideally, lying in bed after a cold shower, watching an endlessly unfurling series of nonsense on YouTube.

Before she does that, though, she has to cook this beef. Alex has experienced enough rotten-food disasters to know that she is not to be trusted with raw meat. If she cooks up her burgers now, even if she burns them, at least they can go in the freezer and remain safe to eat, rather than becoming an oozing bacterial breeding ground.

As she steps into the kitchen for the first time, she wonders how a shorter person would be able to operate in here. Everything, from the stove to the counters to the microwave, is up astonishingly high. She stretches up on tiptoe, opening and closing cupboards, searching for a nonstick pan. She finds it in the last cupboard she opens, the one directly above the shiny gas stove. Of course. She is glad that no one is here to observe her lack of common kitchen sense.

Now she turns her focus to the stove. Gas stoves make her nervous. She has always been terrified of dying in a fire, and she has read too many news stories about accidental carbon monoxide poisoning. One accidental nudge of the dial with an elbow, and your home is filled with deadly gas before you even know it. Surely whatever uniquely potent cooking properties the flames possessed weren't worth the ever-present risk of accidental death.

She takes a moment to rally her courage, then turns the dial on the burner. It clicks twice, and then a small blue flame leaps up under the pan. She drops a frozen patty onto the hot pan. It sizzles immediately, and Alex's stomach roars its approval.

The kitchen sink, much to Alex's delight, is motion-activated. She washes her hands, then pokes around the kitchen for any cooking implements she can find. A drawer houses shiny metal cooking tools, including a burger flipper. A cupboard in the kitchen island is home to dozens and dozens of identical white ceramic plates and bowls. Alex pulls out a plate, arranges a pair of buns with lettuce on them, slices up half a tomato. Then she turns to the stove and flips the burgers just as one side was about to burn. The delicious smell fills the kitchen, and Alex is extraordinarily proud of herself. Here she is, in a new place, cooking her own meal.

The only thing she wishes is that the kitchen had a seat. There is no dining area, no bar stools around the kitchen island, and nothing kills her ankles faster than standing in place. So she does little laps, padding around the island as the meat cooks, gradually speeding up until she gets slightly dizzy. She used to do this when she was a kid, spinning in circles in the centre of the living room until she fell over, running around the dinner table until she crashed into the wall. She thought everyone else found it as entertaining as she did. She loved to wear a flouncy skirt, tie strings and ribbons to her wrists so that they flowed out behind her like the tail of a kite. That was what she did the second time the paramedics came for her mom: "Look!" she said, and spun, arms out and eyes closed, and by the time she opened her eyes again, she was lying on the floor and everyone was gone.

The smell of the meat begins to take on a slightly burned quality, so Alex stops, steadying herself against the kitchen island, her vision a little blurry. She wobbles over to the stove, turns the gas off, jiggles the dial a bit to confirm it's not on. Two of the burgers she lifts onto her prepared buns. The rest she plops into a bowl, covers with a plate, and then promptly shovels into the freezer high above her head.

The wind seems to have picked up outside. The thick glass blocks out most outside noise, but Alex can just hear the shimmering sounds of cedar branches in the wind. She walks outside, freeing her hair from the ponytail, and the breeze rifles its fingers through her heavy hair. Through the grass, she walks all the way up to the edge of the cliff, where she sits, her legs dangling down.

The tide has pulled far out, exposing the beach beyond the large rocks. Craggy, darkened with mussels and barnacles and seaweed, there are tide pools carved in the stone. As the beach extends farther out, it turns to gravel, the big rocks growing more scattered, fewer and farther between, until, right where the waves are lapping up against the shore, Alex can see the bright gleam of soft ocean-floor sand.

She takes a bite of her burger — delicious, perfectly cooked, exactly what she needs right now — and ponders how she could get down to the beach. Scaling the cliff is an obvious no-go. But there has to be a path somewhere. Otherwise, why would Ella's parents keep all these kayaks and paddleboards on hand? The path to and from the parking lot didn't seem to have any other trails extending off it. She'll have to consult Ella's map. Out in the water, the lighthouse stands tall, and Alex wonders if she'll have to walk all the way over there to get down to the ocean.

For now, the breeze and the view and her picnic are enough. She eats slowly, savouring her meal. When her plate is empty, she lies back in the grass, her feet in the air over the cliff's edge, and with her eyes closed, she listens. To her own breaths, slower and steadier by the second; the quiet, distant movement of the ocean; the cedars, still whispering; the occasional song of a bird, the cry of a seagull out on the shore. Sometimes she hears crunching leaves in the bushes, but she reminds herself of the deer, how they're everywhere here on the island because there is nothing, save people with guns, that will kill them. When the huge empty eyes of the deer appear in her memory, she sees them, looks at them, and with an exhale allows them to melt away.

Shadows pass across her face, too, sometimes moving quickly, other times lingering. There are clouds in the sky, soft and white, pushed across the sun by the wind off the ocean. There is nothing to be afraid of. She is completely safe here. And the longer she lies there, the sun warming her skin, the more she begins to believe — deep and warm, in her mind and her body — that it's true.

—

The sky is alight when Alex sits up, the sun blazing above the horizon, so bright that it hurts her eyes even behind her sunglasses. She has no sense of how long she's been lying in the grass. But here, she reminds herself, she doesn't have to worry about wasting time. It's not like school with its relentless stream of work, or like work, where any moment of reprieve was considered as bad as theft. With a yawn, she stretches her arms upward, tilts her neck gently left and right, the tight muscles loosening. A few mosquitoes are beginning to buzz around her; she can hear the nauseating whine in her ears as they get close to her face. Time to go back inside.

When she steps back into the house, she is surprised by how dark it is. Having slept through the parts of yesterday that would have been sunless, she has no idea how to turn any of the lights on. She makes a beeline for the stairs. There's no way she's contending with the possibility of having to scale them without sunlight. Going down on her butt made her realize that crawling might be the easiest way to get back up, so that's what she does: crouched like an animal, hands on the stairs above her, clambering as fast as she can around and around the spiral until she reaches the top, out of breath, her toes throbbing.

Alex is tired, but she doesn't want to go to sleep quite yet. There's still plenty of day ahead of her. She'll have to figure out how to get some light working in here. She scans the room for light switches but finds none. The bathroom's lights turn on automatically when she opens its door, so she takes refuge in there, bringing the envelope with Ella's cheat sheets along with her. Flipping through the pages, she remembers that 709 is a smart home — that she can, in theory, simply talk to it in order to turn the lights on. Sure enough, at the bottom of one of the pages, Ella has written, VOICE ACTIVATION: SAY, *709*.

Alex steps back out into the dimming library room. She looks up at the ceiling, as if she'll be able to see the device listening to her. "709," she says loudly.

Nothing happens. Maybe she has to pair it with a command. "709, please turn the lights on."

The lights turn on.

Despite herself, Alex is frightened by this: this not-alive, unthinking entity that cannot speak, that can only take commands, and yet, if it were to malfunction, would be capable of locking her in this house in complete darkness with no means of escape. Cautiously, she lies down in the bed, burying herself under the quilt, in disbelief that a genuine piece of art could be this cozy, shaking off the sense of being watched. She is about to open her laptop when she remembers that the bed is one of the weird electronic dead zones in this room, where the Wi-Fi doesn't reach and her phone has no reception. In her pocket, her phone starts vibrating.

For a second, she only wonders who might be calling her. Then she remembers why she had just groaned. Was the dead zone only a first-day thing? Had 709 fixed it once she interacted with it for the first time? She takes the phone out of her pocket. The number on the cracked screen doesn't have the normal ten digits; the number is far shorter.

Alex answers, confused. "Hello?"

"STAY INSIDE."

"What?"

"STAY INSIDE." The voice is robotic, inhuman. The syllables seem to have been cut together from snippets of other words. They are choppy and insistent, and the words keep repeating. "STAY INSIDE. STAY INSIDE. STAY INSIDE. STAY—"

Alex throws the phone away from her. It crashes into the chair and falls silent. She stays completely still, as if whoever was calling would start calling again if it sensed life in her. There are bugs crawling under her skin.

"What the fuck?" she says, even though there is no one listening.

Rigid, barely blinking, Alex stays awake long into the night. The lights stay on.

———

For as long as she can, Alex stays inside. Once a day, she makes the precarious trip down the stairs to the kitchen, heats up a burger, eats it as quickly as she can. When the burgers run out, she eats salted rice sprinkled with frozen peas. Sometimes a shake, sometimes a protein bar. Then it is back to the library room, back into the tub or under the covers. She lies on the floor and watches YouTube videos on autoplay, the algorithm taking her to increasingly bizarre places. A blond woman scoops handfuls of bees out of a rotting wooden box. A man in near-total darkness reviews mealworms. Alex stares at them, struggling to focus, pushing away the bright water beckoning outside her window.

She has thoughts of contacting Ella's parents, to see if they had any explanation for the threatening call. But to bother them with her paranoia so early in what was supposed to be a summer-long gig — no, she decides against it, and her mind is made up even more when the first deposit from them hits her bank account. It's not much, but it's far more money than she's had since January, when her second-semester student loan funding hit. And this was just the first week.

So she doesn't call them, though she does write a note on her phone, now with a sizable chunk chipped off the screen, for her planned recounting of the summer's events to Ella. Not that she can imagine forgetting that phone call, the terrible voice in her ear. But there have been a lot of things in her life that she thought she'd never forget, and she can't remember most of them.

Other than her daily trips to the kitchen, her days pass in silence. She had worried about the kinds of noises she would hear staying alone in a house in the forest. Instead, it is the utter absence of noise that oppresses her, the insulated walls and sound-eliminating glass keeping everything out and sealing her in. The only voices she hears are the ones coming from her laptop, and her own, once every few hours, telling 709 to turn the lights on or off. She tries her best not to have thoughts about anything: not about the house, or the outside world, or the voice on the phone, or Adam, or worst of all herself, her abject failure, sealing herself in this house for what? Because she's afraid of nothing, afraid for absolutely no reason at all, unable to free herself from the fear she created on her own. She can't even take a step out onto the balcony, give herself a single breath of fresh air. Unreasonable and extreme and overdramatic, like she's been her whole life, and all the more foolish for believing that the mere fact of being on this island would change her some-how. She is alone because she has never listened, not to her dad, not to Adam when he tried to help her become better, and really, it's all that she deserves: to be trapped in here, unable to move, both jailed and jailor. She might as well be in the hospital, lying in her little room behind the locked doors. The messages hit the right target.

Sometimes she thinks she can hear a mechanical hum from deep inside the house, like a running engine. She considers reading one of the books on the bookshelves, but many of them aren't in English, an assortment of classic texts in German and French and Russian, and the ones that are in English are either hopelessly dense or unbearably boring. Her drugged sleeps are silent, too, and she wakes up with nothing in her head but a sense of unease, like there is something she should know by now that she doesn't.

———

One day, she finds a pair of binoculars on the bookshelf. She hadn't noticed them, but as she was thinking again about hauling the telescope up, there they were, like an answered wish. Presented with the gift of enhanced sight, she spends hours observing the lazy pace of life on the water. Paddleboarders passing by, sometimes shaky, then tumbling off with great clumsy splashes; she thinks she can see them laughing out there. Seagulls flying up from the shore, starfish crammed in their beaks. There's a seal that keeps bobbing up and down, up and down, and Alex sees its glistening head turning, taking in all the aquatic goings-on. Fishing boats, too, speeding along on their way to deeper, better spots, and at one point, Alex spies a young eagle perched on the railing of the lighthouse, eyes fixed in search of prey. She visualizes the trail map she's been studying, the one that shows the way down to the beach: a fifteen-minute walk to the south, then a hard right down a steep staircase to the shore. Just like the beach back at school.

She can't unhear the voice. STAY INSIDE, it told her. But as the sun reaches its noon peak and begins its descent toward her, and as she watches the eagle as it stands patient on its high vantage points, sees the gleam of its dark eyes, she is reminded of the deer she saw when she was coming in on the ferry, the way it stared at her, the way it jumped straight into the water and seemingly didn't resurface. She had wondered whether there was an explanation for that, and all along, she has had the ability to find one. She forgets, sometimes, that the internet can be a source of actual information.

She flips the open tab on her laptop away from the cursed video she fell asleep watching and searches: "deer jumping in water pacific northwest." The first result is a video thumbnail that seems to show exactly what Alex had seen from the ferry: a deer, small and black-and-white-tailed, splashing into the waves from a rocky cliff.

It was real, then, not just a figment of an overactive imagination, and more than just being real, it was an explicable phenomenon. These deer swam between the islands, in spite of the deep chill of the water and the often great distance between them. She watches the videos, a thrill running through her. They are so small, the deer, and ill-suited, one would think, to swimming in the open ocean, and yet they do it anyway, with such frequency and ease. The more she watches, the more she begins to see the deer not as aberrant in the water, but as beautiful, natural features of it: the antlers, soft and hard at the same time, their points jutting upward like beacons in the waves, and their shining eyes as they looked onward to their destinations. How could she have ever thought that this was some kind of bad omen? How could she see this as anything other than a sign of welcome?

When she takes her eyes off the video, turning her face once again to the windows, something has shifted within her. Whatever had called her, whoever did, it was probably just a scam call. She got them all the time in the city. Probably everyone in her area code had gotten the exact same thing, that urgent injunction to STAY INSIDE, and wouldn't the pranksters be just so tickled to find out that someone had actually been stupid enough to let it scare them into isolation. And even if it was meant to threaten her, specifically — which, as she'd already established, it wasn't — it's not like whoever was calling her could see what she was doing. If they actually had access to her, then they would be fucking with her directly, not wasting time with phones. No, there's no reason to be afraid, no need to even check the number online to confirm the nature of the calls, and already she is standing, putting the binoculars into her backpack, taking off the shirt she's been wearing for the last four days and putting on a new one, slipping her bare legs into a fresh pair of pants. She puts her sunglasses on, ties her hair back.

She will go to the cove today, on the bike; she will buy fresh new food, try cooking a different meal. She will go to the café and ask Leo what he's learned about the posters — ask him, too, how he knew her name. Maybe, now that she has all this money, she'll buy that turkey vulture shirt. A tidepool guide to take to the beach. A disposable camera. And then she will ride back home while the sun sets, and she won't be afraid anymore. She will be brave enough to go back to the security room and run the cameras back. She will no longer allow herself to be trapped.

---

After so long spent in a temperature-controlled room behind tinted glass, the light and the heat outside 709 are blinding. Alex needs time to get her bearings, making sure she has plenty of water in her water bottle, before she heads over to the gear shed to unlock the bike. It is so bright, and she is so determined not to be afraid, that she almost doesn't notice the turkey vulture sitting nearly at eye level in the tree in front of her.

Alex has never seen a turkey vulture this close before. Until she researched the birds on the island, she didn't even know that they lived on this continent. Now, since she's learned what they are, how common they are in the summer, she sees them everywhere:

far above her, wings outstretched, silent and faceless in the distance. This one is not faceless, not when it's this near. Atop its sheathed black body is its small red head, the skinfolds, the bright eye over the bone-white beak. At pains not to startle the bird, she reaches into her backpack and pulls out the binoculars. Up close and in focus, she can see the tufts of hair around the vulture's neck, the bloodstains around its beak, the holes of its ears, and how alert the eye: unmoving, like glass, but alive.

Behind her in the bushes, a branch breaks loudly. The vulture turns its head. When another branch breaks, it alights, the massive wings unfurled, ascending until it disappears into the treetops.

Alex turns toward the noise: heavy, human-sounding footfalls through the shrubbery. She is frozen in place. This is no hallucination, no startled deer. There is a large living thing moving steadily toward her. She knows she should run to the door, flee to safety, but she can't. She has to see what it is, this thing that approaches. She can't spend any more time in the unknowing.

Before she sees it, she sees its shadow, widening out of the bushes, and then it emerges: a crew-socked, Birkenstocked foot on a hairy leg.

It is a man. Not just a man, but a bear: a short bear in tiny pink shorts and a white muscle shirt, brown-skinned and black-bearded, twigs and leaves clinging to his arms and legs, a green bucket hat on his head. He is holding in his hands an expensive-looking camera with a telephoto lens. He looks to the sky, squinting, before taking one very small hand off the camera and trying, vigorously and without success, to brush himself off. Then he looks at Alex, and with the same very small hand, he gives her a tiny, hilarious wave.

"Hey there!" he calls, grinning widely. "Did you happen to see where the vulture went?"

# 3.

Alex is dumbstruck. She can't formulate a response. The bear starts to walk toward her, his Birkenstocks slapping against the ground. She doesn't know what she expected to see coming out of the bushes, but whatever it was, this was not it.

As he gets closer, the details come into view: painted nails, bird tattoos on his left arm, the electric blue frames of his sunglasses, his smile growing progressively bigger. Finally, with the bear almost upon her, she manages to squeak out some words.

"Yeah, actually, it went, like—" She waves her hand in the direction the vulture flew. "I couldn't really see where it went, though."

"Too bad." The bear laughs. "Let's hope something dies around here soon so we can lure it back." He peers at the binoculars in Alex's hands. "Nice bins!"

*Bins?* "Thanks?"

He holds out a small, soft hand. "Can I check them out?"

Alex, barely conscious of her own actions, gives him the binoculars. "Uh, thanks. They're—"

"Oh, shit!" The bear holds the binoculars up to his face, incredulous. "I'm sorry, but are these the fucking Monarch HGs? Excuse my language." He holds them up to his face again, spinning around in wonder like a kid with a kaleidoscope.

"I'm sorry," Alex says. "I actually don't know what they are."

"Oh, so you're like, *rich* rich." The bear seems fixated on the water. He adjusts the focus on the binoculars carefully. "Like, 'I don't even care what it is, just give me the best ones' rich." He extends the binoculars back toward her, and as soon as she takes them, he is pointing his camera toward whatever is out there in the ocean, squinting intently into the viewfinder before he sighs and takes it away from his face. "No, it's too far away. That sucks."

"What is?" Alex asks, before remembering to clarify: "These aren't my binoculars."

"I saw a marbled murrelet out there. Or at least I think I saw one. I don't know, I'm not an expert or anything." He sighs again, dramatically. "Little black birds in the ocean. They could be the rarest bird you've ever seen, or they could just be a seagull in weird light. Who is out here lending you their thousand-dollar binoculars?"

"They weren't lent to me, exactly." Alex is a little nervous now. If she'd known they cost a thousand dollars, she wouldn't have just hucked them in her backpack. "I'm house-sitting—"

"Where?"

"There." She points to 709.

"No way." The bear's jaw drops. "You're lying."

She can't think of anything to say to this, but it doesn't matter: the bear has seen, in her silence, a response. "Holy shit, you're not lying. You're house-sitting in that monstrosity? They don't have a team of armed guards in there?"

"Nope," Alex says, "just me. Sorry to disappoint."

"No no no no no," the bear says, and he is on the tips of his toes with excitement. "This is fucking amazing! When did you get here? I'm Amara, by the way. Who are you? How long have you been here?"

"I'm just Alex," she says apologetically. "I think I got here, like . . ." Her mind goes blank. How long has it been? "I got here in mid-June, I think."

"And how long are you staying?"

"The whole summer, hopefully."

"Alex," Amara says, "can I give you a hug?"

Alex hates hugs. She hates being asked if she can give a hug. But for some reason — maybe the fact that she hasn't seen another living person in so long — she opens her mouth to say no, and what comes out is "Yes."

Amara, camera in hand, throws his arms around her. His hug is fully committed, strong and bracing, even with an occupied hand. Alex, herself holding the binoculars awkwardly, finds herself squeezing back. When they separate, Amara is beaming at her. Then he checks his watch, and his eyes widen.

"Shit," he says, "I gotta run."

"Oh." Everything is happening too much, too fast. Alex is still reeling from the hug. "Uh—"

"Do you want to meet me later?" Amara is already hustling back toward the bushes whence he came, the slap-slapping of his sandals echoing around the clearing.

"How?"

"Will you be here? Can I knock?"

"Uh, sure?"

"Awesome!" He stops one last time, and with his free hand gives Alex another comically tiny wave, rippling his fingers so his nail polish gleams in the sunlight. "See you later, Alex!"

And Alex, feeling like she's just taken a hit of something strong, waves back.

Alex bikes to the village in a daze. She barely even notices the view this time. Cars rev up behind her and speed by, almost grazing her shoulder, and she doesn't flinch. At the grocery store, she throws ingredients into her basket almost at random — shallots, portobello mushrooms, saskatoonberry jam, a box of chickpea pasta — and pays without even processing the value of the food she's bought. All she can think about is Amara. Where he came from, manifesting almost out of thin air in the forest; where he rushed off to; why he wanted to see her again, what he wanted them to do together. Why he was so excited to see her. Why he gave her a hug. That's what spins her head the most as she cruises back to the cape, her backpack heavy against her spine: there was a familiar quality to that hug that she couldn't quite identify.

She is almost back at 709 when it dawns on her that she forgot to go down to the café to talk to Leo. Neither did she buy any of the things she wanted from the knick-knack stores. Too bad, because Amara would have loved the turkey vulture shirt, and then she shakes her head. Why is she, knowing nothing about him, considering what Amara would like? Why has she decided, without even thinking about it, that whenever he shows up at her door, whatever he asks her to do, she is going to say yes?

There is no one standing outside the house when she returns, no evidence of anyone having been there. Alex half-expects Amara to pop out of the bushes again as she scrolls through the notes on her phone, searching for the code for the front door. She punches it in, pauses before she turns the handle. No sign of anyone or anything. She is a little disappointed, then a little annoyed at herself for being disappointed.

In the cold light of the kitchen, she is baffled by her choices in groceries. She has no idea how to cook portobello mushrooms. She has no bread on which to spread saskatoonberry jam, and she doesn't particularly like jam without peanut butter anyway. There is chickpea pasta and a jar of organic pesto sauce: that, at least, could make a coherent dinner. She packs the rest away into the fridge and the freezer and fills a large steel pot with water.

Now to wait. "You know what they say," she can hear her dad saying. "A watched pot never boils." He said this every time she tried to boil water. He genuinely thought it was funny. Alex resents him for planting the phrase in her head, because now, as she stands watching the pot and the flame beneath it, she grows extremely restless. She paces around the kitchen island again, but she doesn't want to get too dizzy, lest she be incapacitated and unable to stop any possible fire. She stands on one leg, then the other, but doing so only makes her ankles hurt more. She checks the water — a beginner move, and she knows it. Sure enough, it is nowhere close to boiling. The floor, then: cross-legged on the cool tile, she at least won't be able to stare at the water's placid surface. She traces the grain of the tile with her fingers. It looks rough, but it's smooth, and the contradictory texture is mesmerizing.

A knock at the door. Her heart rate spikes and an image appears in her mind: Adam, waiting outside the door, waiting, angry that she's making him wait. She shoves the thought away. Adam is not here. It's Amara. Should she invite him in for dinner? But she doesn't actually know if she's allowed to invite people into the house. A knock again, much louder. She turns the stove off regretfully, the time watching the pot gone to waste, and walks over to the door, grabbing her shoes out of the closet, her binoculars from her backpack.

Amara has changed outfits since she last saw him. The bucket hat is the same, and she notices now that there are tiny birds embroidered on it. Instead of pink shorts, he is wearing green ones. It is the polo shirt that is pink now. He is already smiling at her.

"Sorry to bother you at this hour," he says, "but I had been told that someone named Alex has recently taken up residence here."

"You heard right," Alex says, stepping outside and closing the door behind her. She focuses on the ground, trying to conceal what she is certain is a very dumb look on her face.

"And where might I find this Alex?"

"Be careful," she says. "You might not want to find out the answer to that question."

He laughs. He is so nice, and she's a bad person. Standing here awkwardly in front of the door to a mansion she lives in, not even letting him see inside. "Sorry I can't invite you in. I just don't—"

"Oh, no problem, I figured." Amara waves his hand in the air. "I have literally never seen another living person enter this house. I honestly thought it was abandoned. So no expectations of you running raves out of it or anything. Actually," he says, his face alighting with excitement, "I came here to apologize to you."

"What? Why?"

"For running off on you so rudely earlier. I was on my lunch break, and lost track of time, but that's no excuse. And so, as an apology, I have come here to invite you to dinner."

"Oh my god."

"What?" He seems concerned.

"No, no, it's nothing bad." She laughs. "It's just that I hate cooking. Like, I hate it, I'm so bad at it, and I've been staring at this stupid pot of water for pasta that I don't even really want to eat, just praying for it to boil, and it wasn't boiling. So this is—" She laughs again, unable to believe her luck. "This is amazing. Like, yes, please, give me dinner. I would love to have dinner with you."

Amara's smile widens. "Thank god. I was worried you were going to tell me to fuck off and like, slam the door in my face. And then bring out the armed guards." He takes a few steps forward, beckoning her to follow. "But now, I not only get to do penance for my earlier sins, I'm doing an act of charity for a tall, dark stranger in need."

Before Alex can think of a response, Amara is swallowed up by a bush. Her immediate thought is of ticks, but she powers through, emerging on the other side into a place that almost resembles another world entirely. Like a cathedral: the trees reaching up and forming a towering, arched roof, beams of light streaming in, bending on the shiny green leaves as though through stained glass. The sound of the waves has faded, and she can just make out the hammering of a woodpecker somewhere up in the trees.

"Isn't it amazing?" Amara says. "It took me like four months of wandering around the woods like an idiot to find this place. But it was so worth it. And right beside the beach, too? Ugh."

"Yeah. It's perfect."

She's been here before. Somehow. She knows this place.

"Oh, you haven't seen perfect yet. Come on." He forges ahead, following a lightly worn path through the trees, so natural that you might not see it if you didn't know it was there. Occasionally

Alex spots pink tape tied to tree branches: Amara, or perhaps someone else, clearly wanted to remember this trail.

"Did you put these markers up?" she asks. "Just out of curiosity."

"Me? No." He pauses. "Like I said, I'm an idiot. Total dumb city kid. I wouldn't even have thought to do something like that. Good thing someone else did, though!"

"Huh." Alex grimaces, thinking longingly of her walking stick.

Amara frowns. "Are you doing okay?"

"Totally." She forces her face into a smile. "Let's keep going."

"Don't worry. We're almost there."

Just up ahead, a small clearing emerges. There's a car parked there, a tiny silver Toyota, and beside the car an equally tiny house: bright red, windows left open, wind chimes pinging outside the doorway. As they get closer, Alex sees a woefully unused fire pit in front of the house.

"Here we are!" Amara stands on the threshold, his arms spread out, almost as if to hug the little house. "Home sweet home."

———

HOME SWEET HOME, reads the cross-stitch hanging on the inside of the door, its friendly serifed text underlined with a row of embroidered flowers. The space is small, the kitchen only a small counter with a sink, bookended by a fridge and an oven, at one side of the living room. Two plump armchairs, afghans thrown over them, face two big windows; in front of them is a cedar-slab table almost identical to the one in the library room. Indeed, this room might very well be an extension of the library room: its warmth, the way the colours contrast and harmonize, the sturdiness of everything. On the windowless wall, behind the chairs, hangs a massive oil painting depicting in dramatic lashes of pigment the round, blankly observant face of an owl. A narrow pair of stairs, so slight that they might as well be a ladder, lead into a small opening in the ceiling.

"Well?" Amara is busy at the kitchen counter, removing a hefty ceramic bowl from the fridge, shaking various spices into it. "Do you love it?"

"I do love it."

"I can't take credit for the furniture. But everything else I take total credit for." He gestures toward the chairs. "Sit down! The choice is yours. Dinner will be ready in literally one minute, I promise."

Alex sits in the chair with the simpler afghan, striped with bright purples and greens and blues. She sinks into the seat, grateful to be off her feet; the cushioned back of the chair is soft, and she throws her neck back. "I'm sorry," she says. "But as much as I like what you've done with the place, these chairs are the stars."

"I know." Amara walks over with a bowl in each hand. He puts them down on the cedar slab, sliding one over to Alex's side. "They're the best. I knew as soon as I sat on one that living here was going to be worth it." He gestures to the bowl. "Go on! I can't eat until you've taken a bite, and I'm starving."

Alex picks up her bowl. It's full of all kinds of things: fresh mango, grilled chicken, greens, a small grainy pasta that Alex has never seen before. It smells like lemon and pepper and salt. Alex crams one of each thing onto her fork before she takes a bite.

Amara watches her as she chews. "Am I a good cook?" he asks, and she can tell that he's actually a little nervous.

"So good." It is delicious, and Alex has barely finished chewing before she puts another forkful in her mouth. "Oh my god. I'm so glad you brought me here. This is way better than what I would have eaten."

Relaxed, Amara begins to eat as well. He laughs. "And what would you have been eating, alone in that mansion of yours? Pasta, you said?"

"Chickpea pasta. With pesto from the jar. And nothing else, because I didn't buy anything else I know how to cook."

"Oh, honey." He seems to be on the verge of elaborating, but instead he leaps from his chair, startling Alex. "Oh, shit!" He runs over to the kitchen.

"What's going on?" Alex sniffs the air for smoke. "Did you leave the stove burning?"

"No! Oh my god, I am such an idiot."

Alex can't see what he's doing, but she hears the telltale crack and hiss of cans being opened. A few seconds later, Amara returns with two tall glasses of a sparkling amber liquid.

"I can't believe I almost forgot," he says ruefully. "That would have been so tragic."

Alex takes a sip from her glass. It's sweet and spicy, with the characteristic nasal bite of ginger. "This is good," she says. "What is it?"

"It's a fermented ginger thing." Amara takes a gulp from his glass. "I made it a few days ago, specifically because I was planning to drink it with this meal. And to think I would have let us go without!"

"I mean," Alex says, taking another sip, "this is really good. But honestly, the food is good enough that I don't think I would have missed it that much."

"Aww, you flatter me," Amara says. Without his sunglasses and hat on, the gleam in his eyes is obvious. "Hey!"

"Hey."

He raises his glass. "We should do a toast."

Alex raises hers. "Okay, but you have to come up with it."

"What? But you're my honoured guest!"

"As your honoured guest, I choose to do what I want while I'm here. And what I want is to not come up with a toast."

"Fine, fine, fine." He clears his throat. "To meeting weird strangers in the woods."

As they clink their glasses, the hair on Amara's arm brushes against hers. An invisible shiver runs up her arm.

In an attempt to distract herself, she drinks deeply from her glass, then turns to the owl painting. As the two of them eat in comfortable silence — Alex, in spite of her hunger, picking away at her bowl, Amara going back for seconds and thirds — she keeps her eyes fixed on it. It is even more impressive up close: the eye is around the size of Alex's face, and gleams with life even at this distance.

"I *love* this painting," she says after a long time, hitting *love* a little too hard. "Is it, uh."

She can't remember what she was about to say. Too much time has passed, and she's fallen out of the rhythm of speech, and at some point Amara must have put on music, because quiet, delicate piano fills the air. She takes another sip. "Did you, like—"

"Oh, this little thing?" Amara scoffs. "Yeah, I painted it."

"For real?"

"I really like birds. You might not have noticed that about me. Many people don't."

"Are you an artist?"

"It's not 'what I do,' if that's what you're asking."

"What do you do, then?"

"Spreadsheets, mostly."

Alex is incredulous. "What are you in the woods for, then?"

Amara shrugs. "For funsies."

She turns from the painting. She can feel how flushed her cheeks are, but she doesn't care. Amara is grinning at her.

"Explain," she says and crosses her arms.

"Or what?"

"Or I won't leave."

"That's not much of a threat. Have you already forgotten what we toasted to?"

She is about to protest, but he laughs — a barking laugh, straight from the chest, with his full body. "There's just not much to explain, really." He puts a hand on his chest. "Look, I'm a simple man. The lease was up on my apartment, my job started offering fully remote, and so I was just like, fuck it, I'm gonna go look at some birds. And even though there are never rentals available here, the listing just happened to go up the day I started looking. Never even had to set eyes on the people who own this place. They were just like sure, yeah, whatever you want, man. So here I am, month to month, saving tons of money, in total privacy, and I can just go back to the city whenever I want." He pauses. "Or, I guess, not *total* privacy."

"Oh," Alex says. "I get it."

"What do you get?"

"So you're, like, *rich* rich."

He laughs again. "Just a little rich. Like, if I had kids on this salary, I definitely wouldn't be rich."

"Isn't that kind of sketch?"

"What, kids being expensive?"

"No. Sorry, I was just thinking about what you said before that, about renting from people you never met. Or, I guess, people are very often renting from people they've never met, but without ever interacting with another human being about it. No property manager or anything."

He shrugs. "Yeah. But it's worked out so far. It's also kind of sketch to invite random people into your lonely little house in the woods for dinner the day you meet them, but that also seems to be working out so far."

"I mean," Alex says. "I hope so."

They both take sips from their dwindling drinks. Amara's eyes run over her face, searching.

"What are their names?" she says.

"Whose names?"

"The people you rent this place from."

"Okay." He sighs. "I know you already said that this whole arrangement sounds shady to you. And you're going to think I'm a total dupe for saying this. But I honestly have no idea."

"How can you not know? You pay them every month."

"Yeah, but it's just, like, a company. The listing was posted on behalf of the company, all the emails were company emails with no signatures, the pre-authorized debit is to a company account. Whatever individuals were actually interacting with me were acting on behalf of the company."

"Weird."

"A little, yeah."

"I was just thinking," she says. "Before I came here, I was reading about the way these plots of land on the cape were divided up. And it's almost impossible, just based on where we are in relation to 709—"

"709?"

"The mansion I'm staying in. But, like, this has to be on the same plot of land, right? So—"

"So you think the people who are paying you to stay in their scary-ass fortress are the same people I'm paying to stay in my wonderful little cabin in the woods." He strokes his beard.

"Yes." Following this train of thought has exhausted Alex immensely. She sinks lower in her chair, face turned upward. "Basically, yes."

"Well, do the people you're house-sitting for own Balthius Holdings Limited?"

"I have no idea. I know they're the Smiths."

"So you know them personally?"

"Yeah."

"Huh."

Alex remembers the NO TRESPASSING signs. She'd read about some company buying up almost all the land on this part of the island, gradually, in pieces, over the course of decades. How people were worried about what was going to happen here: whether it would be clear-cut for mansions and helipads, transformed into a place for only the wealthy. People were scared. Was that all Ella's parents? Was that why they were so concerned about people coming near the house?

But this is not a good line of thought to pursue. This is a spiral. "Ugh, I'm sorry. I don't know why I got so fixated on this. Let's change the subject."

"No, I get it," Amara says. "It would be kind of fucking weird if these people sent you to house-sit for the entire summer and didn't tell you about the bearded guy living in the woods."

"So," Alex says, sitting upright. "What birds do you have tattooed?"

"Oh, you really want to change the subject."

"Is that a puffin?"

"Close." Amara extends his arm. The bird in question is right above his wrist, its wings outstretched, webbed feet grazing the surface of the water. "This is actually a surf scoter."

Alex loves the bird's face: a white-ringed eye, a chunky orange beak shaped like a smile. "Could I—"

But Amara has already scooted closer to her, extending his left forearm over the arm of her chair. "And there above it, that one flying — that's a double-crested cormorant. I'll have to show you a picture of one — during breeding season they get these, like, amazing blue-green crests and eyelashes, it's stunning. And up here —" he points now to his bicep, where a tattooed tree extends its branches "— this tiny one is a brown creeper. Turkey vulture, of course. This one flying is a lazuli bunting. And this pair of love-birds are western tanagers."

The tanagers are both a bright yellow that culminates in a bright red around their heads, and in the tattoo, they seem to be dancing together in the air, wings outstretched.

"This is my gayest tattoo by far," Amara clarifies.

"They're really beautiful." She wants to reach out and run her fingers over them, but she holds back.

"Thank you." Amara moves his arm back to his chair. "I think so, too."

"Why do you like birds so much? Sorry." Alex cringes at herself. "That was such a dumb question."

"It's really not. But," Amara says, his gaze turning to the disappearing light outside the window, "it has sort of a long answer. And if you hang out here much longer, you will actually be staying here, because there is no chance I'll be able to find the trail in the dark."

Alex hadn't even noticed how much the light had faded. How long had they spent eating without speaking, with her staring at the painting like she was in a gallery? She's too used to being alone; she doesn't know how to measure out interactions with other people anymore. She rises, her head swimming. "You don't have to escort me," she says. "I'm good."

"Are you sure?"

"Yeah." She picks up her bag, slips her shoes back on. "I just have to be quick. But it'll be fine. I'm good at trails."

"Are you absolutely, one hundred percent sure?" Amara stands up, too. "Because if I don't come with you and you go missing, I'll never forgive you."

"Yes. Absolutely, one hundred percent." She senses his concern, and it makes her want to give him a hug, even though she's sure he already thinks she's a weirdo. "Thanks so much for dinner," she says, "and for the drink. It was—"

Outside the window, the shadows move.

"It was what? The suspense is killing me."

"It was amazing."

"You're not just saying that because I have you trapped in my house, right?"

"No. Really."

And before she can stop herself, she hugs him. He stiffens at first, surprised. But then he eases into it, his strong arms around Alex's back.

"Wait!" Amara says, right as she is about to open the door.

"What?"

"Can I give you my phone number?"

A vision of the brutally cracked screen of her phone flashes before her eyes. "Can I give you mine?"

Amara offers up his phone, and for a few horrifying moments, Alex is convinced she's forgotten her own number. She types and erases the same three digits over and over. Everything beyond is a blank, a pressure behind her forehead.

"I can just give you my number."

"No, sorry, just a second —"

It comes rushing back. She enters the number, sets the contact name as Alex. As a final touch, she adds a little blue bird emoji.

"I really have to go," she says.

"I know. Thank you, Alex."

"Thanks."

"I'll call you!" Amara yells, standing in the doorway, the warm light from inside the house framing his small figure. Then the door closes, and Alex is alone.

—

There is just enough light left for Alex, as long as she hurries, to make it out of the forest before it gets dark. Her joints do not take well to hurry. But she hustles along anyway, conscious of how rapidly the light is dying, how the light that was coming from every direction on the way here was now a narrowing band on the horizon. She is thankful for whoever marked the trail. Without the pink beacons outlining the bends of the path, she is certain, even after only a few minutes of walking, that she would already be lost.

—

Back in 709, Alex waits for the bathtub to fill, compulsively check-ing her phone. She tries to space it out. No more than once every two minutes, she chides herself; any more than that is desperate, an unacceptable level of clinginess. But she can't stop herself, even as the notifications continue to be empty. She worries that she did forget her own phone number, that her clumsy fingers entered it in Amara's phone wrong. Or maybe he just wasn't that interested. Or maybe he was, and he was leveraging the power he had, being the only one capable of initiating contact. She drops her clothes on the ground and climbs into the tub.

She considers taking some of the sleeping pills but decides against it. If she's going to be talking to Amara, which is entirely possible, she wants to know what she's going to say. Part of the fun of the sleeping pills, back when she was a regular daytime user, was the way it erased all memory of what she'd said while she was high; the only way she knew what she'd talked about were reports from other people or backreading the texts she'd sent, which tended to be long and involved rambles about bodily disintegration. One time, after waking up at Tingting's apartment, Tingting had told her she'd talked about turning into a pile of insentient flesh ooze, played Twinkle Twinkle Little Star extremely slowly and poorly on the piano, eaten half a jar of peanut butter, and passed out on the floor. Tingting seemed more concerned than amused, but Alex was convinced that if she ever completely stopped being high around people, everyone around her would only find her boring and sad. If she had to be sad, she could at least be sad in an entertaining way.

But she wants to be in control of herself now. She doesn't want to be a comical mess. She returns again and again to his forearm extended over the side of her chair, the delicate, colourful outlines of the birds on his bicep; when their hands touched slightly, a warm jolt against the cold of the glasses. Part of her wants to talk herself out of believing that he's attracted to her. The evidence, though, suggests otherwise. And it's fun to be doing this little wordless dance, the nervousness tugging in her chest. It's been such a long time. If the Smiths had been concealing Amara's presence from her, maybe they were only doing so to make the surprise all the more delightful.

She is deep in thought, brainstorming clever responses to various hypothetical texts from Amara, when her phone buzzes. A call. She reaches instinctively to answer it.

But then she remembers what happened the last time she answered it, the empty void of fear and the self-imposed imprisonment, and now she is afraid to even look at the caller ID: what if it's the same strange, short series of numbers that told her to stay inside? If it's Amara, she can check after the phone is done ringing and call him back. She lets the buzzing continue, on and on and on, until it abruptly stops. She takes a deep breath, in and out. There is nothing wrong; she's not in danger. It's just a phone call.

But seconds later, the phone starts buzzing again. It keeps buzzing, buzzing, buzzing — the vibrations clattering unbearably against the side of the tub, holding her hostage.

After nearly an entire minute, it stops buzzing. Alex doesn't believe it at first; the buzzing lingers in her ears. When it becomes clear that the silence is going to stay, she breathes a sigh of relief.

One short, final buzz. Someone has left her a voicemail.

"Hey, it's me," Amara says. "Just wanted to make sure you made it home alive. This is my third call, actually. So, like, call me back, otherwise I'm going to be worried, and then I'll stay up all night, and then the next time I see you I'll be all grouchy and sleep-deprived."

Alex could scream with frustration. She should have just picked up the phone. Amara's number is private, so there's no way she can call him back, and no guarantee that after several failures he'll bother calling back again tonight. She can go to his place and apologize in the morning, but she doesn't know what time he starts working, doesn't want to interrupt him. And even if she did smooth everything over, if she explained her ridiculous fear of the robocalls, they would continue on with her dogged by guilt, knowing she'd repaid him for the wonderful evening by dodging his calls and making him sleepless with anxiety, and him probably questioning her sanity. She keeps refreshing the call log, as if by repeating the action the outcome will change. A minuscule fragment of glass, corroding from one of the broken edges of the screen, lodges itself in her finger. She yelps with pain, and the phone buzzes again.

"Oh my god, you answered," comes Amara's voice, crackly and dim, from the speaker.

"I am so sorry," Alex says.

"Did you have your phone on silent or something? Or did you actually get lost?"

"No," she says, leaning back into the tub until everything but her face is submerged. "No, I didn't get lost. I told you, I'm totally fine in the woods. I'm sorry."

"Okay, so you're a phone-on-silent person. Good to know. Next time I won't call five times."

"I'm sorry."

"No, it's fine, don't worry about it."

There is a moment of uncomfortable silence as Alex wracks her brain for something to say. All that she can think of, though, is the STAY INSIDE call. She can't go on like this: she has to know where it came from. "Can I ask you maybe kind of a weird question?" she finally says, a little hesitant.

"Please."

"Have you been getting, like, weird robocalls?"

"Like what, like phone scams?"

"Yeah. Kind of."

"I don't know what you mean by 'kind of,' but no." He considers. "Actually, the first week I got here, I got, like, five scam calls a day, but I never picked them up, and they only left these creepy silent voicemails. But since then there's been nothing. Blessed silence."

"Okay," Alex says, "because the second night I was here I got this really fucking weird robocall. That's why I missed your call. I was worried it might be the same people again. And then I couldn't call you back because your number is private."

"I can tell you my number now, then."

As she enters the number into her contacts, she can hear rustling on Amara's end. "So what was the scam?"

"That's the thing. I don't know if it's really a scam. It's just—" There's no way to say this without sounding foolish. "It's just a call with a robotic voice saying the same thing over and over. 'Stay inside, stay inside, stay inside.'"

Amara laughs. "So definitely some kind of prank then. Like—" He affects a high-pitched voice. "Ooooh, so scary, the mysterious machine voices don't want me to leave my house!"

Alex forces herself to laugh along. "Yeah, it's really dumb." She notices drops of blood in the water. "I was just annoyed."

"Did you look up the number online? They have these whole forums now where people report scam calls. The future is now."

"That was another thing that weirded me out about it. The number wasn't a normal phone number."

"Maybe it was one of those emergency mass alerts, then."

"But there was no emergency. And then, wouldn't you have gotten one?"

"Maybe I wasn't here that night. I do go back to the city sometimes. Who knows?"

Alex hears, in his repetitive answers, that he's growing bored. She shouldn't have brought this up. "I guess," she says, trying to think of how to get herself out of the conversational hole she's dug.

"Well, maybe next time they call I'll be with you, and I can scare them away with my *man voice*." His *man voice* is a full octave lower than his speaking voice, to the point that it sounds more like a rumble than anything resembling actual speech. For some reason, he adds a vaguely Southern drawl to it, too, and Alex can't help laughing, even as she attempts to pull the shard from her hand with her fingertips. She disturbs the glass and yelps again, her movement sloshing the water.

"Hold on," Amara says. "Are you in the ocean or something?"

"I'm having a bath."

"Without me?"

"Yes. I am alone in this huge, spa tub, lounging in the hot water."

Amara groans.

"There are jets, too," she continues. "So I'm getting my back massaged, my feet massaged."

"Why are you torturing me? That sounds like heaven."

"It is." Relieved as she is to be off the topic of the phone calls, she can't help twisting the knife. "It's too bad I'm all alone, because you could probably fit two people in here easily." Her efforts have only embedded the glass deeper in her finger. It is visibly swelling. "Even two big people."

"Oh yeah?" There is more rustling. "And what might two big people get up to in one tub?"

"Nothing scandalous. Just sitting, relaxing their muscles, letting the jets work out any tension under the skin . . ."

"So is this what we're doing tomorrow? Tub date?"

"I wish." The fantasy evaporates. "I'm sorry. I honestly just don't know if I'm allowed to let people in here. I have no way of checking, and there are cameras everywhere outside the house."

"I know. I get it." A pause. "But you do want to hang out tomorrow, right?"

"Don't you have to work?"

"Honey, tomorrow is Saturday."

Right: tomorrow is Saturday. She would never have known; she's not kept track of the days of the week since she was in the hospital. "So we can just hang out whenever?"

"I leave it entirely up to you." He yawns loudly. "God, I don't know why I'm so tired. I guess it was an exciting day."

Alex stares at her throbbing finger, the flesh around the wound whitening around the edges. It reminds her, strangely, of the disappeared posters in the kiosk.

"I have some errands to run in the morning," she says. "But I can come by your place at, like two or three? And we can just play it by ear."

"Beautiful," he says, and yawns again. "It seems like I have to go to sleep now."

"Goodnight, then. And sorry again. And thanks for not giving up on calling me."

"Thanks for not getting lost in the forest." His voice is slow, a little muffled. "It would have really, really sucked if I never got to see you again."

"Yeah." She smiles. "I'll see you tomorrow."

"Goodnight," he says, and then he hangs up.

—

It is foggy in the cove when Alex glides down on the e-bike, a chill that seems to have dulled the entire island. Last time Alex was here, the road was packed with cars, the café spilling over with tourists. Now, the road is nearly empty; only a few locals are around, sitting at the tables with their meals and their mugs, appearing muted, as though they've absorbed the fog into themselves. Inside, the woman stands behind the register. When she sees Alex enter, she stiffens.

"Do you need something?" she says before Alex can even approach.

"Hi!" Alex says it with such stress that her voice cracks at the end of the syllable. "Could I please get a large drip coffee, black, to go?"

The woman says nothing. She fills a paper cup from the coffee machine, her eyes never leaving Alex, before sliding it across the counter. Alex takes the cup and nearly drops it: it is boiling hot, searing her injured finger.

"Could I maybe get a sleeve for this?"

"No sleeves."

"Okay." Alex pays for the coffee, at a loss as to how she'll carry the thin paper cup without scalding herself. If she can take it far enough that she's out of the woman's view, maybe she can pull her shirtsleeve down over her hand as a protective layer. The transaction goes through, but the woman remains in the same place, statuesque. Alex considers smiling at her, then decides against it.

"Where did you say you were staying again?" the woman asks, before Alex can inquire after Leo.

"709 Cliff Drive," Alex says, and no sooner do the words leave her mouth than she realizes the enormity of her mistake. The woman's expression doesn't change, but her eyes go steely.

"The cape, huh."

"I'm not the owner or anything," Alex says, as if anyone would have thought she was. "I'm just house-sitting."

"Huh." The woman folds her arms. "Lot of strange people around lately."

Alex doesn't know how to respond to this.

"Yeah," the woman continues, talking to herself but staring straight at Alex. "Lot of strange stuff. Theft. Vandalism. All those dogs, gone."

"Mmm," Alex nods, looking for a way into the monologue.

But the woman isn't done. "Not too long ago, I knew every person who lived on this island. Every single one."

Alex finds this a little hard to believe, given that at least a thousand people lived on the island at the last census, but she nods again, hoping she appears sympathetic.

At last, the woman breaks her position. A worn, heavy sigh escapes her mouth.

"Things really are changing," she says, and she no longer sounds stony: just old, old and unhappy.

"Could I perhaps talk to Leo?" Alex says tentatively. She's not sure if this is the right time to be asking favours, but if she lets it get away, she might not get another one. "I mean, if he's here today."

The woman sighs again. "As long as he isn't doing anything." She disappears into the kitchen. When she reemerges, Leo is there beside her, his beanie and sweater much more logical than they'd appeared the last time Alex saw him. He waves, and she waves back.

"Do you want to sit outside?" he says.

———

Leo leads Alex past the watching islanders at the outside tables, back around the building, to a hidden yard, full of green grass and apple trees, enclosed by a rough-hewn driftwood fence. There's a picnic table underneath the boughs, and Leo sits down, stretching his legs. From his pocket he pulls out a smushed chocolate chip cookie. "Do you want some?" he asks Alex.

"Uh, no thanks."

"Mmm." His mouth is already full of cookie. "So Alex—"

"How do you know my name?"

"How *do* I know your name?" He seems confused until enlightenment hits. "Oh, my boss was talking about you before you came in the other day, and when I saw you I knew you had to be the Alex she was talking about."

"She was talking about me? What was she saying?"

"Just that she'd never seen you before."

"Just that?"

"I mean." Leo is sheepish. "She's not exactly happy about all the people who've been coming to the island lately. She thinks it's going to cause crime, make the housing prices go up. Basically every bad thing. And —" He stops. "I feel really bad saying this."

"Just tell me. I know it's not you coming up with it."

Leo casts a furtive glance back toward the café. He lowers his voice to a half-whisper. "Again, I feel really bad saying this. But she was saying that she could kind of tell you weren't from here."

*Oh, so she's racist,* Alex immediately thinks, but she holds herself back from saying it aloud. There's no point arguing with a teen about whether his boss is racist. "I get it, I get it. Did you find anything out about the posters?"

"Oh, yeah." He looks sheepish again. "She just shredded them. Sorry."

So that was that, then. Alex stands up, unable to hide her disappointment. "Well, thanks for all your help, Leo. I really appreciate it."

He stands up, too, hastily. "No problem! And if there's anything else you ever need help with, you know who to call."

"Oh, I did want to ask you something." It's shady, but she has to. "Do you know a guy living on the cape named Amara?"

"A guy named Amara?" Leo casts his gaze heavenward, as though the information will be retrievable somewhere in the mist. "Not ringing any bells, no."

"He's a short, big guy with a beard. He would have been living here for about four, five months."

Leo shakes his head. "Nope. And I don't think anyone else working here knows him either, otherwise I would have heard about it. A huge bearded guy named Amara, new on the island, living on the cape — yeah, I'm sure he would be a hot topic if anyone knew he existed."

"Okay." She is about to leave, but before she does, she stops. "Can I ask you one last question?"

"Hit me."

"Why are you being so nice to me?"

He shrugs. "I try to be nice to people."

The simplicity of this statement is delightful to Alex. "That's really cool of you, dude."

"Also I go to school in the city, and lots of my friends are gay. And so is my sister."

Alex stifles her laugh.

"Well," she says, rising from the picnic bench, "I'm sure they're glad to have such a great ally in their midst."

"Thank you!" Leo says, and she can tell by the proud look on his face that he's being completely sincere.

The fog has only gotten thicker over the road as Alex begins her journey back to the cape. The moisture in the air makes breathing difficult, even with the e-bike on maximum boost. The world is concealed — Alex can hardly see the trees on the other side of the road, so dense is the mist surrounding them — and in combination with the lack of life around the cove, it makes her profoundly uneasy. Every ghostly movement around her catches her attention, and the more she is distracted, the more unsteady she is on the bike. Her focus must remain on the road ahead, largely invisible though it is. She visualizes the way forward: the steep ascent, then the levelling through the trees as it narrows, taking hard curve after hard curve; the section that goes by the farm, the one that advertises fresh eggs, and then the other farm with the black-and-white sheep, the chickens wandering down the driveway. Then another steep climb past the lake before the plateau, perfectly placed to enjoy the view, before the descent again into the trees, back to the abandoned parking lot, the way back to 709 — and now, too, the way back to Amara, to all the tantalizing unknowns he represents.

So successful is Alex's attempt at visualization that she doesn't notice the pickup truck inching along behind her as she slows on the steepest part of the hill. Without warning, the pickup truck revs its engine, noxious and aggressive, picking up speed until it is right on her tail before braking hard.

Alex nearly tumbles off the bike. But there is nowhere to pull over, too steep to try to stop and get off. All she can do is keep pedalling: faster — with the fear pulsing wildly through her — than she has ever pedalled before.

The heat from the front of the truck touches her back.

I'm going to die.

These people are going to kill me.

And as the thought appears in her head, as if she has summoned it, the truck swerves out until it is running right beside her. The window is rolled down, and leaning out is the young man with the black sunglasses. His mouth is open in a red, toothy smile.

Time seems to slow down as the truck starts to move again, achingly slow. Alex sees only a shape, vague and grey, spinning toward her. All thoughts fade away, all instincts other than self-preservation, and she bails, hard — first her hip hitting the pavement, then her bent elbow with a crunch, and then the heel of her wrist, the most painful of all, and as she cries out, she hears the sickening crunch of a large chunk of cement, hitting the ground just a few yards past her.

Then the laughter, the laughter that seems to surround her, stretching back through her. This is exactly what she was always afraid of. That it would never stop happening. That no one would ever care enough to stop it: that, really, everyone enjoyed it when she was in pain. Everyone thought it was funny. They did this on purpose. They are laughing at her, and now the rubber screeches against the pavement and they speed away, leaving her there at the side of the road.

She lies there for a while, crying softly. A few cars pass by; she can hear them slow down, and every time, after a few seconds, they speed up again, continuing on their way. Then nothing but her own halting, shallow breaths. Pathetic. The cement lies wordless on the ground beside her. If only she hadn't bailed. She could have let it hit her. Then everyone would have gotten what they wanted.

Instead, she is conscious, fully conscious of every terrible sensation in her body. She opens and closes the hand that hit the ground, and when she tries to form a fist, knives unsheathe themselves in her wrists. A chunk of skin has scraped off where it met pavement, exposing white and pink flesh underneath with little pieces of asphalt buried inside. Her elbow is probably scraped, too, though it at least had her sleeve protecting it; the same goes for her hip.

She rolls onto her other side, and from there she painstakingly props herself up to the point where she can get on her knees, then the balls of her feet, and finally upright, her vision spinning. The e-bike lies on the ground, some paint chipped off, a pedal slightly bent where it hit the ground. She picks the bike up with her left hand, the glass in her finger angry, and prays, as she hoists her leg over the bar and her right foot onto a pedal, that the electric motor isn't broken.

It starts, but she almost falls backward anyway, starting at zero halfway up the hill. So she dismounts, and for the next fifteen minutes, she trudges, pushing the handles with only the heel of her left hand and only fingers of her right.

It is horrible work. But Alex is somewhere else. She is crying, sobs audibly escaping her mouth; tears are running down her face, blurring her vision; every part of her is in excruciating pain. Yet it is impossible to conceptualize the person who bears this pain as herself. She is not the one pushing the bike up the hill. She is suspended somewhere, not inside her body but around it, observing dispassionately. Someone might have just tried to hurt her. Just a few minutes ago, she reminds herself — he leaned out the window, so many teeth in his mouth, red and white like a hellhound, and then ten pounds of concrete flew at her head. She can barely remember it; it didn't happen to her, but to this trembling, shuddering body, the one that has now crested the hill and is getting back in the saddle, crying like an idiot. This ugly body, this obvious aberration. That must be why people keep trying to kill it.

But it didn't happen to her. She didn't feel a thing. The moment of impact has already disappeared, and in its place is a cool, placid nothing: an empty, untouchable space, the surface of a lake that can never be disturbed.

—

Alex does not turn into the abandoned parking lot. She carries on straight down the road. Something compels her forward, some fear she is pushing down. Maybe she simply can't stop, because as soon as she stops, she knows she will return to the fullness of her pain. In her mind, the shadow of 709 looms, a vision of her crawling up the spiral stairs only to tumble back down again. No one would ever know if anything bad happened in there, not for months. So she keeps going on into the forest, not knowing where, her mind turning every few minutes onto its side to be smoothed over once again.

After a few hundred metres, the paved road abruptly stops. The dirt road that carries on ahead of it is blocked by a hanging chain between two poles. Alex swerves around the chain dangerously: what's the worst that could happen, her falling off the bike? Her legs are heavy and numb and slow. It doesn't matter that she doesn't know where she is going, and when she sees an even more narrow dirt road extending off to the right, she takes a hard turn, plunging into deep forest.

In an instant, a deer jumps out onto the road a hundred yards ahead of her. Alex squeals to a stop, her tires nearly spinning out. It's a young buck, its budding antlers velvety and small. It regards her curiously, but not with a great deal of concern; its little black-and-white tail steadily flicking mosquitoes off its flanks, its ears facing Alex, then turning, then facing her again. It chews on a branch, the end of a leaf extending from its lips.

Alex gets back in the saddle.

"Sorry to bother you," her far-away voice says, "but I can't stop long."

She turns the pedals once, the gravel crunching under the tire treads, and the deer flicks its tail pointedly. Disappointed but clearly not surprised, it bounds lightly into the bushes. And in the space it occupied, Alex sees Amara, walking absently up the road, eyes on his phone. She screeches to a halt again, fighting the urge to duck into the bushes. She doesn't want him to see her like this; it would be better if she just disappeared; that way he would only remember her drinking gingery sparkles in his chair and laughing, and not as a corpse dragging itself through the forest on a two-wheeled vehicle. But it's too late. He notices her, and at first seems pleased to see her. As he comes closer, seeing her more clearly, his joy is displaced by horror.

To be seen by someone, and then to know that the more they see you, the worse it is for them. The pain is starting to bloom again.

"Alex?" he says in disbelief. As he comes up beside her, Alex sees his furrowed brow, hears a new note in his voice that she's never heard before, and her knees almost buckle. She steadies herself, wobbling, the pedals scraping her calves, but now Amara is holding the handles with one hand and her shoulder with the other.

"Here," he says, "I've got it," and Alex, aware that she is sniffling, her whole face leaking, disentangles herself from the bike. When he is sure that she is standing, Amara slowly rolls the bike away from her, kicks out the kickstand. Then he turns back, extending a hand outward.

"Are you okay?" he says, and when he puts the hand on her shoulder again it burns like the fiery thousand-needle sting of a jellyfish. The glass wound is bleeding; the scraped hand is swelling; she tries to open it, but it is locked in place by the knives.

"I'm fine," she wants to say, but what comes out of her mouth is a half-muffled wail. Her legs shake, and Amara quickly places his other hand around her waist, ready to catch her if she fell. This hand burns, too, but she can't tell him; she doesn't understand how she can want to be held so desperately only for it to hurt her so much when someone does, how the sensation makes her want to scream and throw herself on the ground, to smash the places on her body where other people have touched her. But she is crying, and she can't speak, and she can't move.

Amara stares at her, unblinking.

"Let's go back to my place," he says, and his voice has transformed. It is cool, placid, smooth. His eyes are the same: flat and unwavering.

"How?"

"I can carry you."

"I don't want you to hurt yourself."

"I'm not going to hurt myself."

"Okay."

"Tell me if anything feels uncomfortable," he says, serious, and Alex almost laughs — has he seen the state of her? — before she is swooped with ease into the air, an arm under her knees and another around her back. At the end of the road in the middle distance, the little house and the silver Toyota approach, and Amara's breath is steady on her skin. They move together, Amara on the ground and Alex in the air, Amara's arms sturdy, both of them looking only forward, neither of them speaking.

———

After Amara sits her down in the chair she was in last night (was that only last night?) he promptly disappears, running down the road to fetch the e-bike. When he comes back, he is out of breath, his face no longer the quiet lake it had been when he picked her up. He shakes his head as he wheels the bike into the house, parking it by the door. "I don't trust anyone," he says. "Even in the forest. A deer could run away with this bike if you turned your back on them long enough." He walks over to the kitchen counter again. "Do you want a cup of tea? Lemonade, maybe?"

"Oh, fuck!"

"What?"

Alex laughs, which, after crying as much as she has and biking as long as she has, really hurts. She coughs. "I just realized. I went all the way down to the cove to get a cup of coffee, and I left it on the fucking counter without drinking it." She cough-laughs again, aggravating soreness of unknown origin around her ribs.

"I got coffee." Amara brandishes a shiny bag of beans. "Small-batch roasted. Notes of cocoa and French vanilla. Do you want some?"

"Sure. Thank you."

They are both quiet as he grinds the beans, pours water into the coffee maker, sets it to brew. He faces Alex, leaning on the counter.

"Do you think they're real?" he says.

"What?"

"Coffee flavour notes. And wine flavour notes, for that matter."

"Absolutely not."

"Okay, good. Because I have had so much of this coffee — and I love it, it's amazing coffee — but I have never once been able to taste any French vanilla."

"Wine notes are faker, though. Wine just tastes like garbage. Like rot. Even if there were notes of sandalwood or whatever, I'm always too busy trying to choke it all down to find out what the deeper flavours are. I'm not going to be swishing wine around in my mouth."

Amara is entertained. "Strong feelings about wine over here."

"It's just so bad. It makes me feel like I'm crazy. Not drinking wine, but that fact that so many people seem to enjoy it."

"I do love a sparkling wine. Or a nice white." The coffee is beginning to pour into the coffee pot. Amara disappears into the bathroom.

"Honestly," Alex says, letting herself be distracted, "it's fun when you're partying, but I could probably live the rest of my life without drinking."

He reappears wielding a first aid kit. "Mmhmm?"

"I just never find myself craving alcohol, you know?" she continues. "I'm not going around like, oh, it would be so amazing if only I had a beer right now."

"What do you find yourself craving, then?"

The question unsettles her. What does she crave? "Water."

"That's it? Water?"

She wants to say sedatives, but doesn't. "Coffee, I guess."

"You really know how to walk on the wild side."

"So I've been told."

"Could you give me your hand?"

"Which one?"

"Whichever one is worse."

She extends her right hand. His fingers soft, Amara takes it and examines the damage with a grimace. Then he begins to clean the exposed flesh with a damp cloth, talking through it as though nothing is amiss. "I was thinking about what we could do today."

"Ow!"

"My initial thought, obviously, was that we could go to the beach."

The alcohol stings. Alex grits her teeth. "The one down here?"

"Yes. But obviously, circumstances have changed. I don't think you want to be walking all the way past the lighthouse and down the rocks in this condition." Already, he's removed almost all the dirt from the scrape on Alex's hand. With a piece of gauze, he dabs ointment on it.

"No," Alex says, watching his focus. "I don't think so."

"I've narrowed it down to two other options." He presses a Band-Aid over the wound. "Other hand."

Alex obliges. "This one has a piece of glass in it," she says, apologetic.

"Oh, so you were really out there having fun." He examines her swollen finger. "I think I can get this out."

Visions of metal tweezers digging in her wound appear in Alex's mind. "It's okay," she says hastily. "Just put some ointment on it and leave it."

"No, no," he says, "I think I can see it." He picks up a roll of medical tape from the first aid kit and tears off a piece. He lowers the sticky surface onto the place where the glass has punctured Alex's skin; then, gently but quickly, he lifts it straight up.

"Ow!"

"Got it," he says, showing her the almost-invisible sliver now stuck to the tape. The coffee machine beeps, and he leaps up. "There, perfect timing."

Though Alex can't confirm whether the coffee has notes of cocoa or French vanilla — now that she thinks of it, she really has no idea what the difference between French vanilla and normal vanilla is — it smells delicious. With her left hand, minus the now glass-free index finger, she picks up the flowery bone-china mug that Amara puts down on the table, allowing herself to enjoy the aroma. "Mmm."

"Wait until you have a sip. It's the best thing I've ever tasted, I swear to god."

And it is: rich and complex, like drinking life back into her body.

"Okay," she says. "I'm healed now. Let's go to the beach."

"I was thinking," Amara says, "maybe I could take you to one of my secret spots."

"Secret spots? While I'm physically incapacitated? Tell me more."

When she puts down her mug, Amara takes her hand again. "Sorry, this needs a bandage. I'm a completionist. Anyway, my fucking friends, who I love, are lazy as hell and never come to visit me out here. They're like, oh, the ferry's too expensive, I'm scared of driving into the woods, I can't pay for gas. Boo-hoo. I've spent a lot of time just driving around, going down all these random dirt roads to see what I can see. And in doing so, I've found all these secret spots. They're always at the end of these, like, super potholed paths where you're not sure if it's actually a road or a private driveway into some recluse's lair, and you're going to get shot for trespassing at the end of it. But I haven't gotten shot yet, and there's one place in particular that I think you would love to see."

"Why, what's it like? How do you know I'll love it?"

"I don't want to give too much away. It's more exciting if it's a secret. Or," he adds, "we can just chill here. Given that you've obviously had your own adventures today."

"Hey," she says, realizing something.

"Hey."

137

"You haven't asked what happened to me. Like, why I'm so cut up. Why I was riding down the road to your place."

"I guess I thought if you wanted to tell me, you'd tell me."

"In fact," she says, realizing something else, "you haven't asked me pretty much anything about myself at all."

"I mean. Attractive young stranger shows up in a terrifying mansion by the sea, alone, claiming that they're house-sitting? Surely there's no story there."

He's joking, but she can tell he's actually a little worried.

"No, no, I'm not mad about it. It's actually . . ."

She thinks about Ella: how, even though she loves her, their conversations always turn back to Alex's shitty life, how Ella seems to believe that the secret to enlightenment is buried somewhere within Alex's suffering. And not just Ella, but Aisling, the dozens of doctors and counsellors and advisers she's seen, even people like Em sometimes: the way she is always under the microscope, expected to open herself up for investigation at a moment's notice, regardless of the effect that it might have on her.

"It's actually refreshing," she says.

"Yeah," Amara says, relieved. "I'm sure everyone, everywhere you go, is just dying to know all about you."

"Last night," she says, "you were going to tell me about the birds. Your bird tattoos."

"You really know how to change the subject."

"You said it was a long story."

"Did I?"

"Well," she says, lifting her hands up, "you've got a captive audience."

"I lied. It's not actually that long of a story." He takes a dramatic, slurping sip of his coffee, then leans back. "Basically, when I was a young teenage sort of person, I did all kinds of crazy shit."

"Like what?"

"You name it. Going insane at parties. Breaking into construction sites, drinking on playgrounds, fighting people, blah, blah,

blah. Pretty much the stereotypical, you know, 'I'm closeted and my family sucks and I'm acting out' stuff."

"That all sounds familiar. Except I was out in high school. I came out when I was twelve."

"Well, I didn't. I was an extremely normal and fine heterosexual teenage girl." He laughs, and then scans her face, gauging her reaction. "But that doesn't surprise you, obviously."

Alex shakes her head. "Nope."

He brings his hands up to his cheeks, pressing them together. "Was it my hands? I have such clocky hands."

"When I was a kid," Alex says, "the other girls used to make fun of my hands because they were so big. I mean, they made fun of a lot of things about me. The hands were just the first. Then, you know, puberty, and it became 'Alex has no boobs, Alex has such huge shoulders, Alex is so hairy, Alex is so tall.'"

"And then you came out? With all that going on?"

"I just felt like I had to. Like, they all knew already. Before I did, even. Just based on my body. I'd already been assigned the role of, like, scary gross lesbian, or girl who isn't *really* a girl. So I was like, fuck it, yeah, I'm a scary gross lesbian. What are you going to do about it? And I leaned into it. It was the only way I felt like I had any control over how people were perceiving me, I guess." She considers. "It didn't make me any friends, but it helped me get laid, so that was a plus. And then—"

"See," Amara interrupts, "I always find that so impressive, because I could not deal with that shit. Like, obviously no one was coming at me for having big hands, but being small and weird and ambiguously brown? In the suburbs? Middle school was not a cool, fun time for me. And also there was no way I ever could have mistaken myself for a lesbian. So I went all in on, like, body hair removal, boob shirts, makeup, two hours a day straightening my hair."

"And now look at you."

"Now look at me." He runs a hand over his shaved head. "But it took my mom dying for me to really stop giving a fuck."

Amara was so unlike her, so free and unburdened. He walked solidly, not like her; the way she would be suddenly crushed under an invisible weight, then just as suddenly spun out of her body. Was that not true? But no. No, she is looking at him, even after saying what he just said, and he is the same as she thought he was: grounded, whole, easy.

"I'm sorry," she manages to say.

"It's okay." He laughs. "It was twelve years ago. And we didn't get along. She had a lot of problems, and then she got cancer and died before she could fix any of them. That's life. But this—" He taps his forehead. "This is getting us back to the bird story. Because after my mom died, people were really like, oh, shit, we better make sure this kid has something constructive to do, or else things could *really* go off the rails. So the summer before senior year they put me in this summer job placement for at-risk youth."

"I am so excited to see how this ends up being about birds."

"I'm getting there! The whole point of the program was to be getting kids out there and working with small, community-type businesses. Most of which were in the vein of, like, florists, and ladies who sold hand-painted silk shawls. Definitely not the vibe I was giving off. So they kind of went off-book. They sent me to basically be the personal landscaper for this old rich guy. This old queen, Lou. He had a tiny house, but a huge, huge garden.

"And Lou did not cut me any slack. I came in there all sullen, tossing my hair around, pouting, feeling like there was no one in the world who had it worse than me. Just a miserable, miserable person. And he would just calmly tell me to go trim the branches off his apple tree — but in this very, very specific way. I never did it right the first time, or the second time. I got so frustrated with how bad I was at it, but he never did. Just very, very calm, showing me how to do what he wanted me to do.

"So one day a few weeks into the summer, after I'd been mowing the grass, he kind of beckoned me to come inside. I thought he was going to try to give me some kind of lecture. But instead, he led me to the window that faced over the garden. He had this huge camera set up there, and a telescope and a pair of binoculars, and he handed me the binoculars and told me to look at one spot in one of the trees — somewhere on the trunk of the tree, in the bark. It took me forever to find what he was talking about, but eventually I spotted it: this tiny, tiny brown bird, moving up the tree all haphazardly like a bug. I thought that was it, but then I noticed it ducking into this crevice in the bark. There were baby birds there. A whole nest full of baby birds, just under the skin of the tree. And I never would have known had he not pointed it out to me.

"For the rest of the summer, I would spend all day doing all this hard, physical labour, and then we would sit and watch the birds. He'd put so much thought and effort into this garden over the years, and he planted everything specifically to attract local species. So there was a little pond where the summer songbirds would splash around. There were evergreens, and the apple tree, and the cherry tree, and each one had different little friends that it attracted. I learned all of their names, their songs, where they came from. And for pretty much the first time in my life, I was spending time away from groups of people and their expectations. I was just absorbed in quietly working on this space, learning about it, listening to it, this whole massive alive world around me that I'd completely ignored for the entirety of my life before that. I didn't have time to worry about other shit, like, about what other fucking teenagers thought about me. Or, for that matter, what my mom thought of me. I was so difficult, and I think she felt like the way I was reflected some kind of failure on her. She was always the one telling me to lose weight, to try to look prettier, otherwise no boys would ever want to date me. I can sympathize with that now, looking back as an adult. She was an isolated immigrant with a shitty white husband. She probably didn't want me to end up living her life. At the time, obviously, I didn't think of it that way. I found it painful and annoying.

"But she wasn't around anymore. So I stopped straightening my hair, and then eventually cut it all off. I told myself it was because it was getting in the way while I was gardening, and that was true, but that was only part of it. I didn't bother waxing anymore, because no one was really seeing me, so no one was going to shame me for having body hair or whatever. It felt comfortable, and it felt right. I felt connected, really, for the first time — to the world, and to who I wanted to be.

"I wish I could have stayed in touch with Lou after that. I was too scared to contact him after the summer was over. I honestly don't know if he even actually liked me, or if he was just a really polite person. But he must have known about everything that was going on with me, and he was never weird about it. I'm sure he must have lost people, too. An old man in an empty house. But his garden was full of life, and he made it that way. I guess that was something."

Amara exhales, as if he's just undertaken a great journey. He has a distant look on his face.

"Anyway," he says brightly, "two summers after that, after my dad died—"

"Your dad died too?" Alex blurts, unable to contain her horror.

"Oh no, it's fine. I mean — not fine for him. He had a heart attack. Just keeled over one day while watching CNN."

He is so calm about this. How is he so calm about this? He is leaning back in his chair, drinking his coffee, like nothing in the conversation has changed.

"But it was a long time ago. And he was a whole other can of worms. I don't want to get into it. I was nineteen, completely alone in the world, with a little bit of money that was left for me, and I was free. There was just no reason not to want what I knew I wanted. So I started hormones a few months later. And I kept looking for birds."

Alex is silent.

"I guess that was actually kind of a long story," Amara observes.

"My mom also died," Alex says.

Amara's eyes widen, then quickly settle, searching again in Alex's face.

"I'm so sorry," he says softly.

"Yeah." She curls and uncurls her fingers around the mug handle. "But it didn't free me or anything. I was seven. She drove forty kilometres to work every day. She was also an immigrant with a shitty white husband. It was the winter, and she was in an accident." She speaks carefully, focusing intently on every syllable, but she is starting to cry anyway. She looks up at Amara, who is not moving: only observing her, his attention not leaving her face.

"My parents were divorced. I saw my dad on the weekends — he had another family. A baby, way younger than me. I had to move in with them. Everyone hated it. They all hated me. And everything was my fault." She hasn't thought about this in so long; the dam holding the flood back has become, with time, even more fragile, not less, and her continual reinforcement of it, the practised turns of conversation, the lying and stonewalling, now seems like nothing more than scattered handfuls of sand. "And my mom—"

Her mom. If Alex had never been born, her mom would still be alive. She would have gone back home. But she never got to. She never got to say goodbye to her family. She was sick, and she had to spend every waking hour working, and then she just died on the side of the fucking road in the dark. Alex shouldn't be alive. That's why everything fell apart. She couldn't be happy. She couldn't make Adam happy. She couldn't run. She couldn't be the daughter anyone wanted. She couldn't even be trans properly. And now she was here with all of this handed to her, this summer, and she's fucking ruining it.

"I'm sorry," she says, and she can't speak anymore. She curls up into a ball on the chair, face buried in her knees, shaking as the silent sobs wrack her body.

She doesn't know how long she's in there, in the shadows of her own form. Her breathing is so erratic, so painful. She starts gasping, and it is then that she feels Amara's hand on her shoulder.

"Hey," he says.

It takes her some effort, but she says it back. "Hey."

"Is it okay if I bring you some tissues and some water? You don't have to say anything. You can just nod."

She nods.

"Okay."

She can hear him walking to the bathroom. It is good to have a sound to focus on: the slap-slapping of his sandals against the wood floor, getting farther away and then coming back again.

"Here. I'm putting them on the table, whenever you want them."

In, two, three, four.

Out, two, three, four.

Alex lifts her head up. Amara is back in his chair, watching her. She takes a Kleenex, turns to the side, and blows her nose noisily.

"I'm sorry," she says.

"It's okay. I sneeze like a car horn. Very few nose noises are shocking to me."

She laughs a little. But it fades fast, the reassurance from Amara's lightheartedness, because she has regained some measure of control over herself, which makes her prior lack of control more cringeworthy. Just like dad: holding it back until the storm comes, leaving someone else to pick up the damage. She would cry again with this knowledge of what she's doing, the pattern she's repeating, but to do so would be to make things worse. Instead, she forces herself to smile, excusing herself and walking to the bathroom, where she splashes water on her face and stares into the mirror, attempting various means of contorting her face into something human.

"Don't worry," she says under her breath, rehearsing an easy tone. "I'm sorry. It was just nothing. I'm just tired."

"Pardon me?"

"Sorry," she calls back, forcing another laugh. "Just talking to myself."

"Okay. Nothing bad about me, though, right?"

"Of course not." She takes her frizzing hair out of its ponytail, shaking it out over her shoulders. Its size, at least, should help distract from the horrible appearance of her face. She takes off her stained glasses, wiping them on the hem of her shirt, then puts them back on. She gives herself a thumbs-up in the mirror. It's okay, she says, making sure she is speaking silently this time, only her mouth forming the words. It's okay. It's actually funny. We all think this is funny.

When she steps out, Amara is staring at nothing. His body is still, but his foot taps a jumpy rhythm against the ground.

"Back to normal," Alex says, and sits down. "So are we still going to go to the secret spot?"

Amara is taken aback. "Are you sure you want to?"

"Yes. Obviously." She wants to sound playful. "I mean, not that you ever let me actually answer the question, since you went on for so long with your allegedly short story."

"You're the one who changed the subject back to birds!" he says defensively, and Alex breathes out. She hasn't ruined it; he isn't going to ask her questions, make her explain, keep her here until she can convince him that she's stable. He's not trying to figure out how much pain she's in, or why she's in it. This is still fun.

He chugs what remains of his coffee and stands, grabbing his car keys from off the table and his hat from the back of the chair. "You wouldn't happen to have those binoculars with you?"

"No. Sorry, I left them at the house."

"That's okay," he says, and grabs his from where they sit by the window. "These old things will do just fine." He reaches out to her. "Do you need someone to lean on as we walk out to the car? I promise that where we're going you pretty much won't have to walk at all."

"No, no, no," she says, and she walks toward the door, slowly, trying to conceal her hobbling and doing a poor job of it. He lets her walk by herself, but he stays close to her, vigilant. She manages to make it to the silver Toyota without tripping and falling on any tree roots. He holds the car door open for her.

"Your ride." He bows extravagantly.

"Much obliged."

Alex can count the number of times she's been in one over the last five years on one hand. Amara has a medal of some kind, a tiny saint etched into it, dangling from the rearview mirror, attached to a bright red rosary, and one of those wood-beaded car seat covers is draped over the driver's seat. Other than that, though the car is clearly old, it is sparkling clean. There's hardly even any dust on the dashboard.

"How do you like my baby?" Amara says, patting the steering wheel lovingly.

"Most of the cars I've been in," Alex says, "have, like, McDonald's wrappers stuffed into every crevice. It's a real change of pace."

"This car was the first major purchase I made after I started working full-time. I swear I'm going to make it last the next twenty years." He turns the key in the ignition. "We've had a lot of adventures together. And we're always happy to have travelling companions."

"Is that a frequent occurrence?"

"Honestly," he says, as he shifts into gear and begins to drive gently down the dirt road, "not as much as you might think."

"Oh really?"

"My ex wasn't super into adventuring. And we were together for eight years, so. You do the math." They emerge out onto the road, and Amara takes a right, deeper into the woods, where Alex has never been. "There were a lot of impromptu solo road trips."

"Eight years is a long time."

"Yeah. It really, really is."

And for the first time, Alex hears a strain in his words, a simmering underneath the surface. She searches for a way to change the subject, but Amara seems distracted, distant somewhere in his own mind, and outside the window is only a green world, passing in blurs, the grey-white mist growing thinner the farther they get from the house.

Eventually, Amara shakes his head. "Ugh, I'm sorry," he says. A strained laugh. "We just broke up last year. I'm still not completely over it, as much as I wish that weren't true."

"I know what you mean."

"Right? Like, two years on hormones, you think you've finally figured it all out, and you find some guy you love who seems to love you back. And it's like, oh, shit, I gotta lock it down, otherwise what if I never find anything like this again? And you spend all these years worrying, making yourself sick, trying not to do anything that might make him leave you. To the point where you can't remember who you really wanted to be before. Every possibility gets closed off, and the only door that's still open is the one where you somehow become who he wants you to be. Ah, fuck, sorry." He rubs his neck, his arm tense, eyes on the road. "You don't need to hear this."

Alex wants to hear it, though. She wants to hear everything he has to say.

"Look." He eases the car to a stop. "We're here."

———

Alex steps out of the car onto sand. Not the sand she is used to on the beaches here, the pieces of granite tumbled and crushed over centuries into small, hard-edged stones. This is soft, light sand, the kind that fills the well left by your foot as soon as you raise it, where you can see the ripples the waves left in it as they roll back into the ocean. A whole beach of this, spotless, extending out from the dense forest like the mouth of a river, framed by the elegant twists of the arbutus trees. From here, there are no islands visible: just open water, and beyond that, the blur of the horizon. It is as though the beach has had a blanket cast over it. Even the waves are soft, their murmuring quiet, the surface of the water glassy-smooth as it catches the sun. Alex takes off her shoes and walks, almost in a trance, out toward the sea. She stops just at the water's edge, where the water laps up against her feet, cool and gentle. She reaches down, letting her fingers trail in the waves, and the salt doesn't sting. She sighs, and the ocean sighs with her.

She hears the sand shifting behind her, and Amara appears next to her, barefoot as well, binoculars around his neck. He is not looking at her, so she looks away, too, imagining herself as part of the water. When she sneaks a glance at Amara, she sees his eyes dart away from her.

"How did you find this place?" she says, hushed, barely breaking the quiet.

"It's funny," he says, and if she wasn't listening for his voice, she could almost have lost it among the waves. "One of the first days I was here. I was just . . ."

He trails off. Alex can hear him swallow heavily.

"I wasn't doing well," he continues at last. "Just holed up in the house, thinking about everything that went wrong. Everything I might have lost in the last decade of my life that I could never get back. It was either drive or claw my own skin off. So I drove, and I ended up right here. Like I was meant to, somehow. Like the universe was saying yes, you deserve peace. You're on the right track."

Now he is looking at her. "I know that sounds crazy," he says, sadness in his voice.

She meets his gaze. "No," she says. "I know exactly what you mean."

Behind his sunglasses, she can't tell what he's thinking. They hold each other there, both unwilling to be the one to break. In the end, it is Alex who does. She can't take it. Something is in the air between them that is unbearable to sustain for much longer. She looks back down at her feet, focusing on the cold water.

"Do you want to sit?" Amara says. His voice is no longer so hushed. "I brought a mat."

Alex turns around. So he did, and it is already spread out there on the ground a couple of yards behind them. There's a sun umbrella, too, folded up on the ground, and a big jar of iced lemonade with plastic cups. Where did all of this come from?

"I had it in the cooler in the car," he replies to her thought, as if reading her mind. "I was packing for our beach hangout when I heard you there on the road and walked up to see what was going on."

She sits down on the mat, unable yet to form words. Amara pours her a glass of lemonade, and she sips at it: perfectly balanced, tart with a sweetness that lingers on her tongue. Her legs crossed, she watches the flight of a cormorant, speeding over the surface of the water until it's out of sight. Beside her, Amara lowers himself onto the mat, his legs unfurling. He leans back on his hands, his breaths deep and steady, and as they sit, Alex's breaths slowly come to align with his.

The pain is there, but not isolated, throbbing or stabbing as it usually does in individual joints. It is diffuse, like some of it is disappearing into the air, the water, the sand underneath her.

Alex closes her eyes again. She allows the surface of her mind to go completely still.

"I know exactly what you mean," she says again, "because I was feeling the same way." As long as she doesn't look at him she can be calm, even, quiet. She can tell him about it as long as she can't see him. The horizon is the only thing she's talking to. "I broke up with someone last year, too," she says. "Or, I guess, he actually broke up with me. And it wasn't last year. It was right after New Year's."

The rain at midnight. Running in the dark, sightless and crying, out into nothing.

"We were only together for two years, not eight. I can only imagine what that was like. But I really believed that it was going to last forever."

Her head on his chest with his arms around her, listening to his heartbeat grow faster.

"I had a lot of problems in high school. Like you, I guess. When I graduated, I took a year off and worked before I went to school. Community college. I did a year of that, and I was doing okay, but then things were bad again, worse, even, and I ended up in the hospital for a long time. After that, I just was like, fuck it, I'm going to do what I want to do. And it felt good. I was running more than ever — I was a runner, I don't know if I told you that. I was going to parties, meeting lots of other gay people, dancing and being an idiot. I cut off my dad and transferred schools, put a body of water between us. It was kind of like how you said you felt without your parents around, I guess. I felt really free. And I got top surgery. I really was nervous about all of it, actually. But I knew.

"I knew I was doing the right thing. It was kind of shocking, realizing just how much of my life I'd been spending just dissociating into the atmosphere. But now I could feel everything. I *wanted* to feel everything. It was like everything that didn't make sense about me finally clicked. And then I met someone."

From across the bus, he looks at her.

"This guy. No one else I'd ever met understood me like he did — when it came to the mental health stuff, the family stuff. Everything that I'd never talked to anyone about before. He knew what it was like. And he took care of me. When I was with him — I felt like through being with him, through seeing him, I was becoming more myself, seeing myself more clearly. And then—"

Nothing. A blank space. She is crying — when did she start crying? How did she get on the ground, and why Adam is above her, his face stone, his chest heaving?

*If you tell anyone about this—*

"He never," Alex starts to say, but her voice is shaking. She clears her throat, and as she does, as she sees in the corner of her vision the earnestness of Amara's expression, the concern and anticipation, she knows she can't tell him. She had thought she could, this time, here on the beach in the sun, having been pushed to the edge of her capacity for concealment by the battering waves of shock and fear and pain and relief. Especially because he seems to like her so much — especially because she wants him to like her. And from what he'd told her, he knew, too, what it was like. Some of it, anyway. But it was the same as it had been with Em, with all of her friends from before. It was the reason she had to cut them off. How could she explain having her whole self-concept changed by someone that much? After living with her dad, after high school, to allow someone else's idea of who she should be to fundamentally alter the way she thought of herself. Adam said he respected how she felt about herself, but he thought of her as a girl. And she'd thought that the more time they spent together, the more he understood her, that understanding would grow naturally out of knowing her. He would have to come around. Instead, it was her who came around, who became uncomfortable when people they-themed her, who stopped even thinking of herself as trans. It seemed, when it happened, inevitable. Her dad, most of her teachers, almost all the hospital staff — everyone, really, who had been in any position of authority in her life — she was just proving them right. She thought she knew who she was, and it turned out she didn't.

"You're living in a dreamland," her dad had said. It was the day she thought she was leaving him behind forever. She was walking away, and he was standing in the doorway of the grey apartment where she grew up, yelling at her back down the dim hallway. "Someday, you'll have to come back to the real world with the rest of us."

She can't stand the idea of Amara feeling sorry for her. She can't stand the idea of explaining to him that she isn't really who he thinks she is. After how open he was with her, it would be tantamount to a betrayal: to begin to say, *I'm like you, I understand,* only to take it back at the end. She doesn't have the right to talk about any of this, anyway, to make it all seem so straightforward. Not after what she said to Adam at New Year's — the whole reason why she's in this situation in the first place. She doesn't deserve, really, to be talking to anyone about anything.

A seagull cries out, somewhere unseen.

She doesn't know what she was about to say. "Sorry. It doesn't matter." She forces a smile. "I'm here."

"You're here," Amara says, and she turns to face him. The sun, sinking in the sky, has cast its light on his face. He's glowing, like there's a halo in the air around him. When he raises his hand, his fingers glitter like jewels.

As his fingers touch her face, a hoarse, guttural shriek splits the quiet. Alex nearly jumps out of her skin. It happens again, and then more shrieks join it, creaking and groaning like the gears of some horrible machinery. Amara looks up, somewhere above Alex's head, and begins to laugh.

"What the fuck is that?"

Amara hands her the binoculars. "This," he says, "is what I took you here to see."

At first, when she points the lenses of the binoculars upward, she sees nothing: just the blue sky, vaguely blurry. She adjusts the focus, turning haphazardly to and fro, until she sees a great creature soaring through the sky into frame: thin, small legs dangling behind it, broad, sharp-edged grey wings, and a knife for a mouth with a lively eye behind it, a wisp of feather flying from its head like a hairpiece. It opens its beak, sending forth another terrible screech.

"A heron!" Alex says, and as soon as she says it, she sees that it's not just one heron, but two, three, four, five, small ones yelling and clacking their beaks, all coming to alight eventually deep in the branches of a tall tree. There, their screeching turns to a harsh cackling, sounding like laughter coming from some bizarre peanut gallery. The nests come into view, monolithic arrangements of sticks among the branches. Sometimes the little herons jump around, flapping their wings, the whole time cackling. All the while, the parent stands upright, its lively eye trained on the water, undistracted by the cacophony of its offspring from its perpetual mission of finding food for them.

"There's a colony here," Amara says. "That first time I came here, I only saw the nests. They were just starting to come back. I've watched them the whole time, from when they were laying eggs, to when the babies were first sticking their beaks up from the nest. And now look at them. They're almost grown up."

"They're amazing." Alex listens to their cackling, watches them wobble awkwardly, their dinosaur necks ever extending to beg for food, and she starts to laugh and laugh and laugh. "Oh my god! They're amazing!"

She turns around to see Amara smiling, admiring her delight. "Thank you," she says.

"Thank *you*. If you hadn't come along, I wouldn't have had anyone to share this with."

Alex can't stop thinking about how much she wants to kiss him. There is a manic energy running through her that she hasn't felt in a long time, that she thought she might never feel again. She doesn't know what to do with herself. But she can't kiss him. That would be too fast. Too much, too fast. That was the mistake she made with Adam.

She jumps to her feet, disregarding how much doing so hurts. "Amara," she says, "we have to go swimming."

"What?" He's a little spacey, not fully there with her. Then he laughs. "Sorry, where is this idea coming from all of a sudden?"

She points at the ocean. "Look at the water. I bet it's so warm."

"Saltwater? With all your wounds?"

"How bad could it be? It's water."

"And what are you going to swim in, your clothes?"

She hadn't considered this: her long-sleeved shirt, her long biking pants. They would drag her down in the water, get heavy and stiff when she emerged, and that's not what she wants right now. She wants the water to bear her up. She wants gravity to fall off of her.

"You don't mind, right," she says, but it's not a question, and she's already taken her shirt and her glasses off, and her pants follow soon after, and she is running, running down into the waves. The sun is hanging low over the sky, and she's immersing herself in it, the heavens and the water all at once. The cold is a shock when it hits her belly, but she doesn't care. She dives in, and even though the salt stings in her eyes and her cut-up hands, she doesn't care. There is no difference between her and the ocean. She *is* the ocean.

When she surfaces, her hair tangling around her face, she can see Amara's blurry shape, sitting on the mat, lemonade in hand.

"Water's great!" she calls. "Are you going to join me? Or do you just like to watch?"

"I don't mind watching," he calls back, and he rises, taking off his shirt and folding it, placing it neatly on the mat: not like hers, in a heap on the ground and probably full of sand. "But it's always nice to be invited to join."

He splashes toward her, and when he comes into view, Alex is desperate to touch him again — his broad chest covered in soft hair and gleaming in the sun, the pale swoops of his scars, his round belly. Instead she splashes him. He nearly topples over.

"Hey! That's cold!"

She dives in again, making sure that she's angled so that he'll get the full brunt of the water kicked up by her feet. She swims as fast as she can, getting winded after about three strokes — it has been years since she's gone swimming. But Amara is a stronger swimmer than her, and he catches up to her quickly: first pulling up alongside her, then catching her around the waist, pulling her in to where he is standing. She wriggles, laughing, but is unable to escape, even as she splashes water in his face as a distraction.

"You'll never get me alive!" she says.

"Big words from the person who I have currently very much gotten alive."

"For now. You'll never see it coming," she says, panting. "One day you'll look up and I'll have slithered away. Like an eel."

He pulls her closer. "Oh yeah?" he says. There are beads of water on his skin, and she feels the up-and-down rise as he breathes hard, his hand warm against her skin in the water. "That's too bad. I thought having you trapped here was going to be really fun."

She runs her hand up his body, from the band of his shorts to his collarbone, his neck, his beard. Her mouth tastes like salt.

She can't take it anymore. She has to do it.

"Can I kiss you?" she says.

He takes her face in his hands.

Behind them in the trees, the herons cackle, their beaks wide, hungry, anticipating.

# X.

Alex wakes up in bed. Disoriented and bleary, they blink, grasp around for their glasses beside the pillow. They put them on. They are in a white room with a huge, blinded window, nothing but a closet and a black TV screen and the bed they're in: large, too large for just them, firm, draped in satiny grey sheets. There's a space beside them that's still warm. They look around, but there's no sign of anyone. The door is slightly ajar.

"Hello?" they call. They are wearing only boxers, and when they run a hand over their head, the longer hair on top, the part that's not buzzed off, is spiking out in all directions. They catch their reflection in the TV screen. They look a mess. Their mouth is dry and stale-tasting; they would do anything for a glass of water.

"Hello?" they call again. When no one answers, they sit up. There are bite marks on their neck. There is something important that they are not remembering.

"Good morning," says a deep voice, and from behind the door emerges Adam, a towel wrapped around his narrow waist, his hair wet. He grins at them, closing the door behind him. "You really slept in. It's almost noon."

"How do you know?" they say without thinking.

He furrows his brow. "What do you mean?"

"I mean." What do they mean? "There's no clock in here, we can't see outside. How do you know it's almost noon?"

"There are these things," he says, sitting on the bed beside them, "called phones." He leans down and kisses them on the mouth, soft and slow. "What do you want for breakfast? Or lunch, rather. Or perhaps brunch? We could go to Nancy's and get waffles."

He is so beautiful. Alex slides a hand across his smooth chest, then across his face, the tips of their fingers catching against the rough golden stubble that he won't shave. They're glad he won't; they love it, love the sensation of it scratching across their own skin when he grabs them by the back of the head and presses his tongue hard into their open, waiting mouth. They kiss him again, and there is a painfulness to their longing that gives them pause.

"What's wrong?" he says.

"Nothing."

"No, you have to tell me. I can feel it. You're tensed up, and you're not telling me something."

"I feel like I'm not telling *myself* something. I feel like there's something wrong that I need to fix, and I didn't fix it, and now I've forgotten about it. And I'm trying to remember what it is."

"It's not me," Adam says. "You don't have to worry about that. Because I forgave you."

Something is wrong.

"You forgave me?"

"For New Year's." He smiles.

*Oh no.*

"No, you didn't," they say, slowly. "No. That's not what happened. I begged you to forgive me, and you said no. And then you refused to speak to me. Even after I nearly fucking died."

"*I* nearly fucking died," he says, "and you still said what you said."

"Adam, I told you—"

"But that's all in the past now." He smiles again. "We can move forward. Together."

"No."

"Even though you're clearly still harbouring some unhealthy resentment toward me."

"I shouldn't have said what I said. I know that. I knew it as soon as the fucking words left my mouth. That's why I said sorry. That's why I fucking ran down the street in the middle of the night in the pouring rain to try and find you. It was wrong. I'm sorry."

"Stop yelling at me. You don't have to yell at me. I'm right here."

"I'm not yelling!"

"And I already forgave you."

They cover their face with a pillow. "If you forgave me, why do you keep bringing this up?"

"I love you," he says. "I'll always love you. You're hurting, and I want to take care of you."

He puts his arms around them, and it's like it always was: like returning home after a long time away. How could they not believe him when he says he cares? How could this not be the rest of their life?

"I didn't tell anyone," they whisper.

"Are you sure?"

"Your friends wouldn't have heard us. They were drunk, and they were downstairs. And I thought they knew, anyway. I thought they knew and they just didn't care."

"I'm not talking about my friends."

"I didn't tell anyone. Who would I have told? It's not like I talk to Em much anymore."

"Amara," he says, and they remember.

The knowledge freezes them in place. They want to run out the door, but they can't. They are half-naked, and they are wrapped in his arms, and they want to leave, and they never do. In this exact bed, the same scene repeating endlessly. But at least, they think, at least he isn't running away this time. At least he isn't dying. He is talking to them, not in the dead voice, but like he always did: deep and rich and alive, like they were the only person in the world he spoke to this way.

"I didn't tell him, either."

"But you gave him an idea."

"I don't think I did."

"You made me out to be this one-dimensional villain of gender repression."

"What was I supposed to do? Lie?"

He is stroking the nape of their neck, where the prickly buzzed hairs meet their skin.

"Is it lying to tell both sides of the story?" he says. "The situation, as you laid it out, was totally without nuance. I was this horrible evil man who destroyed your self-esteem, isolated you, pushed you back in the closet. You were an innocent little flower whose glorious blooming was cut short by your relationship with me. That's what you told him."

"That's not fair."

"We agree, then."

"No, I mean I told him about what I loved about you." Did they? "How you took care of me and understood me. I told him that."

"Only as window dressing to my alleged cruelty. You wanted to spice up the narrative. Make it more tragic-romantic. I know you love that stuff."

They look at the image reflected in the screen. Adam sitting upright, his hands stroking them, his body supporting their weight. So many times they thought there was nothing else they wanted more than this. That there was nothing more to desire in life than this. He's right, they think; he's right. They wanted the tragic romance. They wanted the burning, the eternal flame.

"Did you tell him," Adam continues, "about all the times you kept me up at night trying to talk you off the ledge? All the time you spent burying me in narrations of your poor self-image, begging me to make you feel better about yourself? Going on about how you were ugly and worthless and you didn't deserve me. Dumping your mom trauma and your dad trauma and your sick trauma and your crazy trauma straight onto my head, expecting me to be your saviour. Not only about that, but about the rest of the stuff we did together. All the nights we spent just talking and talking and talking. The night we walked along the beach in the snow."

They were a little drunk, and the snowflakes kissed their skin, and in the pocket of Adam's big winter coat they held his hand tightly. The streetlights were like stars.

"Because if you don't tell him that, you're not telling him the full story. It's called codependence. It takes two to tango, Alex."

"But you." They can't say it. "But you—"

"You're making excuses for yourself."

"You told me not to tell anyone. And I haven't." Their own eyes in the black screen, hollow. They can't see Adam's. "Doesn't that count for something?"

"You always have to be the victim. Even when you're not."

"I'm sorry." The tears roll onto his chest. "You're right. I'm sorry."

"You don't even know what happened to me."

They can no longer lie in place. They try to twist upward, but his arms are closed around them. They can only look up at his half-smiling face.

"What happened?" they say, pleading. "Tell me what happened."

"You don't want to know."

"But I do. I tried—"

"You just want to use me for this web of tragedy you're spinning around yourself. And I'm not going to let you do that."

They watch the motion of his hand on their neck, back and forth, predictable like the hand of a broken clock.

"That's why I'm staying with you," he says. "It doesn't matter what happened anymore. Because it's what we promised, right? We need each other. I'm sorry I made you feel like I was abandoning you. I only did it because I was feeling abandoned. Not that that's an excuse. But I'm here now. I'm not going to leave anymore. It's just you and me. Like it was always supposed to be."

Back and forth. Back and forth.

Tick tock.

"I don't want to be here," they say.

"What are you talking about?"

"I don't want to be here," they say, louder this time, and they strain against his arms. "Let me go."

"I thought," he says, his voice tightening, "you would do anything for this."

They are stronger than he is, and when they press their arms outward, his collapse. They spin away. "I don't want it anymore."

"You said you would do anything for me to talk to you again. You said that the last time we saw each other."

"I want to go back." They look around the room for something to cover their body. There is nothing but the sheet on the bed, so they whip it off and drape it over themself. They grab the handle of the door. It is locked.

"Did you fucking lock this?"

"I didn't do anything," Adam says. He is lying in the same position on the bed. He is entertained. This is funny to him.

"Well, can you open it? I'm leaving."

"You're strong," he says with a mocking edge. "You're so strong, Alex. Why can't you open it?"

They rattle the doorknob, turning it hard one way and the other, twisting their wrist, bracing their feet and pulling. Nothing gives. "Fuck!"

"Why are you yelling? The door is inanimate. It can't hear you."

"Shut the fuck up!" They are actually yelling, not caring if he's hurt. They remember Amara glowing in the ocean. They remember the look in Adam's eyes as he stood over them. *If you tell anyone—*

They take a few steps back from the door. Then, with all the strength they can muster, they leap at it, barrelling forward, leading with their shoulder. They slam into the door, expecting no effect other than their shoulder bursting with pain. But it is the door that crumbles, splintering easily, like a thin sheet of balsa for a model plane. They nearly topple through it.

Alex looks back at Adam. He is stricken, no longer laughing.

"Alex," he says, "I don't use this word lightly."

"Fuck off."

"But you're crazy."

They step over the threshold, out the jagged hole in the door, where there is nothing but an enveloping whiteness.

# 4.

Alex wakes up without sight. She blinks painfully, trying to see, trying to remember where she is, but everything is white, and everything behind her eyelids is angry red. She grasps around the pillow for her glasses, and instead puts her hand directly on someone's face.

"Mnfm?" Amara says, still asleep, and pulls his arm around her closer.

Alex slides one hand out from under Amara's and uses it to shield her face. He has to get blinds in here, or at least a blanket to pin up over the skylight. Based on the strength of the sun beaming in, and on the degree to which the little loft has the temperature and humidity of the inside of a rice cooker, it must be around noon. Did she make him miss work? But no, they think, no, it's Saturday. The two of them can sleep in as much as they want.

In this heat, though, it is high time to escape the loft. Alex gently pokes Amara in the shoulder. "Hey," she says. "Wake up."

"Mfnfgh," Amara grumbles.

Fine, then: he can sleep if he really wants to. Alex carefully lifts his arm off her torso, replacing it on top of the blanket. Then, as quietly as she can, she grabs her glass from the other side of the pillow and rolls away, stepping lightly so as not to activate the house-shaking creaks of the wooden steps as she climbs down to the living room. The temperature here seems to be ten degrees cooler, though it remains on the verge of unbearable. Alex cracks open the window, breathing in the fresh air of the forest. It is nearly as hot outside as it is inside.

She leaves the windows open as she walks to the kitchen, fills a mug with tap water to sip, and begins to prepare her coffee. Normally, Amara is awake far before she is. She never has to worry about bean-grinding disturbing his rest. But she figures it won't be a disaster if he gets woken up by the grinder this late in the day. It'll save him a few minutes roasting in the heat of the loft.

She pours the last few spoonfuls of beans left in the bag into the grinder a little mournfully — there will be no afternoon brew today — and grinds away. She listens for the sounds of disturbance up the stairs. Nothing but Amara's normal sleep mumbles. She pours the grounds into the coffee maker, fills it with water, presses the button. It beeps dutifully. Now all she has to do is wait.

It is strange being here in the little kitchen without Amara a few feet away, or Amara hovering over her, telling her what to do, groaning good-naturedly at her culinary ineptitude. The mornings already feel routine: waking up to the bright light in the loft, coming downstairs to see Amara sitting in his chair with his laptop, headphones on. Sometimes he'll be on a call with his coworkers, loudly discussing things that make no sense to Alex — data sets and code and trends. If she checks the counter, she'll see coffee, most often, already ground for her, some kind of little breakfast snack prepared: a bagel with peanut butter and jam, or a fruit salad; she told him how she doesn't like to eat too much right after waking up. Then she'll sit in the chair beside him with her coffee, poring through one of his bird books, or she'll take the e-bike out for a ride. Not to the cove or the village, but to the heron beach, the road through the forest so familiar now that she barely has to look where she's going.

Every time Alex goes to the beach it is exactly as magical as when Amara took them the first time. It doesn't matter what time of the day it is, how hot the sun is, where the tide is. The herons fly, roost, sometimes fish, chattering all the while. Eagles, too, soaring high above the herons' tree, checking from their great height for any opportunity to snatch up a gangly heron baby from the nest. The herons alight, all of them shrieking louder than Alex has ever heard, and fly far out over the ocean, out to where the blue fades into the sky and she can no longer see them. The eagles pause at the very top of the trees, the branches swaying in their taloned clutches. Then they, too, fly away, out beyond the treetops, where their hunt might be more successful.

Alex has gone to the beach almost every day. It is the most she's been in the water since she was a kid. At first, she swam nervously, breathing shallow, in a shirt and boxers, staying only where her feet could touch the ground. But it doesn't take long for her to grow bolder. She dives to the seafloor, eyes open and blind and stinging, and lets her hands trail across the ridges of sand. She takes the shirt off. No one is ever there — no one is watching — and if she does hear the stirring of the engine down the road, she knows it will be Amara there to admire her, to lift her out of the water and tell her that it's time for dinner. It's natural, all of it: deep in the water, taken back home.

Natural, too, has been having sex again. Alex was scared that she wouldn't want it, that it had been too long, that getting fucked would be too much, that she wouldn't be able to take Amara's touch without her body going limp and pleasureless, her body retreating to that distant empty place. She told him as much, unable to look him in the eyes. He said it was okay if they stopped. It was okay — he wouldn't be mad. He understood.

But Alex's fears never manifested. She found herself wide open, begging to be filled up, conscious and present in every nerve. Her face buried in Amara's thick hair, her tongue stroking his cock, moving up and down at the will of his hand inside them and his mouth licking her ass. When they were finished, she couldn't stop kissing him: not on the mouth, but little, light kisses, all around his face, sitting on his lap with her legs wrapped around him as they both laughed in pleasure. Alex didn't remember that she'd fallen asleep when she woke up the first morning, the sunlight stream-ing through the skylight. Amara's heavy, slow breaths rose and fell in his chest, and Alex felt them against her own. It seemed real again, the dream that they'd once had. To see yourself reflected, brighter and more beautiful, in someone else.

She slipped out of bed, creaking down the stairs, and in the bathroom, she stared at her body in the small mirror. The worn-out face; the hair, messier and coarser than ever. The fading, sloping scars, the defined muscles that were once in her torso and arms nearly gone. They pushed their hair back. And they realized, standing there in the unlit bathroom, the door left open absently, that they were not seeing their body as the body of a failure, an incompleteness that could never be fully her. It was hers, even though she didn't love it, even though it had so many obvious flaws, so much pain whose source was unknowable. Within it, she recognized herself.

Now, Alex looks at the empty counter and has an epiphany. She should cook Amara breakfast.

The more she turns it over in her mind, the more it resembles a perfect plan. She's observed him cooking enough over the past days that she feels confident in her ability to make a simple meal. Fried eggs and toast and a little salad. Nothing crazy — just classic and delicious. And he'll be so surprised. He'll never see it coming.

When they open the fridge, though, it is barren. There are only two eggs left, a bit of wilted spinach at the bottom of a bag. Some leftover rice noodles from last night. No bread anywhere — the fridge, the freezer, the counter, the microwave. Okay, so fried eggs it is. Fried eggs and a little spinach, one egg for each of them. It's not much, but it's the thought that counts, especially when you're talking about breakfast in bed. So she takes out the two eggs. They turn on the cooktop, pour a little oil in a clean steel pan. She watches the oil as it spreads out, beginning to shine. So far, so good.

The eggs, now. The worst thing would be to crack it too lightly, crumbling the shell and increasing the likelihood of shell mixing in with the egg. Or no, wait: it would be worse to crack it too hard, smashing the egg in her hand, wasting it, and leaving only one egg to cook for Amara. And Amara wouldn't let her go without. So, after taking a deep breath, she hits it against the edge of the counter almost in the same motion as an injection: gentle but direct, like throwing a dart.

It works. The egg is broken, but not collapsed. Alex opens the shell above the pan, and the egg falls out, sizzling as it hits the pan, the yolk unbroken. The other one is cracked and placed in the pan with similar ease. The whites start to set, and Alex admires her work with pride. She might actually learn to cook while she's here.

The stairs creak horribly behind her. "Is that food I smell?" Amara says, yawning. He comes up behind them, catching her by the waist and planting a kiss on the back of her neck. "Is the notoriously bad-at-cooking Alex frying up some eggs?"

"They're all that's left in the fridge."

"Oh, shit, really?" Amara opens the fridge and groans. "God, I'm going to have to go into town soon."

"Why not just go to the village?" Alex has avoided mentioning the village. She doesn't really want to go back, not after what happened the last time, and Amara hasn't expressed any desire to return, either. It has been easy, then, to imagine that the entire world of the island is just the forest and the beaches and this cottage, and them the only two people alive.

But the threat of Amara leaving her on her own is even more potent than her fear of seeing other people again. Every night she has been here, long after Amara falls asleep, she has laid awake, her heart pounding, attuned to every small noise. The darkness and the silence surrounding the cottage is unlike anything she's experienced before: not a comforting contrast to 709's mechanical sounds, but a new kind of fear, an anticipation of interruption. She wakes up to greet every bright day exhausted, like she hasn't slept at all. With Amara here, it's easy enough to forget during the daylight hours, to imagine that the open-eyed nights have all the significance of a half-forgotten dream, but what would happen if she had to be alone?

"You think I'm going to the village?" Amara fills a cup of water from the tap and points it at Alex, a little water splashing over the rim as he does. "Let me tell you what happened to me when I went to the village. This was the second day I got here. I got out of my car and stood at the crosswalk to cross over to the grocery store. Very normal, very citizen-like behaviour. This elderly lady comes up behind me. And so I step to the side and smile at her, because that's what a nice young person does, right? And I keep smiling, even though she's full-on staring at me with her lips pressed together and her eyes bugged out like she's super mad. And then she says, in this really suspicious voice, 'Are you from here?' And I'm like, no. Then she goes, 'Are you from the city?' So I'm like, yes. And then, finally, like she's some kind of bridge troll and I have to answer her three riddles before I can cross the road, she comes in with the kicker: 'Are you gay?' So, obviously, I'm like, yes. Yes, I am gay. And then, right as the traffic clears up enough for me to cross, she shakes her head and, like, mutters to herself: 'What a world.'"

"She was so right, though. What a world."

"And then when I left the store some guy in a truck drove by and yelled at me. So I was like, yeah, that's enough excitement in the village."

Alex stops laughing. "Was he wearing sunglasses?"

"I didn't see him. Why, were you hatecrimed too?"

"Yes! Literally as soon as I got here. Some guy in a truck also drove by and yelled at me."

"Jesus Christ." He puts a hand on Alex's shoulder. "I wonder if he has a quota he has to hit, like every day he has to identify someone to harass."

Alex is about to tell him about the other thing, the rock flying at her head, the fear that made her come crawling to him in the first place. Something stops her, though, a bit of hesitation in her throat: the knowledge of how she might come off, how much she would derail the lighthearted tone of their conversation, just like she had that first time they talked on the phone. Someone looking for violence in every interaction. A victim.

Before she can push it aside, Amara furrows his brow. "Are the eggs okay?"

"Oh, fuck!"

Alex turns around. There is smoke swirling up from the pan, and the outer edges of the eggs are crisp and black. Panicked, she turns off the burner and attempts to slide the eggs out of the pan and onto a plate with a spatula. The scrapings pile up on the plate in a messy heap, and thick unscrapable chunks of egg are burned to the pan.

"I think they're edible," Alex says mournfully, offering Amara the plate.

"It's okay," he says, picking a tiny piece of non-burnt egg off the plate and eating it with his fingers. "We can pick up sandwiches from that farm when we go to the lake in an hour. And besides, it's the thought that counts."

"The lake?"

"Oh, yeah." He is peering into the fridge, moving containers around. "God, I need to do a cleanout. Yeah, my friends are coming to go to the lake. They're supposed to be on the 1:10 ferry. You don't have to come if you don't want to, though. Aha!" He emerges, triumphant, with a container of Greek yogourt and a spoon.

"Where did that spoon come from?" Alex asks. Panic grips her chest.

"It's a fridge spoon. I keep a spoon in the fridge."

"That's fucked up."

"So, the lake?" He shovels yogourt into his mouth. "I mentioned it, right? I must have. It's a huge deal that their lazy asses are coming out here. They've been complaining about how much it costs to take a car on the ferry for two weeks."

Alex has no memory of this plan, but if Amara remembers mentioning it, then he must have. How can Alex trust her mind over anyone else's? Not after how many times it had proven itself useless. Worse than useless: actively antagonistic to the cause of her leading a bearable life. "Sorry," she says. "Remind me what your friends' names are?"

"There's gonna be Mel and Tristan for sure. No more yogourt," he says mournfully, looking into the empty container as though he can will away its emptiness.

"Okay." Alex waves their arms, an ineffective attempt to waft smoke out the open window. "I really should go check on the house, though."

Like the village, she has not mentioned 709 to Amara the whole time she's been here. She has not made the walk back through the cathedral to the house. She's been wearing Amara's clothes, loose enough to hang off her body like dresses. She's been eating Amara's food, sleeping in Amara's bed. She has thought sometimes, guiltily, about their responsibility to Ella, to Ella's parents — but then she remembers the days spent in there, the horrible voice coming through the phone speakers, the cliff and the smell of death. The shadow on the screens in the security room. The painful crawl up the stairs: would it even be possible with her injured wrist still hurting? The house was empty long before she got there. Surely, it would be fine without her for a while.

But she has to go check at least once. At least to get her clothes. She can't wear Amara's clothes around his friends. She can make sure everything is clean, check the security footage. Once she goes back, once she demonstrates to the irrational dread that has taken root in her brain that nothing bad will happen, then it will be okay. Once she knows it's fine, she'll be free to check in every once in a while and leave afterward, the house not casting a shadow in her mind over every moment spent away from it. And while she's there attending to her tasks, she won't have to sit here with Amara waiting for his friends to arrive, imagining all the while what they're going to think of her, how little she'll have to say to them: how little, in the well-worn grooves of conversation between old friends, she'll exist.

"That makes sense," Amara says over the sound of running water and scrubbing. "Just be back in an hour if you want to come along."

"Okay," Alex says. She stops at the door, waiting, before she slips out.

———

Alex is always surprised by the speed with which the temperature can change in the forest. Even in today's otherwise suffocating heat, as she walks among the trees, the pink trail markers sometimes waving lightly in the shallow breaths of the breeze, a chill runs through her. Like someone is walking over her grave: that was another saying her mom always liked. Or maybe it wasn't. Alex is unsure, sometimes, what she really remembers about her mom, how many of the things she thinks she knows about her are mere transpositions, the patches applied, subconsciously and haphazardly, over the holes in her childhood consciousness. She has the feeling, as she does often, that she used to remember more. The memories come to her in flickers, like small flames, and to move too quickly toward them snuffs them out before she has a chance to feel their quiet heat. She follows the wavering pink ribbons, and in the heat and wooziness of oversleeping, the forest seems to waver along with them.

As she drags her heavy feet over the soft forest ground, as the world shimmers and warps around her, she focuses on the trail markers. A bolt-bright thought, clear and sharp, pierces through her cloudy mind: Years before she ever arrived here, she knew this place.

———

In all her years of running trails alone, Alex only got lost once. People were often dismayed to find out that she didn't wear a GPS band, that she carried only a decade-out-of-date Blackberry with her. The real reason she didn't have better devices was that she couldn't afford them: the money that she did spend on running she put into shoes and clothes and race fees, which she figured were much more important. But she explained it to others as a desire to fully engage her senses as she was running, to take everything in, eyes open and ears listening, attuned not just to the rhythms of her body, but the shape of the world around her.

James shook his head. "Alex, no offence," he said, "but that sounds like bullshit."

It was. Alex knew the trails better than anyone. She had an innate sense of direction; she learned to read the moss on the trees, the position of the sun in the sky, the sound of water. And she didn't push the limit, not when it came to running in places where the trails were unmarked and the weather could change in an instant; that was why she felt safest close to the ocean. But there was a part of her, somewhere just below her conscious mind, that believed if she was going to get lost, she was meant to get lost. How many times, after all, had she tried and failed to take her mortality into her own hands? Every earnest attempt at controlling the ultimate outcome of her life had gone awry. Maybe, then, this was the right way to go about things, to let the mountains determine what was going to happen to her, ceding all agency to a power far greater than herself.

A full year after the bad suicide attempt, the one she doesn't think about, Alex felt strong — truly strong — for the first time. She was beginning to believe, in fact, that she was a little bit invincible. She would party until the club closed, sleep for a few hours, and then wake up with the sun for a morning run before work. She was doing well enough in school; with student loans and her income from her job, she had started to put money away.

Everything felt like it was exactly where it should be, her life flowing out ahead of her: a vast, unobstructed river.

One late-fall Saturday, early in the morning, she stood out at the beginning of her habitual trail: facing the ocean, the mountains towering over her to the north. The sky was clear and cold. She watched her breath crystallize in front of her, and beyond the faint cloud of her breathing, the pair of twin peaks glistened in the distance.

I'm going to do it, she thought. I'm going to run the crest alone.

In James's car — at that point, he was basically her personal chauffeur — he seemed skeptical. "You've never run this alone before."

"Nope," Alex said, bouncing in her seat. She took a slug of water. "And after today, I will have."

"In fact," he said, "none of us have ever run this alone."

"Yeah. That's what I'm so *fucking* excited about, James."

"Have you been planning this for a while?"

"Nope."

He looked askance. "Nope? Alex, it's like a nine, ten-hour run. You don't just do this on a whim. We're not professionals."

"Yeah, but we've done it together before, right?" Up, up they climbed, up the mountain road, through the thick trees; the city, when it appeared in the distance, grew smaller and smaller below them. "So I know all the landmarks. And it's an extremely well-marked, popular trail. And it's such a beautiful day. I don't know, dude, I just feel like nothing can go wrong."

"Historically, that's what people tend to say right before things go wrong."

"I mean cosmically." She could see the parking lot up ahead, and she could barely restrain herself from flying out of the seat with excitement. "I kind of feel like nothing is ever going to go wrong for me ever again."

James sighed, pulling into a parking spot just ahead of the trailhead. "That's great. I'm happy for you. But don't do anything

stupid, okay? Turn around if you get tired. Don't drink from pud-
dles full of mosquitoes if you're thirsty. I don't want to turn on the
news tonight and find out they're naming a peak after you."

Three of the five peaks on the trail were named after people
who'd died on it.

"No way," Alex said, already out the car door and beginning
her stretches. "I'll be seeing you down at the bay in ten hours.
Probably less."

And as soon as she saw James's car disappear around the bend,
she began her journey.

The crest trail wound its way up and down five mountain
peaks, passing by lakes and meadows, cols and sheer rock faces,
before descending down to the bay, opening up almost at the ferry
terminal. It ran twenty-eight kilometres, ascending six thousand
feet and descending eight. Certain sections of the trail were popular with day-hikers and runners; certain sections were populated
only by serious outdoorspeople.

This first section, before the hard ascent started, was one of the
popular ones. Alex bypassed groups of older women, people with
dogs, hikers carrying tents and poles: for them, the trail required
an overnight stay. But not for her. When she finally pulled ahead,
the forest quieting around her, the trail growing steep and treach-
erous with roots and rocks, the elation propelled her forward.
This was what she was looking for.

Alone on the trail, Alex had one of the best days of her life. She
watched the sun rising from the first summit she crested; she scaled
the narrow col between the two peaks that had called to her hours
before, back when she was standing on the shore. In a meadow, the
heat starting to bear down on her, she stopped to eat among thousands of purple flowers, thousands more bees humming around
her, and then onward she went: to the lookout where she could
see the entirety of the island laid out in the ocean, a slight descent,
and then upward, upward to the final peak, where a small, crystal-
line lake was nestled into the rocks. After taking off her hydration

vest, putting her poles and pack in a pile on the shore, she jumped in, diving, the occasional trout jumping around her. Her laughs echoed, sounding like the forest was laughing with her.

When it was time for the steep descent, the sun was already beginning to fade. The fatigue was building in her legs. The trail here was steep, narrow, laden with roots and loose earth; with each step, she had to hold herself upright, tense and tired, digging her feet in to make sure they didn't slip out from underneath her. Down and down and down the trail wound, all external landmarks disappearing from view, and Alex, for the first time all day, found her mind wandering. She wondered if James was already at the bay. Having nearly run out of water, she thought about how she would ration the rest for the descent. The temperature was dropping quickly, and the heat from her body was turning into steam in the chilly air. Alex blinked, and then stopped in her tracks. She was lost.

She had been following the trail markers tied in the tree branches, almost without thinking about it. But the dwindling light and a few moments of distraction were enough for her to have veered off course. She leaned over, her hands on her thighs. Her muscles, now taken out of their steady rhythm, began to feel heavy and immobile. Standing in place, she scanned the surrounding trees for trail markers. There were none, none anywhere, and every minute, it was getting colder and darker.

She pulled out her phone. There was no reception, as she expected. She tried to put a call through to James anyway; it was promptly dropped. She was still an hour off the time that they were supposed to meet at the bay, so there was no chance he'd be walking up the trail trying to find her. And she knew well the advice for anyone lost in the mountains, especially when the weather was changing, especially in the dark: stay put until someone comes to find you.

But she couldn't bring herself to do it. She had to be able to get out of here. She had to. She couldn't have gone that far astray. And despite the protestations of her body and the anxiety sprouting in her mind, she decided to find her way back to the trail.

Northwest: that was the way she needed to be going. The sun was no longer a helpful compass, so she studied the moss on the trees. It was only slight, but she thought she could identify a greater density on one side. She faced that side, turned slightly to the left, and set off in that direction. It seemed to be the right choice at first; it was, at the very least, going downhill.

But after about fifteen minutes of continuous walking, Alex hit a deep ravine, dead trees and earth tumbling into a scar in the ground. She peered into it: a trickle of water at the bottom, thick shrubs all around. A groan of frustration. It was impassable.

So she took a right, hugging the side of the ravine, and continued on that way. Now she was no longer going downhill, and her vision was growing more and more limited. She'd taken a headlamp with her, less out of an expectation that she'd have to use it than a belief that having a headlamp was an extremely cool thing to do in all situations, and now she was grateful for her commitment to an outdoorsman aesthetic. The beam from the headlamp flooded over the needle-covered ground at her feet. On the branches around her, though, it revealed nothing but green, brown, green, identical branches on identical trees.

Alex was genuinely cold and getting genuinely worried. She was fully out of water. She had only one nutrition bar left with her, the one that she'd been saving for the car ride back home with James. Where was the trail? How had she gone so far off? Maybe her estimation of the tree moss had been wrong. The ravine took a left, but Alex continued on the same trajectory. It seemed like the only thing to do was to keep on going. She looked at her watch. James would have arrived at the bay by now, and he would be waiting for her. Her phone refused to connect. Dizzy, the ground sloping underneath her. She should have bought a personal location beacon when she thought about it last winter. She should have paid for a better phone plan. She should have just fucking paid attention. She would be back at the car by now if she had just kept her mind on what she was doing. But it was too late, too late to stop moving, and so she kept going on through the darkening woods. When she looked up at the sky, she could see clouds coalescing into an ominous mass. A flash — and then, a second later, a skull-shaking rumble. Rain began to spatter onto her head.

Maybe it would be better to die in a lightning storm than to freeze to death at the bottom of some gully. A tree could fall on her head, or maybe a bolt would strike her directly. Boom, zap, and it would be over. They might never even find her that way. Her chest heaved, and a pain stabbed her guts from all sides, like she was wearing a belt with spikes turned inward. She knew she wouldn't be able to continue walking for much longer. She closed her eyes. She might as well have had them closed since she took the first steps away from the trail.

When she opened them again, she had entered a completely different world.

Instead of the dense, thick forest she had been pushing through, she found herself in the centre of an empty space, where, massive trees arched over her like a roof. Somehow, there was light streaming in, brighter even than the artificial light pouring out of her headlamp. The rain fell lightly, the light catching it in rainbow sparks. It was quiet, and the ground was soft and open.

Like a cathedral, Alex thought, her mind suddenly clear. And at the far end of the clearing, she could just make out a pink ribbon tied to a dangling branch, swaying lightly in the wind.

When she got back to James's car, she was only fifteen minutes late. She never told him what happened. And she never went up the crest alone again. She met Adam a few weeks after that, and memory became unsettled, untrustworthy.

She hasn't thought of the crest trail in years. But that's where she knows this place from. She remembers now. Even though she's never been here before this summer; even though, the last time she was here, she was near-delirious, lost and panicked, on a completely different land mass, living a completely different life. An existence so different from her life now that it's hard to process as being part of her own past. This place can't possibly be the same, but it is. She knows it is.

She stops and looks up. Somewhere up in the trees, the woodpecker's lonely hammer echoes. Below it, Alex hears the faint, clear ringing of a bell.

It is so faint that she believes it's a trick of the forest, some combination of sounds that has deceived her brain, altering the unfamiliar into something familiar for the sake of comfort. But it grows clearer, getting closer. The soft knocking of the woodpecker, steady but slightly irregular like a worried heartbeat, and underneath it the bells, unmistakably there and moving toward her.

An apparition: a bright colour, a blurry shape. Standing in front of Alex in between two trees is a dog. The dog is long-haired and fluffy, with a black and white and grey coat. Their eyes are blue. They have a shiny tag around their neck, and their pink tongue lolls out as they pant in the heat.

Alex doesn't dislike dogs, but she doesn't understand them. She never had a pet growing up, and on the rare occasions that she visited other kids' houses, she found the presence of dogs confusing and inconsistent. The body language of cats was more intuitive to her: most of the time, they just wanted to be left alone, and one was better off not touching them. But dogs were full of noise and motion and contradictory meanings. A wagging tail, a pant, a bark — all of these contextually dependent, varying from creature to creature. Like with people, one had to be attuned to individual nuances of personality in order to establish a safety level. Like with people, to misread an interaction could be dangerous, legitimately dangerous, and as Alex stands facing the dog her breath grows shallow, her mind retreats. She wills her body to be as calm as possible. Never go up to a strange dog: that was another piece of her mom's advice that she always remembered. You don't know where they came from, and you don't know if they might bite.

The dog doesn't move. The dog pants, then blinks. Its tail wags softly. Slowly, Alex's breathing steadies.

"Ella," she says aloud. The beloved friend, missing — maybe stolen — the poster now thrown out, so who would know? Who would know where she is except Alex?

Alex takes a step forward gingerly, bracing herself for a bark, a flinch, a charge.

But Ella doesn't move. She only pants. Alex extends a hand. Her fingers waver, and when she speaks again, so does her voice. "Hi, Ella," she says, moving closer in such small increments that it barely even seems like she's moving. But she is moving, and the dog's face is so close that she could touch it. That's when she stops, her body held still, waiting for the other to make a move.

The woodpecker drums, and the soft cracking of a piece of falling bark nearly makes Alex jump out of her skin.

In, two, three, four.

Out, two, three, four.

She is just about to grasp the shiny tag in her hand when the dog takes off. It is so abrupt, so unannounced by any change in sound or gesture, that Alex doesn't even react. She stands dumbfounded, watching Ella's fluffy tail disappearing into the trees. The faint jingling from her collar grows softer and softer until it disappears and Alex is once again alone.

Alone: alone in the forest, alone in the dripping heat, smothered by a thick blanket that encompasses her from all sides. She can't breathe. She needs to breathe, but she can't. She looks for the trail marker, the bright pink ripple of the familiar, but she can't find it, her eyes can't focus. There is an emptiness, an endless darkness between the trees where the dog once was and is no longer.

Alex runs. She doesn't look at the ground. She looks straight ahead, right where Ella had plunged into the forest. Her toes catch against roots and her ankles scream, but she has to run — she has to — there is no choice, nothing to do but try to get away, and the trees are changing around her, the angles of the light warping and the chill brushing against her arms even as the sweat pours down her back. Ridiculous, she knows she looks ridiculous, sprinting painfully in sandals with this too-big shirt flapping around her, even more so because she doesn't know why she's running anymore: there's no way she'll catch up with a dog who doesn't want to be caught. She is long past the trail markers, but she runs faster, breathing harder, letting the ache of collapse fill her lungs, her whole body.

She won't be able to go on much longer, not with the knives from below, the broken heaving in her chest. When she finally stops, she bends over like her back is broken. Her feet give way to the ground, and her glasses slide off her face.

In the blur of the lens-less world, she can barely understand that what she has stumbled upon is a fence. It is only a few feet away from her, close enough for even her terrible eyes to make out the grain of the wood. She reaches out and touches it, running her fingers along the smooth surfaces of the beams. The wood is oddly cool, and the contrast between its placid surface and the roiling heat of her own body makes Alex shiver. She moves closer to the fence and rests her face against a beam. Half-formed questions bubble in her mind: Where is she? What is this fenced-off place? Who lives here? They float away as quickly as they appear. They are not real. The heat and pain of her body, the cool solidity of the fence: those are real, and she trains her focus on them, the tactile sensations of her physical reality.

But as her breathing relaxes, the thoughts don't slow in tandem. Instead, they bubble faster, building pressure against the backs of her eyes. The chill returns, this time running along the base of her neck. Like she's being watched. Is she being watched? Who is watching her? No, stupid, no one is watching her. She's being paranoid. But she can't force the thoughts away, can't calm the rising panic — not with the texture of the wood, not with any counting of breath. She has to check. She has to make sure.

She reaches for her glasses. They are so smudged, covered in sweat and tears and clinging dirt, that putting them on makes barely any difference to the clarity of her vision. She rubs them on her shirt frantically, which at least gets the dirt off them, and puts them back on again. Bracing herself against the fence, she stands and faces the world beyond the fence.

There is an uncanny sense that she is gazing into a pocket dimension. Outside the fence, the forest is tall and evergreen, but within are the bright, feathery leaves of short and manicured deciduous trees. On the ground, surrounded by smooth grey stones, are occasional little flowerbeds, their vivid colours at odds with the warm brown tones of the forest floor. Pulling the strangeness of the landscape together are tiny cottages painted bright white with brick-red shingled roofs. The place is clearly meticulously maintained, but as Alex stares, there is no one in sight: no human, no animal, not even a sound. There is only her.

In the window of one of the cottages, something moves.

Alex sees it only out of the corner of her eye. She faces the window straight on. It is one of the cottages farther away from her, and her glasses are so blurry, but she needs to make sure. At first, squinting, it seems to have been nothing. A darkened window, a curtain mostly drawn. She stares for a long minute. Nothing.

She becomes aware of how long she has been on this detour from her original plan of going back to 709. Doing so now seems impossible. She will have to find her way back to Amara's and find some excuse to explain why she disappeared only to go nowhere. This place must be connected to the road, so if she follows the fence all the way around, she should be able to make it out. Heading back into the forest would be foolish.

She begins to follow the fence to her left when, out of the corner of her eye, she sees the movement in the window again.

This time, it's not fast enough to evade her sight, even with the blurriness of her glasses. It is a person, most definitely a person: a person in black, a person with a shock of blond hair.

———

The dirt of the road leading up Amara's house has new tracks on it. Alex can't quite tell how long she's been walking along the road back from the pocket world, but she knows it's long enough for the heat and the sweat and the dirt to have formed a layer over her skin. Her hair, too, must be so tangled. And she's wearing Amara's clothes. His friends are already here. She doesn't want to think about it. She hears their voices echoing through the woods as she walks up, the overlapping ripples of laughter. She pulls her mouth into a smile, practices a silent laugh. At least she can be prepared in that sense.

Amara's friends' car is small and silver and inoffensive, a recent enough hatchback from which no distinct personality traits can be discerned. From inside the house, Amara and someone else, a warm, nasal voice, yell over each other, their interruptions competing and escalating. A softer voice laughs continuously underneath them, a gentle, harmonious counterpoint. When Alex used to hang out with people, Em's friends, before she met Adam, it was so much like this: the yelling and laughing cascading in on each other, often audible even through closed windows as Alex walked up to the old house where they all lived with each other, the blue house with the unkempt rhododendrons out front. Em lived in the attic. Lisa and Marielle shared one of the three bedrooms, Fen had the master, and the other was what Alex called the chaos space: part guest bedroom, part art studio, part work-from-home office.

Maybe it was still just like that, even after three years. Maybe they didn't get renovicted like Fen kept worrying they would. They might still all be there, with Em lying on the floor like they always were for some reason, and Fen taking up the entire couch, and

Lisa and Marielle crammed onto the hideous armchair, laughing and yelling and screaming at each other just like they had before they ever met Alex, just like they probably continued to do after she faded out of their lives.

Alex pauses outside the door. She can make out what they're talking about, but she can't understand it, full of references to things that they were doing in high school, names that she doesn't recognize. She's not sure, at this point of familiarity with Amara and the house, whether it would be more polite to knock and wait for an answer or to simply let herself in. After some consideration, she opts for the latter. She will open the door and slip in without being noticed.

It doesn't work. The conversation stops as soon as she steps in, and three pairs of eyes stare at her. A blue-eyed white girl in a comically floofy dress is sitting, presumably cross-legged, on the floor. A moustachioed guy, dark-skinned and bald, in what could only be described as a normal-guy uniform sits in the armchair Alex has been sitting in. And then there is Amara, whose eyes are red and puffy as he rubs the laughter out of them.

"Oh my god, Alex," he says, "I've been murdered."

Alex can't think of a funny response to this. "Oh no," she says weakly. Standing awkwardly with nowhere to sit, feeling the eyes on her, the stoppage in the conversation that her entrance created, she fights the urge to cover her face with her hair.

Amara gestures toward his friends. "These are the murderers I've invited into my home. Tristan—" He waves to the guy on the chair, who waves at Alex. "And then there's Mel." Mel flashes a peace sign.

"So you're the famous Alex," Tristan says: the softer voice.

"Am I famous?" Alex says nervously.

"Are you kidding? You appeared out of nowhere from the fucking forest to sweep Amara off his feet, of course you're fucking famous." Mel laughs, then stops. Something has occurred to her. "Do I know you from somewhere?"

"I, um." Alex wracks her brain, fighting the urge to avert her gaze to a random corner of the room. She can't place Mel's face at all. "I'm not sure. My memory isn't great, though."

Mel squints again, then shakes her head. "We'll table it for now. But I'm watching you."

"Okay," Alex says, and looks at the floor.

"Lake!" Amara cries, leaping from his chair. "It's finally fucking lake time."

Mel leaps from the floor with equal vigour and four times the drama, her dress swooshing upward around her. "Shotgun."

"At this point, there's no need for you to even verbalize calling shotgun," Tristan observes, taking his plain grey baseball cap off the top of the chair and putting it on his shaved head. "You've been doing it for, like, twelve years."

"Yeah, and you won't catch me slipping now," Mel says, already out the door Alex had forgotten to close.

"Do we have drinks? Food and drinks?" Amara takes a step toward the fridge.

"Yeah, of course we do. Cooler in the trunk. Who do you think we are?" Tristan now has sunglasses on. He extends an arm. "Can I carry anything?"

"No, no, go sit in the car. I've just got towels."

As Tristan walks out, Amara sidles up to Alex. "So you're still wearing my shirt," he observes. "And you have nothing with you, and you look like you just ran a marathon. Was the house that bad?"

"I got—" She is about to say, *I got lost,* but is struck with how pathetic that sounds, how much context she would then have to provide. "I got kind of sidetracked," she continues instead. "With checking everything I needed to check. I didn't have time to go upstairs and get my clothes."

"Ah, well." He wraps an arm around her shoulders and squeezes. "No matter. It's lake time. Shall we?"

"Of course," Alex says, and hopes that he can't sense her shakiness as they walk to the car together.

Alex's legs are cramping. Tristan's sensible car isn't very big. She imagines herself as a crumpled spider, half-dead and twitching, positioning her unwieldy limbs in a way that doesn't cause them to snap and break. Tristan, much smaller than any of the others, is thankfully disengaged from Alex's wriggling. He stares contemplatively out the window as Amara and Mel babble in the front seat about some friend of theirs whose wedding was called off. It sounds like a great story, and Alex wishes she could focus on it. But it's too loud, and she's too uncomfortable, and they are in motion, speeding up and down hills to a new, distant part of the island, and everything is happening at the same time.

"So," Tristan says, "how are you liking the island?"

It takes Alex a second to notice that he's talking to her. "Oh," she says quickly. "Yeah, it's beautiful."

"I could never live here," he says.

"You don't think it's beautiful?"

Outside the window, Alex sees the flash of another NO TRESPASSING sign, then a bare patch of ground cut out of the forest, a graveyard of stumps and felled trees pushed to a perimeter, all of it fenced in by sharp wire.

"Oh no. I think it's incredibly beautiful. But it's so . . ." He looks upward, like he has a word written on the roof of the car. Eventually, he snaps his fingers. "Isolated! It's so isolated." He smiles apologetically. "Sorry, it can take me a minute to find words sometimes."

"Me too," Alex says, suddenly endeared to him. "Yeah, it is isolated, I guess. Maybe it's different if you live closer to the village."

"Maybe. You guys don't, though. You and Amara, I mean."

"Yeah, no. We really don't."

"I was honestly—" He leans toward her, speaking under his breath. "I was honestly pretty worried about Amara living alone out here."

"Really?"

"Yeah. He loves nature, obviously, but he has zero survival skills. And he's so impulsive. Obviously. That's why he ended up here in the first place. I was afraid one day he'd, like, chase a fancy bird too deep into the forest and fall down a hole like Alice in Wonderland."

Alex laughs. "He still might."

"Or just have a tree fall on his head. Or get struck by lightning. And we can't come visit that often. It's so far, and it's so expensive. So," Tristan says seriously, "I'm glad you found him."

"Me too," Alex starts to say, but her voice is drowned out by Amara and Mel's hysterical laughter.

"What is going on up there?" Tristan pokes his head between the front seats. "You two shouldn't be left unsupervised."

"Nothing, nothing, nothing," Mel chortles.

"Mel is an evil person," Amara says. "An evil, evil, sick freak of a person."

"Please don't crash the car." Tristan rolls his window down, letting his fingers trail out in the rushing breeze. His hat nearly blows off, but he catches it just in time. "No matter how evil Mel is."

"What are *you* talking about back there?"

"You."

"What could you possibly have to say about me?"

"About how," Alex chimes in, "we worry you might chase a bird and fall down a hole like Alice in Wonderland."

"And so what if I did!" The car slows and turns right onto a crunching gravel road. "It would be worth it."

"Yeah," Mel agrees, "the only reason Alice had a bad time was because she made stupid decisions. If you had common sense, you would have a great fucking time in Wonderland. But," she says, pointing a finger, "Amara has no common sense."

"It's Wonderland! Lack of common sense would be a positive quality!" Amara shakes his head. "All of this slander of the person who, as of right this second, has delivered you unto the promised land."

And as he speaks, the car slows to a stop. He turns the engine off, turns to face Alex, and grins. "You're going to love this."

---

As Tristan, Amara, and Mel haul out the coolers and blankets and towels, as they laugh and chat, Alex stares out over the lake. Even under the hazy sky, it is jewel-blue and glittering. There are patches of lily pads scattered throughout little coves. A small dock floats deeper out in the lake, and much farther away, the small forms of people kayaking dot the water. There are infrequent houses, with infrequent private docks; those, too, are dotted with the forms of people, though so far away as to be difficult to make out. She stands perfectly still, inhaling the smell of water.

"Are you going to come sit?" Amara calls. The three of them have already set up their little lakefront picnic spread. Tristan has lost his shirt and is slathering sunscreen on his top surgery scars. Mel has produced a comically large floppy hat and cat-eye sunglasses from somewhere. Amara has kicked off his Birkenstocks and is wiggling his toes in the water, can of cider in hand.

Alex wanders over. She perches uncomfortably on the edge of the blanket between Amara and Mel, her legs crossed and twisted, wondering how long it would be socially appropriate to wait before she disappears under the water's beckoning surface and swims away.

"Sunscreen?" Tristan offers her the bottle, which she silently, gratefully accepts. It occurs to her that it would be incredibly unwieldy to swim in this too-big shirt. She'll have to go shirtless. She sunscreens her own scars, keeping the shirt on. Perhaps she can find some excuse to sneak away before she goes swimming.

The placid lake seems to have chilled even Amara and Mel, and the four of them sit largely in quiet, sipping their beverages and munching on the various snacks that Mel and Tristan brought in from the city. Amara and Mel occasionally have some laugh-filled sidebar conversation, and Tristan occasionally chimes in. None of it really registers to Alex, who remains fixated on the small, distant actions of the lake: the kayakers, the people on the docks, the infrequent flash and ripple of leaping fish. Sometimes she hears more laughter coming from the people across the lake. Sometimes she hears a ringing bell. She pictures herself as one of the people on those docks, or as one of the kayakers, or — best of all — as a fish, shining underwater, cold and in constant motion, leaping into the light only for a half-second before being submerged again.

———

"Hey!" Mel says.

Alex has no idea how long they've been at the lake. The light has changed since the last time she noticed it. The kayakers are gone, and the air has an orange glow.

"Hey!" Mel says again. "Alex!"

"Hi," Alex says, startled. "Sorry."

"No, no, it's okay," Mel says. "I think I just solved a mystery, though."

"Oh, really?"

"Were you ever friends with Fen Rosen?"

"Um." Her mind goes blank. "Um. Yeah. I was."

"Holy shit, so *that's* where I know you from!"

"Oh my god," Amara says, "so you do really know each other."

"Yeah!" Mel is thrilled, and her speech is rapid-fire. "I must have met them at one of the parties at Fen's house. You remember the house?"

"The blue one," Tristan supplies. "With the rhododendron hazard."

"Yeah, yeah, yeah!" The brim of Mel's floppy hat bobs up and down. "Yeah, this is the Alex who dated Fen's roommate Em for a while. Jock Alex."

"*You're* Jock Alex?" Tristan says incredulously.

*Jock Alex* — that was what they called her. They were all artists, and she was the only person they hung out with who was into a sport, who was studying something sport-related. That was part of what drew Alex to them. She had never entertained any ideas of being an artist, not since their dad found their little folder of poorly drawn comics in the eighth grade and mocked them for an entire week. All of those people, though, Em and their friends, seemed to be bursting not only with ideas, but with belief: that they would be some of the few people who would make it, whatever that meant, or that, at the very least, they would be able to create what they wanted around the periphery of a normal working life. When Alex found out Adam was a writer, that he worked in a medium so alien to the way they related to their own thoughts, they were even more taken with him. He would read her stories he wrote sometimes, as if she had anything meaningful to contribute in the way of feedback. He could command so many different voices. For Alex, who struggled to summon even a few words to describe how she was feeling, who felt most at ease in situations where she wasn't expected to talk — where she *couldn't* talk — it seemed impossible, an impossible power for someone to wield.

Mel turns to Alex. "Holy shit, this is amazing. I know Fen from art school. Like, a thousand years ago. We were both in animation. Did you keep up with Em after you broke up? Sorry if that's a sore spot, but, you know, it's been a while. I feel like the statute of limitations is up."

"Not really," Alex says, digging her fingers into the rocky ground.

"Oh, that's too bad!" Mel is leaning toward them, fully engaged. "They really liked you. So did Fen, by the way. How old are you again?"

The leaps between topics and questions are becoming hard for Alex to follow. There is a rushing sound building in her head. "I'm twenty-four."

"Yeah, right, that's why you were still in school. Just a youth."

"An innocent," Amara says fondly, and wraps his arm around Alex. The sensation that has been so comforting for her over the past few days is now inhuman, unrecognizable, a weight dragging her down. She wants to wriggle away, but instead she stays still, as still as she can.

"You should talk to Em again." Mel is clearly so happy, so excited, and Alex wishes that she could make her own face and body respond in kind. "Like, Fen is going to be so shook when I tell them I ran into you on this fucking island, of all places! Em and all of them would be so excited to hear from you. I mean —" Her voice changes. She pauses.

"You mean what?" Amara pokes her in the shoulder.

"I'm so sorry again if this is, like, a sore spot." Mel grimaces. "But you're not still with that guy, are you?"

"No." Alex's voice seems to come from outside of her.

"Okay, good. Thank god. Because everyone was honestly kind of scared of him. Like, Fen told me about that time he showed up outside the window—"

"I don't think they need to rehash that," Amara says.

"Right, right, sorry." Mel covers her mouth with her hand. "But wow! I love how, like, every transsexual in this city ends up knowing every other one somehow."

"It's inevitable," Tristan says.

The conversation continues, but Alex can't hear it. Their voices meld together, a wall of mounting noise. Amara's arm is still around her and she wishes it wasn't. It's too much: the memory of Em and Fen and the house, the dark shape of Adam outside the window. Warm skin against her skin. Jock Alex. *I don't think they need to rehash that.* Had Amara heard of them before they met? Alex trains their eyes — no, her eyes — on a single spot of dirt on the picnic blanket.

In, two, three, four.

Out, two, three, four.

In the window, a black hoodie and blond hair. Watching, silent, waiting for them to leave.

"I'm going swimming," Alex says, and runs away.

———

Alex can't actually run anymore, not after the running she's already done today. She walks as fast as she can out of earshot of the picnic, willing herself not to overhear anything anyone might be saying about them. She focuses instead on the pain that radiates up her legs with each rocky step on the lakeshore, and on the promise, so near, of the cool water around her swollen feet.

She pauses after rounding a bend, listening for the sound of voices. They are present, but faint. She is far enough away to be alone without being lost. There is no one else visible. So she kicks off her shoes and socks, takes off her shirt — Amara's shirt — now sticky with her own sweat and a layer of dirt. She can't tell from here how deep the lake is. The rock of the shore extends down a couple of feet before being absorbed by an echoing darkness.

Alex takes off her glasses. She takes a step into the water, then another. The temperature change ripples through her. She closes her eyes so she can feel it better. Then, without looking, she dives.

When Alex was a kid, she could hold her breath for a minute at least, maybe more: not from swimming, but because she decided at some point that it was a skill she needed to practise. Now, even after the swimming she's been doing at the heron beach, it's still only a few seconds before she needs to surface. Every second in the underwater world, though, is precious to her. The water holds her close. She reaches out blindly to see what else is down here with her — the long stems of a lily pad, maybe, or rocks, or silt, or even a fish. But there is nothing, cold nothing, and her hands move through the water easily as she pulls herself up out of the water and to the surface, where she emerges, gasping, throwing her heavy soaked hair out of her face.

There is a thrill that comes with being blind in the water. It's not safe: people die all the time in lakes, complacently running into hidden hazards, hitting their heads or getting tangled in plants. But Alex doesn't care. The trees, the sky, the water, their body: All of them are one, a single mass breathing together, and it seems impossible that anything bad might happen.

There it is again. *Their* body. It is theirs, not hers, theirs, their world, their little pile of clothes and glasses barely visible on the now surprisingly distant shore. It keeps happening lately, this slipping back into the old pronouns, the ones they used back when they envisioned a life extending into the future. The dreams of who they used to be. They've been trying not to let the memory of that person creep back in. It's painful, like the space on a shelf where some now-lost memento used to stand.

But maybe it's okay. Alex flips over onto their back, the heat of the sun on their face, gleaming on their bare chest. *Their* face. *Their* chest. Maybe the secret is to stop fighting, to let the water bear them upward. Maybe they can just float.

—

"Alex!" someone yells from far away.

Their ears half-muffled by water, Alex can't make out the voice. They turn upright, treading water. They can't see anyone, and they've almost convinced themself that they were imagining it when they hear it again.

Squinting at the shore, they try to identify the source of the sound. It can't be Amara and his friends, because they're nowhere in sight; Alex has drifted even farther away from them. There are no more kayakers. The only place it might be coming from is a private dock some small distance away, where shapes perch that might hold humans.

Alex swims closer to the dock. Even though they are at home in the water, they are slow: they seem to get winded so easily, and their lungs are tired from the run. As they get closer to the dock, they see someone waving at them.

"Alex! Hey!" the voice says more clearly this time, a voice Alex's brain can now identify as familiar. They try to place it: not someone from home, not someone they know very well, friendly and energetic—

"Leo?" they yell back, their voice raspy. They cough. "Leo?"

"Yeah!" The blurry shape on the dock stands up, revealing bright red swim trunks. "Come sit with us!"

To sit with two different groups of unknown people in one day seems like a lot, but Alex figures they're committed to this course of action; it's too late to turn around now that they've yelled back. There's another person on the dock, too, someone in a black bikini with a buzzed head dangling their feet in the water.

Panting, Alex arrives on the dock. Leo and the other person stare at them. They had forgotten, in their state of floating, that to appear shirtless on this dock was equivalent to immediately outing themself.

"Hi," they say, fighting the urge to jump straight back into the water and paddle away.

"This is my sister Anna," Leo says, gesturing to the buzzed-hair person. "Sorry, I didn't know you were trans. What are your pronouns?"

"Uh—"

Anna scoops a handful of water out of the lake and throws it at Leo. "Dumbfuck, don't just ask someone their pronouns out of nowhere. That's so weird and rude." She turns to Alex. "Sorry about my brother. He's trying to be inclusive."

"Is that not what you're supposed to do?" Leo is crestfallen.

"It's fine, it's fine." Alex cringes. "Don't worry about it. Is this your dock?"

"Yeah, we live—" He points behind him at the shore, where the vague shape of a path weaves into the trees. "Just in there. It's like a ten-minute walk."

"That's a long way to go to the café every day."

"It's not really, though. I just drive."

Alex always forgets that people drive. "Right, yeah."

Silence falls. Leo kicks his feet in the water. Anna takes a hit from a joint she has sitting on an ashtray beside her. She wordlessly offers it to Alex; they shake their head. Anna shrugs. Alex's skin crawls with anxiety. They find themself sitting in their habitual pre-surgery posture, shoulders slouched and knees tucked into their chest, their arms wrapped around their legs.

They are about to open their mouth to announce that they're leaving when Anna speaks. "So," she says, "I hear you were worried about the posters outside the café."

"Oh. Yeah. There were a few things on there that I was wondering about. Like, the missing dog."

Anna sighs. "That shit is so sad. Leo, did Sarah ever find Ella?"

"No. I mean, they took down the poster."

"Oh!" Alex's voice comes out louder than they intended. "I think I saw Ella. Ella the dog," they clarify for some reason.

"Really?" Leo turns to face them. "Are you sure?"

"Pretty sure. I think I saw her today, actually. In the forest near the cape. But she ran away, and I couldn't catch her."

"Oh my god! We have to tell Sarah."

"It's been so long," Anna says, "I was sure the killer had gotten her."

"The, um." Alex gulps, their throat thick. "The killer?"

"Anna," Leo says, "you can't just talk about 'the killer' with no context. You're going to scare Alex away."

"Sorry! Right, 'the killer' sounds dramatic." She looks at Alex apologetically. "Obviously you don't know about the killer."

"The killer," Leo interjects, "is who we think is making all the dogs disappear."

"Over the last year or so," Anna continues, "there have been so many dogs disappearing, and nobody ever has any idea what's happened. People have lots of different theories, like, there's a cougar, or coyotes, or thieves—"

"Can I explain this to Alex? It's not like you've even been here most of the time."

"But I still live here."

"Do you?"

"God, fine, if it's so fucking important to you."

"*Thank* you." Leo resumes his story. "So yeah, people have a lot of different theories. The thing is most of the dogs have never been found, so there's not really any evidence to go off of. *Except*," he says, his voice rising dramatically, "that somebody stumbled across the body of one of the missing dogs in the forest. And even though there's no proof, this person claimed that the dog had been murdered with a rock. Like, a big fucking chunk of rock. It was so grisly. So we think there's a killer on the loose."

"And," Anna says, "our mom doesn't let Bozeman — that's our dog — out of her sight."

"I'm glad Ella's managed to stay safe, though."

"Of course she has. She's so smart."

Alex's body is tense. They remember hitting the gravel shoulder of the road, the rock coming at them. The truck and the black sunglasses and the mocking voice. But maybe it wasn't intentional. And there was no evidence that there was a dog killer.

"Scary," they say.

"Oh yeah." Leo's voice is serious. "And the really scary thing is it could be anyone. It could be an island person, or a new person, or a summer person, or a visitor, or . . . a ghost?" He takes on a goofy tone. "We just don't know."

"I guess I'm a summer person now," Anna says sadly.

"Hey," Alex says, "sorry for the random thought, but do you know any guys who drive a pickup truck around near the café?"

Anna groans. "I wish I didn't. Matt and Liam. I went to school with them."

"Okay. So—"

"They're not the killer, though, if that's what you're thinking. Like, they're for sure assholes, and *super* annoying, and their sense of humour is stupid, and they look like fucking idiots driving that truck everywhere. But they would never actually hurt anyone.

Trust me. I've known them since I was five." She points out into the near distance, not far but too distant for Alex to see. "That's actually their dock right over there."

"Okay," Alex repeats.

"Anna," Leo says, "is in school for psychology."

"Oh, really."

"Yeah, out in the East. She's a big shot now. Too good for us out here on the island."

"Shut up." Anna splashes him again. "I'll come back. That's the whole point of me becoming a psychologist."

"That's what everyone says, and then we never see them again except for in the summer."

"That's not even true, though."

"Yes, it is! Erica said she'd come back, and where is she?" Leo counts on his fingers. "Grace. Amy. Noah."

"Okay, okay, sure, but that doesn't mean—"

As Anna and Leo continue bickering, Alex focuses on the water. They deliberately avoid looking in the distance where Anna pointed. Though they can't see anything very well, the air is changing again, becoming thicker, more unsettled. They wonder how long it's been since they left Amara and Tristan and Mel.

"Hey," they say. "Thanks so much for inviting me over here. It's nice to meet you, Anna. But I think I should go back to my friends."

"Oh, no problem!" Leo seems a little disappointed. "It was cool to see you again, though."

"Yeah, it's always a fun surprise to meet another queer here." Anna waves. "We're here most afternoons, so . . ."

"Come whenever! And come to the café whenever. I'll sneak you free coffee."

Alex laughs. "Thanks." They lower themself down the ladder. The water is chillier now, less inviting. "I'll try to make it down."

Behind them, fading as they swim away, they can hear the faint sounds of Anna and Leo arguing. Their limbs and lungs are heavy, their breathing laboured, focused on the barely visible form of their clothes on the shore.

━━━

The sounds of splashes and yells and laughter float through the air as Alex makes their painful way back to Amara's picnic spot. The blanket lies empty, clothes abandoned. Mel is standing in the shallows, wearing her hat and sunglasses. Tristan is treading water. Both of them are admiring Amara, who is flailing around ridiculously in the deeper water, diving and emerging and diving again.

Mel is the first to notice Alex's return. "Alex!" she cries out. "Can you believe this fucking clown?"

"If you can explain what he's doing," Tristan adds, "please do tell. We've got nothing."

Alex shrugs, sitting gratefully at last on the blanket. "You all know him better than I do."

"I'm trying," Amara gasps, "to improve my underwater breathing capacity."

"Is that how you do that?" Alex says, unable to stop the note of amusement from creeping into their voice.

"Nobody believes me!" He flops dramatically onto his back, sending water splashing onto Mel and Tristan. When they laugh, Alex laughs too.

"Alex," Tristan says, "where did you end up swimming?"

"Yeah," Amara says from where he floats, "you better have a good story to justify abandoning us."

Alex's good humour fades. The killer — the nearby, invisible dock — the pickup truck and the empty gleam of black sunglasses. Did it come off like they were abandoning the group, like they thought they were too good for them? "Oh, I just went to see one of those lily pad patches over there," they say, hoping they don't sound evasive.

"That's so cool," Mel says mournfully. "I wish I could swim."

Amara stands up. "What are you talking about? You can swim just fine."

"I guess I should say I wish I was a more confident swimmer. Obviously I can swim. Who can't swim? But I definitely don't feel good enough about my swimming skills to go all the way out to the lily pads by myself."

"Isn't that dangerous?" Tristan says.

"What do you mean? It's only like a hundred feet."

"No, I mean, Alex, you have to take your glasses off to swim, right? Kind of dangerous to go out in open water, with all those roots, not only alone but blind."

Alex is about to answer, but Amara cuts them off. "Dude, it's fine. Alex is an amazing swimmer. You should see them in the ocean."

"Yeah, Tristan, come on," Mel chimes in. "This is Jock Alex we're talking about. The person who, like, runs up mountains."

Even though the reminder hurts, Alex feels a little surge of pride. Yes, that was them: the person who ran up mountains, the person who now swims blind and alone.

"Speaking of mountains," Amara says, beginning to slosh back up to the shore, "we should probably head back over that one now. I'm kind of getting tired, and I do have to cook us dinner."

"Aww, but we just got here!"

"Do you want to cook dinner, Mel?"

"No."

"Then get out of the water."

"Yes, chef," Tristan says, already grabbing a towel off the blanket and drying himself off. Amara follows. Mel gives the water one final splash before she, too, heads back up.

The four of them work in near-silence as they pack up the picnic. Amara was right to want to leave now: not only does the weather seem to be changing for the worse, but he clearly sensed the group reaching an energy threshold. It's been so long since

Alex spent any time in a group of friends that they had forgotten how comforting it was to be around people who know each other, who knew how to read each other without needing to explain and could let the conversation rest when it needed to.

They pile into the car, and as they pull out of the dirt road to the lake, Alex rolls the window down. They stick their head out like a golden retriever, the wind pushing their hair back off their face. This isn't bad, they think. Even though they didn't contribute much to the conversation, even though they freaked out and ran away, and even though their body hurts. These people, this day: this hasn't been bad at all.

A flash of light sears into their eyelids. When they open their eyes, they see their own face in the passenger-side mirror. The sky has become dark behind them. The light is from a pair of head-lights, huge and with their high beams on, on a silver pickup truck.

"Oh, fuck," they say, rolling the window up.

"What?" Amara peers at them in the rearview mirror. "Oh, did you wake up? Tristan and Mel are asleep, too." And it's true: Tristan is slumped over across the middle seat, and Alex sees the floppy brim of Mel's hat drooping.

"It's the fucking guys," Alex says, struggling to form words through the tension in their chest. "The guys."

"What guys?"

"Behind us. The pickup truck."

"Oh, yeah. These idiots have been riding my ass for like ten minutes."

"You have to speed up." Alex is leaning forward, and the hard edge is creeping into their voice.

"What? No. I'm not giving them the satisfaction. Besides, this road is a thirty, and—"

"You have to speed up," Alex says, "or pull onto a different road or something."

"I didn't know you were such a backseat driver," Amara says, and though his tone is bright, there's a pressure behind his words.

The lights in the mirror are bright and cold and empty. Alex can't tell where on the island they are. It's all darkness, tall trees, a sky that says nothing.

"Amara, you have to fucking pull over."

"I don't *have* to do anything," he says, and there is now the same flatness in his voice that there was when he found them on the road. "*You* have to calm down. I'm driving. There's a truck behind us, there's nowhere good to pull over, and there's no other road to turn on. We'll be back at the cottage in five minutes. Calm down."

"I can't calm down." Alex is frantic. "It's the fucking guys. They've seen us—"

"Of course they see us, they're literally driving right behind us."

They want to scream. Does he need them to elaborate? A chill has descended over him, the freezing, glassy energy that they have sometimes observed in him over these weeks: first when they arrived by his house after their run-in with these men, and sometimes after, when certain topics were broached, or when they inadvertently spoke in a way that conveyed panic. There would be no use explaining further, no point in explaining the source of their fear to him. He was somewhere else, and the more paranoid they seem now, the less likely they are to be understood.

"These guys aren't driving like normal people. They're going to fucking run us off the road or something. Please pull over." Alex tries to level their voice. "Please just pull over."

Amara's eyes in the rearview stay facing forward. Alex can tell he wants to speak, can hear the catch in his throat. But he doesn't say anything. Silently, he slows the car and pulls carefully onto the narrow shoulder. He turns the engine off.

"Thank you," Alex says, their voice small. Amara doesn't respond.

The truck revs its engine, accelerating rapidly. It goes by so quickly that Alex can't make out who is driving it, whether there's a person behind the open passenger-side window. They could swear they hear the voices again: the horrible, indiscernible yelling, the mocking laughter. Then the truck disappears around a bend.

Mel startles awake. "Huh?" she says, half-yawning. "Are we back? Why are we stopped?"

"Almost back," Amara says, turning the engine back on.

"Thank god," Mel says, and Alex sees her hat droop again.

Amara doesn't look back at them.

———

"Hey," Amara says, "Alex."

Alex opens their eyes, expecting to see the little house. Instead, they are in the trailhead parking lot.

"We're here," he says.

"Oh."

"I figured you'd want to go home. It's been a long day, and it'll probably be pretty cramped back at the cottage with all of us. And once these two wake up, it'll get pretty loud again."

He's leaving them here to be alone. He doesn't want them around anymore.

"Oh," they say again. They don't want to sound as fragile as they feel. They unbuckle their seatbelt. "Okay. Thanks."

"It was really fun having you hang out with everyone," Amara says as they open the door.

"Yeah," Alex says, turning their back to him. They are so tired, and so cold, and every step is so painful.

"Text me if you want to hang out tomorrow," he calls as they walk away.

"Yeah," they say, and don't look back.

When they finally arrive back at the house, they are afraid, for some reason, to go inside. They have gotten so accustomed to Amara's cozy house, the clutter and the bright colours and close quarters, that the coldness and austerity of 709 seem even more hostile than when they first stepped inside. The lights turn on without a sound, revealing an environment completely unchanged from when Alex left it. There are buns going stale on the counter, pots and pans unclean — a mess they should probably deal with. Not today, and certainly not right now. There is nothing they want more than to go upstairs and be unconscious.

But they can barely stay on their feet. If they were to attempt the stairs in this state, they would probably just fall right back down and get injured in the process. They consider the elevator, then decide against it: now doesn't seem like the best time to be attempting previously untried and forbidden house exploration.

They curl up uncomfortably on the grey couch. Every mental image they shove away begets a new image. Ella, Amara's friends, the running. The place in the woods and the person in the window. The lights of the truck and the roar of the engine as it went by. The flatness in Amara's voice. When they finally fall asleep, they dream about an emptiness on the horizon, creeping ever closer as they watch, unmoving.

—

A buzzing rouses Alex from their sleep. They are freezing cold, and there is shooting pain in their arms, pain resulting from the vice-like grip with which they have crossed their arms over their chest in their sleep. They also fell asleep with their glasses on, making the lenses even smudgier and blurrier than they had been.

The buzzing rattles their skull again. Is the house's generator failing? Is an explosion imminent? They are weighing what the safest course of action is — to go check the security room, or run out the door, or simply stay inanimate on this couch — when a fuzzy voice echoes through the room.

It's Amara. "Alex?" he says, crackly. "Helloooooo?"

Of course it's a buzzer. Why would this house not have a buzzer? Alex rises as quickly as they can, checking their phone as they hobble over to the door. Not only have they missed a bunch of calls, it's the early afternoon. No wonder they are so withered: sleeping too much is the second-worst thing to not sleeping at all.

Amara is there on the screen, wearing sunglasses and Mel's floppy hat, tapping his foot and presumably humming. There's no time to do anything, no time even to figure out how to operate the buzzer. There is no choice other than to simply go outside and meet him.

Amara seems at first thrilled to see them stepping out the door. It doesn't take long, though, before his face falls. "Did you sleep in these?" he says.

"Yeah." They need an excuse, a reason why a normal person would choose to sleep in someone else's sweaty, dirty, lake-watered clothes, but they can't come up with one. "I was too tired," they say regretfully, "to make it up the stairs."

"Jesus." Amara takes his sunglasses off. He is worried. "I'm so sorry. If I'd known it was that difficult, I would have at least taken you back to the house to give you some clothes."

"No," Alex says, "it's fine."

"How are you feeling now?"

"Fine. How are Mel and Tristan?" they ask, diverting the topic of conversation away from themself.

"Oh, they're gone. They caught the noon ferry. Actually," he says, sounding nervous, "I'm also going back to the city tonight."

Alex doesn't say anything, but their face must betray them.

"Not forever!" Amara clarifies. "Just for tonight. I'm really running out of food. I was planning to go tonight, then stay with Mel tomorrow, and then come back in the afternoon the next day. So I thought, you know, maybe we could do something fun today. I called you a few times, but you didn't pick up, so that's why I showed up here." His cadence is hurried. "Only if you're feeling up to it, though, I don't want to—"

"Yeah, sure," Alex says. "I'm good. Let's do it."

"Do you want to get some clothes first?"

"No," they say, "I'm fine."

"Are you sure? We have to walk back to the car anyway—"

"Let's just go," Alex says, already walking away.

The little car weaves along an unfamiliar road in silence. There are thick, heavy clouds in the sky, even though they seem to emanate a kind of hot light. Alex keeps their eyes firmly planted on the blurry outside world, the vague shapes of trees speeding by. Amara drums his fingers on the wheel in random bursts of chaotic rhythm. Occasionally he half-hums a tune, then stops. Every so often, Alex senses the pricking of his eyes on the back of their neck.

"I just want to say," he says, "I'm sorry if it was kind of uncomfortable for you yesterday. I should have thought about — like, I was just really excited to see my friends, and I didn't really think about how it would be for you."

"It's okay," Alex says, trying to conceal that they're for some reason on the verge of crying, struggling to keep their voice level and calm. "It's my fault for being so weird. Running away and stuff. The truck."

"No, it's not your fault," Amara says, a little frustration creeping into his voice. "Really. Just let me know if you're ever uncomfortable with anything. I promise I won't get offended. I get up my own ass sometimes and lose track of other people. It's good for me to get reality-checked."

Alex wipes their eyes with the back of their hand.

"Mel and Tristan," Amara continues, "really liked hanging out with you."

This makes Alex want to cry even more. They have to get a grip. They remember the excitement in Mel's voice when she talked about Fen's parties, the old house, meeting Alex before, and the grimace and stiffness when she brought up Adam. The dark shape in the window, the dark spaces in their memory and at the corners of the world. How can Alex face anyone who knows?

"Anyway," Amara says with a studied brightness, "I thought we could do some tourist shit before we go."

Alex finally turns to look at him. "We?"

"Oh, fuck! I forgot to ask you. I thought maybe we could both go back to the city. Only if you want to, obviously."

"I'll think about it."

"Okay!" The car slows. "Awesome. Just let me know. I'm not leaving until the second-last ferry, so you have lots of time to decide."

They are stopped in a crowded parking lot. There is a trail-head just up ahead of them: not a trailhead like the one leading to 709, but a fancy trailhead, with a shiny wooden kiosk covered in colourful signs and diagrams and a bulletin board. There are more people here than Alex has seen in her entire time on the island, people who are clearly tourists, with suspiciously pristine summer clothes and huge fancy cameras.

"Where are we?" Alex asks.

"Well," Amara says, "I figured you might be tired after yesterday, and this is a tourist place, so all the trails are really short and accessible. It's the galleries."

The galleries. Alex read about them in the tourist guides: waves carved out of the ancient sandstone by the ocean, a beach sculpted by water and time. As they step out of the car, they can hear the ocean just nearby. Amara takes their unsteady arm as they walk forward, and they lean on him gratefully.

"Thanks," they say, as they make their way along the tidy, level trail.

"Thank *you*," he says. "I kept forgetting to go here until I was trying to think of stuff for us to do. If not for you, I might have neglected the most obvious, well-known cool place for us to visit."

The trail is indeed short, and in no time at all they are looking out over the ocean, sparkling blue even in the haze. Gnarled red trees with glossy green leaves lean out over the carved shore, whose crags and curves lean up in the air. Some tourists are standing inside the galleries, running their fingers on the stone. Most are taking pictures.

Amara gestures to a bench on the viewpoint. "Do you want to sit?"

They sit, a few inches between them, listening to the unharmonious chorus of sounds: the chattering of the people, the dulled, quiet voices of the ocean and the trees.

"It's beautiful," Amara observes after a while.

"Yeah," Alex says. "I see why this place is famous."

Amara seems to be struggling to find words.

"You know," he says eventually. "The guy Mel mentioned yesterday. Was that the guy you told me about?"

Alex's body is brittle board. They watch the gentle waves, the happy people, and they are angry — angry that Amara would bring them to this beautiful place and ruin it by bringing up Adam. Angry that he knows about Adam at all, that he thinks he's entitled to ask them about their relationship. It was a mistake to have said anything. It was a mistake to think any of this was a good idea. They grip the bench, hard, their fingers reddening.

"I don't want to pry," Amara says, and Alex almost laughs: he doesn't want to pry, but he's going to anyway. And sure enough, he continues. "But what you told me before — obviously, it sounded kind of bad. But I got the sense that there was more going on there. And then what Mel said, about how your friends and your ex felt about him, how he showed up outside their house. She said you kind of dropped off the face of the earth. And the way you reacted after that."

"So?" Alex says, unable to keep the bite out of their voice.

"So, I just want to make sure you know that if you're scared of anyone, or if you feel like you're in danger, then you can—"

"I'm fine, thanks."

A long silence.

"Okay," Amara says.

Neither of them look at each other as they walk back to the car, Alex leaning on Amara, their footsteps perfectly synchronized.

―

When they reach the trailhead, Alex stops. Amara nearly trips over their feet. "Are you okay?" he asks.

"Yeah," Alex says. "You can go ahead to the car. I just want to take a quick look at the bulletin boards."

They wait until Amara is out of view, shielded by the walls of SUVs and Jeeps, before they turn to the board. There are shiny placards about the local flora and fauna, about how the sea and stone and winds created the galleries. But that's not what they're here to look at. They run their eyes instead over the bulletin board, whose posters are largely more recent than the ones that had been in the decrepit kiosk outside the café. Their eye had caught on something as they walked up the trail to the beach, a variation in the many shiny, laminated posters of missing dogs. It is right there, beaten-down and faded almost beyond legibility, the photo bleeding past the point of resembling anything. But the number is there, the number remains, and as soon as they see the four digits, Alex grabs the paper off the board and shoves it in their pocket. They walk back to the car with their heart hammering. There it was, the memory that they had lost: 4736. Please come home.

———

Alex can't talk to Amara. The car ride only makes their heart clench harder. It is the same rage that made Alex ghost Em, that made them go cold with Aisling, that made them lie to the hospital psychiatrists to the point of never even mentioning Adam's name. They are vibrating in their seat. How dare he think he knows anything about Adam, that he knows anything about them. This is why they could never tell anyone anything, why they had to lie all the time, lie about even the smallest, stupidest things. They all thought Alex was so pathetic. Alex knew what they thought — that of course their first relationship with a cis guy would be like this. But they didn't know shit. They didn't know how hard it was for them to connect with anyone, how desperate they were to be loved in a way they could feel, and then how easy, how natural it was with Adam, right from the very beginning. None of them knew what it was to be cared for like that. Adam told them they were the most important person in the universe. That there was no one like them. That he would be there for them no matter what. All that stuff that Alex thought was just bad movie cliché — it was real. No one else understood. All they wanted to do was keep them apart, keep Alex from the only person who loved them. And Adam wasn't just the only person who loved them: he was the only person who *could* love them. He knew that they were evil and loved them anyway. It was their fault, their fault that he left in the end, because there was only so much one person could put up with, only so much hatred that one person could handle. Alex was evil, evil, a lying, cold, rage-filled, manipulative person, and here they were again, so angry they didn't have room for anything else inside them, and then the anger sublimating into pain, pain in the pit of their stomach, the enormity of all they'd lost — all because they were disgusting, horrible, unworthy of anyone's love, let alone the love of someone like Adam. They deserved to die. They should have died. That's what they keep thinking, over and over, as the car pulls up to the little house. The reason why they feel like they shouldn't be here with Amara, shouldn't be with his friends, shouldn't be on this beautiful island: They should have died. They should have died.

—

"Are you okay?" Amara says in a quiet voice. They are sitting in the chairs, holding a cup of tea. When did this happen? There is an opacity in their mind, blocking their thoughts. Everything is slow, thick, difficult. The heat from the tea and the heat from the air blend together. The crumpled paper in their pocket weighs them down like a stone.

"I'm—" *Fine*, they start to say yet again, then stop. "Can I take a nap?" they ask instead. "Before we go. I'm really tired."

Amara checks the time. "Sure," he says. "That might be good."

Alex climbs the ladder, the creaking in the steps blending with the friction in their limbs. They pull the blanket over their head.

# 5.

Alex is being cooked alive. The sheets are stuck to their legs and their ass, the sweat acting like glue. It is hot, so hot, and their lungs are full of nothing but heat, and it is suffocating them. The light coming through the roof is reddish and stifling. They sit up with a start, fear coursing through their body. They shouldn't be here. They shouldn't be here at all.

"Amara!" they say, shaking his shoulder. He is fast asleep on the other side of the bed, his mouth open and twitching with dreams. "Wake up!"

He groans. "What time is it?"

"Too late. You have to leave."

He moves to sit up, then flops back onto his pillow. "I feel like something dead that's been lying out in the sun."

Alex is already out of bed. The dehydration is making their head spin.

Amara groans. "God, why did we fall asleep?"

"I don't know." They are crawling around on the floor, grasping, coming dangerously close to toppling down the stairs. "Do you see my glasses? I can't see shit."

Amara runs his hands under the sheets. He pulls out the glasses. "Oh no."

"Oh no what?"

"They're kind of bent."

Alex takes them from him. One of the metal arms is sloping downward. When they put them on, the world appears clear, but at off-putting angles; the frames threaten to slide off their face. They try to slowly bend the arm back up into position, but it won't budge.

"Okay," they say. They put on the wonky glasses, and the blurry, lopsided world makes them dizzy. There it is again: the rush of anger, the desperate need to be alone. "Okay," they repeat, and begin to lower themself onto the ladder.

It doesn't help that Amara seems exasperated, cranky with heat and fatigue. "Did you ever tell me if you wanted to come with me?" he asks, yawning.

"I have to go back to the house."

"Are you sure? That house is still going to be there tomorrow, and the next day, and probably forever, really. It's a fortress. I'm sure it's fine."

"I have to go," Alex says, already at the bottom of the ladder and heading for the door. They don't wait for a response.

———

The sky that is visible above the trees is heavy with dense cloud, and the light behind them is fading fast. The heat on the ground rises up above Alex. Pain shoots up, too, from their ankles, as they turn to follow a pink trail marker up ahead. They can barely make it out, their vision blurring from the strain of their lopsided lenses. They're really running this time, and in the blink of an eye they are coming up on the cathedral, the trees opening up ahead.

There is something alive, sitting centred under the shade of the cathedral. Something with shining eyes.

Alex stops dead in their tracks. They hold their breath.

In the silence, they stare at each other.

Alex, slowly, adjusts their glasses on their face, holding them in place.

"Ella?" they say.

Ella the dog doesn't move.

"Ella?" they call again, their voice pitching up. They resume breathing, crouching low to the ground so they're at Ella's eye level. They extend a hand outward. If only they had a treat, or some food, an offering to get her to trust them. "I'm a friend, Ella. It's okay."

Ella doesn't move.

They move closer, inch by painful inch. "Come here, Ella. I just want to help."

Ella turns and runs.

"Ella!" Alex calls after her, breaking into a sprint, but Ella is too fast. She bounds away, veering off to the right, into trees too thick for Alex to follow.

"Ella!" they yell. "Ella!" But there is nothing, not even the sound of movement anymore.

Then thunder shakes the ground, louder than they've ever heard it before, as though it were coming from within the island and not above. When they think it's done, it shakes even louder, closer, like it's moving toward them. They cower on the forest floor, their arms over their head. Every second between the noise seems to last an eternity.

And then — silence. Dead, anxious silence, waiting to be broken again.

Alex can't wait anymore. All they can do is keep running.

⬤

When Alex reaches 709, there are only three seconds between the flashes of lightning and the thunder that follows. They count, though they don't look up: it is already clear enough in their mind, the jagged, buzzing streaks reaching down toward them, and if they think about it too much they will want to curl up and hide. They can't curl up and hide. They enter the door code as fast as they can, barely able to read it through their phone's disintegrating screen, their frenzied breaths fogging up their glasses. As they open the door, the forest of lightning bolts crashes down over the ocean, just over their shoulder. Then the door shuts behind them.

It is dark in 709. The silence eats all sound.

"709," Alex says, and they can hear the shake in their voice. "709, please turn on the—"

The world explodes around them. Glass shaking, the ground shaking — everything in the thrall of the thunder, everything becoming sound. Alex crouches on the ground, their arms held desperately over their head.

I am going to die in here.

Everything is silent again. As though nothing happened.

Alex doesn't want to speak again. They don't want to hear the sound of their own voice. They will not check the security room. The idea of burying themself deeper in the house, deeper from which to crawl should the walls crash down around them, fills them with horror. They need to get their things and leave — to make it through the forest, back to Amara. Back to safety.

Through the gloom, they hurry to the bottom of the stairs. They take one step and become certain that they can't do it. It'll take them time they don't have to crawl up, even more time to crawl down. They look back at the elevator, the button a glowing circle of red in the grey.

They press it. They step inside the elevator, jarred to see their own self again, again and again repeating: chest heaving, clutching the piece of paper they ripped off the tree. Sweat is soaking the paper, pouring from their face down their neck. They press the red-ringed button to the top floor.

Nothing happens. They press it again, then again. Nothing.

"709," they yell, "unlock the top floor."

The button turns green, and they smash it. They begin to rise. There are no windows in here, no way to check on the lightning:

only their own body, reflecting back at them. They pray that there will be no thunder until they are out of the elevator.

The doors slide open. They step over the threshold with their eyes closed. They hear the door shut behind them.

When they open their eyes, they see nothing. Darkness extending in every direction, tangible darkness, darkness that seemed to have mass and volume. Until, all at once, there is a piercing light from above, mediated by whatever roof holds Alex in the house, twisting and dulling at the same time — a few seconds — and then the world explodes again, this time the blasts of thunder right where Alex is, right beside them, in the very air that is touching their skin. As the air crashes around them, a red halo begins to form above them. It is bent, as though creased in the middle, deformed and bleeding, and in the centre there is a spotlight, a blinding ray of white. It trembles, massive and blinking. It looks alive. Underneath it, suddenly illuminated under the shadowy crisscross of unfinished beams and pieces of plastic sheeting, is what looks like a scale model of 709. But not just 709, standing alone in the forest as it is, but dozens of them, massive, spiky houses perched on their tiny false cliffs, with barely any trees in sight, casting huge, warped shadows over the room.

A siren blares, harsh and insistent and metallic in their ears. Alex runs. Stumbling over their feet, not seeing what is on the ground ahead of them, in every step expecting some obstacle, but instead falling into nothing, their one free hand grasping at nothing, nothing that seems endless until it stops, hard. A door — a doorknob. Alex prepares to fight it, but it opens easily in their hand.

And then they are out, out in the quiet hallway of the top floor, standing outside one of the two doors they never entered, and the door closes itself behind them, and all is still. The siren is no longer audible, even though it rings in their ears. The darkness, the warped, bleeding darkness, is their own every time their eyelids close.

In the library room, they stuff clothes maniacally into their bag. The walking stick lies where they forgot it, all those days ago, and against its white shine the reflection of lightning flashes somewhere outside the window. They keep packing, frenzied, even as the thunder wracks the house down to its bones. They can't stay here. They will have to crawl down the steps; they can't go back to that place, if the door would even open again, but it doesn't matter, they've already been seen, and they will be there in that glass tube on the winding stairs, exposed to the lightning, exposed to the thunder — as if it was by design, all of it. But they have no choice, no choice, no choice, and they are standing on the edge of the first step when their phone rings.

It must be Amara. He must be worried. They pick it up instantly, and they open their mouth to say: I'm coming back, I'm scared but I'm coming back, I'll make it, don't worry about me.

"STAY INSIDE," the robotic voice says.

——

They sit there on the steps, shaking, waiting for the thunder and lightning to start again. They can't move if the thunder and lightning start again. They can't move until it does.

*STAY INSIDE.*

The phone rings again, then stops. Then again.

*STAY INSIDE.*

They weren't free, after all. They should never have left. They had seen the deer. The man in the sunglasses. The woman at the café. The poster, buried, then wiped away. The shadow on the security camera. They should never have left. It was right — they knew what to do. They had known, and they did something else anyway. And now they can do nothing. They are trapped, because they have already been seen.

The phone rings again. They pick it up.

"Alex?" Amara is nearly yelling. His voice is fuzzy; the connection is bad. "Alex, are you there? Are you okay?"

"I'm at the house," they say, almost in a whisper.

"Oh, thank fucking Jesus Christ and all his sweet sweet angels. Did you not get my calls? I've been calling and calling you. I was this close to running out into the forest to look for you. I'm pretty sure lightning struck some trees within, like, five hundred metres of the house." He is breathing heavily. "They've cancelled the ferry, so you can just hunker down where you are. It's stopped for now, but I don't think the storm is gone yet. Oh my god, I cannot express to you how glad I am that you're not out there in the forest, lost and dodging bolts of electricity from the sky. I was going a little insane."

Alex stares at the crumpled piece of paper in their hand. They don't remember pulling it out of their pocket. Its ink is already bleeding out from the sweat.

"Hello? Alex? Can you hear me?"

"I can't leave," they say.

"That's what I'm saying. Don't worry about it. Just stay inside, and I can come over tomorrow morning and pick you up."

"No," they say, hard and cold and sharp. "No. Don't come near here."

"What? Why?"

"I shouldn't have left."

"What?"

"I shouldn't have left the house alone."

"Did something happen to it?"

"I got a call."

"From the owners? Alex, just fucking tell me what's happening."

"One of those calls I told you about."

"Oh." He goes silent. "I actually got one, too, right before I called you. STAY INSIDE. Pretty stupid prank to pull on a night like this, because who in their right mind would *not* want to stay inside right now?"

The crumpled paper trembles. "You got a call, too?"

"Yeah." He laughs. "Like I said, pretty dumb stuff."

"I didn't follow the instructions," Alex says. "I didn't do what it said."

"What are you talking about? Alex, it's—"

"I didn't stay inside. I knew, and I didn't stay inside. I didn't check the cameras. I took the elevator to the top floor. Now they know. They know it's you, too. That I left to meet you. So I can't break the rules anymore. I can't."

Silence.

"Alex," Amara says, speaking very slowly. "I know the thunder is scary. But these are just dumb prank calls, or some kind of mass text alert system error. Remember when they texted everyone in Hawaii that a nuclear missile attack was incoming? No one is trying to send us any kind of weird threats."

"Don't talk to me like that," they say, sharper and colder. "I'm not some kind of stupid infant."

His voice changes, too. "Okay, sorry. It's just that what you're saying is sounding kind of crazy."

Crazy. He thinks I'm crazy.

*If you tell anyone—*

They stand up, their foot nearly slipping on the edge of the stair. "I fucking spent all this time with you telling you about what I have fucking dealt with, and you think you have the right to call me fucking crazy? Crazy for thinking that getting threatening phone calls every time I get back to this house might mean something? It could be some kind of fucking automated system, Amara. Or it could be literal messages from the people who own this house, the people who might very well also own the house you currently live in as well as a quarter of this fucking island, telling me that they see what I'm doing and they don't like it. And I don't have this, if I don't have this job and I get kicked out, my entire life is fucked. It'll be totally, one hundred percent fucked. Or it could be—"

"Alex, aren't those people your friend's parents? You really think people who own mansions have no better, clearer way of communicating with the people they're paying to live in them than to send ominous, vaguely threatening robocalls? You think that's at all logical?"

"I said don't talk to me like that."

"I don't know how else to talk to someone who's not making sense. Look, I just Googled it. It's an alert system thing. I was right. They're trying to stop people from going out and getting struck by lightning. Okay? It's not a conspiracy, it's just unclear government messaging. No one is threatening you. I'm sorry for using the word 'crazy,' but . . ."

Alex laughs. They laugh and laugh and laugh, their nails digging tighter and tighter into the paper balled up in their fist.

"Goodbye," they say.

"Stop!" Amara yells, urgent and loud. "Alex, what the fuck are you planning to do? Just lock yourself in there?"

"I don't know," they say. "I'm crazy."

"I told you I'm sorry for saying that. I really am."

"I didn't tell you," they say. "About how crazy I am."

"Alex, stop."

"I was locked up right before this. I didn't tell you that."

"I'm going to come over."

"I took a bunch of pills. I was trying to kill myself. For, like, the third time. So pathetic."

"The storm has to be gone. It hasn't thundered in like half an hour." There is crackling on Amara's end. He starts to sound far away. "Just stay on the line."

They put the phone on speaker. Uncurling the crumpled poster, smoothing it out with both hands. The number is legible — that's all that matters. "Don't come over," they say. "It's dangerous. The storm isn't over yet."

They can barely hear him. "Wait," he says, and then his voice disintegrates.

Alex hangs up.

———

They dial the number from the poster. The phone rings once, twice, three times. They are not afraid; they know there will be an answer. And sure enough, on the fourth ring, there is.

"Good evening?" says a tight, high-pitched voice. Adam's mom. They had only met twice. The last time was just before New Year's. Alex was Adam's date to a family dinner at a fancy restaurant. It was the first time his family had sat down together, all of them at the same table, in five years. Alex had never been more uncomfortable, and they had never seen Adam look so diminished, so much like a child, waiting for his parents to put an end to their cold war and pay attention to him, even for a second. It didn't happen. They talked more to Alex, engaging in vague, pointed inquiries about what they studied at school, what their parents did. When the table fell silent, they stared at their phones. Adam was alone, and it seemed like the slim, elegant dining chair was swallowing him up.

"Hi," Alex says, with no fear at all that their voice will be recognized. "Sorry to bother you in the evening, but I'm a friend of Adam's—"

"A friend of Adam's?" Alex can hear the sound of footsteps. "Just, give me a minute. Sorry, hold on." The footsteps clatter, then come to a stop.

"I was just wondering," Alex says. "About where the whole situation is at. I was so worried when I heard about him boarding the ferry."

"Yes." Adam's mom sighs. "We had reason to believe that he was going to the island to . . . well, to do something he might regret."

Alex never fails to be amused by the coded language people use for suicide. As if choosing to die can be regretted the way one regrets having another margarita.

"He had left his phone at his apartment," Adam's mom continues, "and didn't seem to have brought anything with him. It was a
very, very worrying couple of days, as you can imagine."

"So he's okay, then."

"Oh, yes. More than okay. He wasn't doing very well when we
did find him, of course, out there in the woods. But, of course, it
turned out he was just at the Cathedral—"

"Sorry," Alex says, "the Cathedral?"

"Oh, you haven't heard of the Cathedral? It's this wonderful
place. What do they call it? An artists' colony — lots of luminaries
have stayed there. Hollywood types. He just wanted some time
to focus on his work, focus on himself. And it's right there on the
island, too. Things just have a way of working themselves out in
life that's so beautiful."

"I think so, too," Alex says.

"I'm so glad to hear that — I'm sorry, what was your name?"

"James."

"I'm so glad to hear that, James. Yes, even if you don't believe in
God, if you believe in the universe, the creator, Mother Earth — I
believe that whatever God is to you, that's what worked in Adam's
life. In our lives."

"Amen."

"Even things that seemed like curses to begin with. Things
that made it seem like we were on the wrong path. I'm sure you
were aware of this relationship he was recently in."

"Of course."

"That person — that person was very unstable. That person
was bringing all kinds of negativity into Adam's life. I'm not sure
of the details — I believe in giving children their privacy — but it
seems like there was a great deal of mental illness involved. Not a
very good family situation. So when it ended, yes, Adam was dev-
astated. But now he's free from that toxicity. And because of that,
he can work on achieving his potential. What seemed to him like
a catastrophe was, in fact, a blessing in disguise."

"Amen," Alex says again.

"So, James," Adam's mom says hopefully, "is there anything else I can help you with today?"

"No. But thank you so much for everything."

"I'm always happy to talk to one of Adam's friends." So happy that she barely knows any of their names, has never met any of them, wouldn't know them from an impersonator. "I'll let him know you say hello, and please, do call again if you have any more questions or concerns, or if you just want to chat."

"I'll do that. Goodbye."

"Goodbye now."

The line goes dead.

They take the first painful step down the stairs.

It's true.

It was my fault.

I'm a bad person.

I knew it all along.

—

They sit on the edge of the cliff, their feet dangling. They would have thought that the storm charging the sky with energy would have done the same to the water. Instead it is utterly, uncannily silent, unmoving. The clouds are lit from behind; the air is hot and suffocating. Like the end of the world, they think. But it won't be. It never is. The changes that they feared and the ones that they searched for, the ones they thought would transform their life — they were all the same, when all was said and done. Their mom died. Their dad hated them. They came out, and then they came out again. They fell in love. They went to school. They ran, then they got too sick to run anymore. They went back in the closet. They destroyed everything, were given an opportunity to start again. Then they destroyed that, too. And here they were. Here they are.

From their bag, they pull out their water bottle, their containers of sleeping pills. Maybe enough, or maybe not. They pour the water into their throat, a deeper well than they've ever made before. They twist the child-locked plastic lids open. They pour one down the well, like a stream of blue pebbles, then the other. They swallow, horrible, bitter rocks down their throat, dry and grating, and they gag as the pills go down. They barely choke back the vomit, both hands tight over their mouth.

Then the wave hits. The familiar wave of emptiness, only this time overpoweringly strong.

Alex lies on their back. Above them, light flickers in the grey, collapsing sky.

―――

"HAPPY NEW YEAR!" the boys are yelling down in the basement. Outside, the chattering and squealing and booming of fireworks. Dogs barking somewhere else in the neighbourhood. The rain pounding on the roof. Standing at Nathan's kitchen island, Alex drinks white Bacardi of unknown origins straight from the bottle. It burns her throat, her stomach already irritated from the pills she took in hopes of blacking out, and she slams the bottle back down on the kitchen island as if to punish it. Rum splashes out from the bottle, or maybe from a crack she's now created in the bottom of it. But it doesn't matter. She doesn't care. She hates drinking. She hates being drunk. She hates Bacardi, and most of all, most bitterly and most passionately, she hates the fucking New Year.

Creaking from the stairs: someone is coming up. She ducks, helplessly, behind the kitchen island, because it is the only way to preserve the solitude she fled the party to find. The footsteps approach, getting ever closer, and then stop.

"Why are you hiding behind the kitchen island?" Adam says.

He is wearing a shiny paper party hat. He's spilled beer on the crotch of his jeans, and his hair is sticking out in random directions.

His cheeks are flushed, and he is laughing a little, laughing at her cowering on some random guy's kitchen floor.

Alex remembers why she agreed to come to this stupid party.

She jumps to her feet, forgetting that doing so will hurt, and forgetting that she's drunk. Her socked soles slide nearly out from under her. But Adam swoops in to break her fall. It is almost a disaster — she almost takes him down with her. But after wobbling around, the two of them manage to steady themselves. Adam has his back against the kitchen island, and Alex leans against him, her feet on top of his.

"We didn't get our New Year's kiss," she says.

"We never get our New Year's kiss. We always miss it."

"Well, we can do it now."

"Midnight is gone. It's too late."

"It was two minutes ago. This should still count."

"No," Adam says sternly. He is extremely drunk, and very serious. "It doesn't count. A kiss two minutes after midnight still counting would defeat the entire purpose of a New Year's kiss. We could have had a New Year's kiss, but you were crouching on the kitchen floor alone like a crazy person. We can kiss now, but it'll just be a normal, regular kiss."

"Fine, fine, fine," Alex says, and she plants a kiss on his mouth. He slides a hand under the back of her shirt as he kisses her back, and she shivers a little with delight.

"Happy New Year, Adam," she says, after they pull apart.

"Happy New Year." He lets go of her, slides his feet out from under hers, and turns to survey the bottles stacked on the kitchen island. "Wow. What happened to the Bacardi?"

Something about the way he lets her go, almost tossing her, makes Alex a little angry. "No idea," she says. "You should have some water first, though."

He groans. "Alex thinks I'm too drunk."

"No, I just don't want you to have a hangover tomorrow."

"No, you think I'm too drunk."

"No, I just—"

"Stop lying to me, Alex." He sighs dramatically. "I just wish you would stop lying to me. Can you do that, Alex?" He pours Canadian Club messily into a plastic cup. "Can you stop fucking lying to me for one minute? As your New Year's resolution, maybe?"

He is being mean on purpose. She knows he means it, too. He might not remember it in the morning, or he might say he doesn't, but right now, he is drunk, and he knows he is drunk, and he knows she is drunk, and he wants it to hurt. Like he did two weeks ago after that cursed, godawful dinner with his parents, which she knew she was invited to only as punishment for what had happened in October. He was drunk, and he mocked her for how she'd acted, the way her voice went girly when she was answering his parents' questions, the way she twisted and untwisted the napkin nervously in her hands. She did what she always did, then: shut down. Rolled over, pretended to be asleep. Said yes when he asked her to say yes and said no when he asked her to say no. Until he was tired out, and then she lay there awake, crying silently as he frowned in his dreams.

Maybe it's the fact that that was just a few weeks ago. Before, they could go a little longer than that without having these kinds of blowups; now they're happening like clockwork. Or maybe it's just that she's particularly drunk, or that it's another New Year and she's fucking miserable. But she doesn't want to lie awake crying tonight. She doesn't want Adam to go back downstairs with his Canadian Club. She wants him to stay here with her. To understand why it was that, as the clock struck midnight, she was up here alone behind the kitchen island, making a mess of the Bacardi. If he doesn't want to understand, well—

"What's your fucking problem?" she blurts out. She is shocked, and so is he. He was already shuffling back toward the stairs, plastic cup in hand, but now he has stopped. He says nothing, as if he's daring her to say more. The fact that he looks so lovable, even now, makes Alex somehow angrier.

"If you want to be fucking mean to me," she says, "you don't have to get drunk to do it. You can just go at me when you're sober. I can take it. I take it all the time. All your sober thoughts on how pathetic I am, how much I lie to you, how much you wouldn't care if I fucking got hit by a car."

He steps toward her. "You don't want to have this conversation."

"You're the one who said it. I'm just supposed to memory-hole it away because you felt bad about it?"

"I was the one," he says, getting louder, "who had to go to the hospital that night. Where you were nowhere to be fucking seen."

"Oh, yeah, Adam, that makes total sense. Evil, evil me for not coming to the hospital for the one night you were in there because I was lying in bed with my phone off, unable to sleep because the person I love more than anyone in the world just told me that he didn't give a shit about me—"

"This victim shit again. Fucking ridiculous." He turns to leave.

"You should take a look at yourself if you want to see a fucking professional victim," Alex says, now unable to stop the words from pouring out of her mouth. She follows him down the hallway. "The way you were at that dinner. Oh, oh, mommy and daddy don't love me, they only give me money and let me do whatever I want, whose life could possibly be worse than mine? You act like you're the only one who's ever been suicidal, you're the only one whose family is shit, you're the only one who's ever fucked their life up and needs comforting about it."

"Fuck off, Alex." There is a dangerous edge in his voice.

"And you know what? I wish I'd never met you," she says. "I really do. You're a nothing. You're worse than nothing. You're a void that's sucking me in. You need me. I don't need you. I had a great fucking life. In spite of everything. I had a great fucking life, and it was mine. You are fucking lucky." Saying it is more of a rush than the alcohol has ever given her. She feels like she could walk on water. "You are fucking lucky every single day that I don't bring up how you—"

He strides over to her, stopping just short of slamming up against her. Instead, he slams his hand on the wall.

"What were you about to say?" he says, very quiet.

Everything goes blank. Smooth, flat. She isn't breathing.

"I don't know," she says.

His eyes are burning. Cold and hard and sharp.

"Just kill me," she says. "Like you said you would. And hey, while you're at it, maybe you can finally kill yourself."

She wonders if he's about to do it.

Instead, he throws his cup on the floor. Before Alex can process what he's doing, he grabs his jacket from the coat rack, slides on his shoes. The door slams — he is gone.

As Alex stands in the hallway, stricken, Nathan stumbles up the stairs. "Hey Alex," he says nervously. "Is Adam still here, or—"

But Alex is already on the move, not even taking her jacket, only her shoes, half-slid on, the backs digging into her heels. "Happy New Year," she yells venomously, and then she is gone, too. Down the stairs, slick with water, down the long driveway and onto the street, where the streetlights — few and far between on these residential blocks — shine against the huge streaks of rain in their air. There is no sign of Adam, not down either block. Up in the sky, the clouds in the distance have parted, exposing a pale sliver of moon.

How lovely, she thinks, and then: something is wrong.

She looks back up at Nathan's house, its gables, the lightless upstairs windows, the brightness and noise from where the basement peeks out above the lawn. Then she looks back at the slick street, clearly in need of repaving. Then back at the moon, becoming more obvious by the second. The rain is starting to fade.

"This isn't how I remember it," she says out loud. The rain has almost stopped.

No. This wasn't how she remembered it, because she barely remembered it at all. She'd been so drunk. She remembered going upstairs to hide. She remembered Adam following her; she remembered standing on his feet, his toes pressing into her heels. She remembered screaming at him; she remembered him running away. And she remembered running through streets that were a black void, rain hitting her face, only abstract streaks of light cutting through the darkness.

Adam told her a week later, when he finally took one of her calls, that she'd said she hoped he killed himself. That she screamed it at him. And she must have, she thought. She must have. She hated herself. She believed she could be that hateful. She apologized, over and over and over. But he said he was done with her. He stopped responding. It was what she deserved: the death she'd wished on him.

The moon hangs over her now. It's as if the clouds were never there.

"Is this what actually happened?" she asks the moon.

"Yes," Adam says. He is standing awkwardly in the door of her hospital room, a stack of books under his arm and a bunch of lavender in his hand. Alex can't get up. There's an IV in one of her arms. She is in a hospital bed, covered by a blanket. She looks under the blanket, and she is wearing the same grey shirt, the same black jeans, as she had been on New Year's. Her hair is still a little wet. But it's short, a high fade getting overgrown on top.

I'm not a woman, they think, trying to make out the date written on the hospital whiteboard. I haven't thought of myself as a woman in years. Why was I doing that just now? What did I just ask Adam?

"But I'm sure she won't notice," he says, handing them the bunch of lavender. "The bush was so overgrown. Along with everything else in her garden, really."

They smell the lavender, its floral bittersweetness filling the tiny room. He's talking about his neighbour, Mrs. Barksdale. That's what they were asking about; they'd asked if he'd stolen the lavender from her. Of course he did. He's right: she'll never notice. Alex has often thought about sneaking into Mrs. Barksdale's garden, appearing as it does to be its own secret world, its hedges overgrown, the tops of willows and maples visible from the street.

"So is it true?" they ask. "Does she have a koi pond?"

Adam puts the books on the nightstand beside their bed. He sits beside them, running his hands through their hair. He looks like he's about to cry. "She does. I didn't get a great look at it because I was trying to go pretty directly to and from the lavender. But it has a little waterfall fountain built up above it, and there were little birds splashing around."

"We'll have to go together sometime. Maybe legally instead of sneaking in. Does Mrs. Barksdale need any work done around the house?"

"If I ever see her again, I'll ask. I haven't caught a glimpse of her in years."

"That's honestly kind of iconic of her."

"Has anyone else been to visit you?"

"My dad came for like five seconds. And Em came for a few hours yesterday, but they were really upset, so it was kind of stressful. I told them they didn't have to come by anymore if it hurt them that much."

"Well, I'm going to be here every day. So they're really off the hook."

"Every day?" Alex sits up carefully. "What about school?"

"Who gives a shit about school? I promised I would take care of you." A tear rolls down his face, and he rubs at it angrily with his shirtsleeve. "And I already failed enough at that."

"Adam," Alex says, and now they're about to cry, too. "This isn't your fault."

"I should have been there. I should have picked up the phone. It doesn't matter how late it was."

"This was going to happen anyway. And it has nothing to do with you. It's just my fucking brain. You didn't know me in high school — this is just the way things are sometimes."

"But it shouldn't be," he says passionately.

He lies down next to them. They turn their faces on the scratchy pillow, facing each other.

"I'm sorry," he says.

"I'm sorry, too. I'm sorry for putting you through this."

"Don't apologize. I'm not the one who's in the hospital."

"Well, I'm sorry anyway."

"Promise me," he says, "that this isn't going to happen again. To either of us. We talk to each other before it gets to this point. That's the difference between high school and now. We were alone then. Now there's two of us."

"I promise," Alex says, and looking at him, they believe it.

"I love you," he says.

"I love you, too."

And it feels, then, like they have just inhaled smoke. They break into a coughing fit.

"Are you okay?" Adam jumps out of bed. "Do you need me to get the nurse?"

"No," they try to say. "It's fine." But the coughs swallow up the words, and the taste in their mouth is bitter and burning.

"Hold on," Adam says, and he runs out the door.

The coughing, as quickly as it started, stops. Alex frowns. They get up, wheeling the IV cart alongside them as they try to peek out the door. They can see nothing through the frosted glass. They wheel over to the whiteboard. Where they thought they could see dates written, chart notes, there are only illegible squiggles of marker. The window, they see now, is partially open. They don't recall opening it. Who would open the window in someone else's hospital room?

They wheel over to the window, pulling up the blinds. It is dark outside. Below them, small waves flicker under the night sky, reddish-grey and hot. Adam is sitting down there on the cliff's edge. He looks back at them, his face worn and tired.

They look at the IV in their arm. Then they yank it out. Nothing happens: no pain, no blood spurting. They climb out the window, one tentative step after another, and find that there's a ledge right underneath, just big enough for them to balance on. The smell of rot is in the air, and a ladder leads down to where Adam is. As they descend, the hot wind picks up their long, tangled hair. When they're a few feet off the ground, they let go, landing softly on the ground, their joints receptive and painless.

They walk over to where Adam is. They sit beside him, a foot of charged space separating them. Adam has his knees hugged into his chest, his arms around his legs. He looks small. Alex spreads their legs out, letting them dangle again, propping themselves up with their hands behind them.

"They're all dead," Adam says after a while.

"Who?"

"The mussels. The starfish. It was too hot today. The sun cooked them alive."

That must be what the smell is. Alex leans out over the edge, hoping to get a look at the carnage, but the water has covered it now.

"That's what caused the storm, too. The heat. The energy coming from the ground. The lightning will start fires, and the cycle will continue. And it's only going to get hotter."

Alex can hear rumbling, somewhere off in the distance. The faint smell and taste of burning wood. A world perpetually on fire. A life spent always on the edge of the cliff.

"You tried to kill me," they say.

They are not sad, or shaking. It is simple. A cliché, a story written by a thousand other people in a thousand other books before.

"About a year in. Or maybe it was six months. I don't remember. I was with Em, at Em's house, and we were playing a board game. It took fucking forever. My phone died, and I wanted to just leave, but that would have ruined the game for everyone else.

"By the time it ended, I knew I was late. I ran to your place. That was one of the last times I ran more than a few metres, actually. I could tell as I ran that I wouldn't be able to for much longer. It felt like my bones were scraping against each other. I got inside, and you were there lying on the couch. You were looking straight up at the ceiling.

"I said hello and you didn't move. I said sorry and you didn't move. I thought, then, for a second, that you were dead. So I took a step toward you. And then—"

The lightning flashes. It is approaching again.

"And then." They take a deep breath of smoky air, then cough. "And then. You got up. And the next thing I remember was that I was on the floor, the narrow strip of linoleum between the chairs and the wall in the dining area. I couldn't feel anything. Just my heart beating, and this insane rush of adrenaline.

"You walked over and leaned over me. For me to have been where I was, you must literally have picked me up and thrown me. I must have hit the wall and the chair. I must have hit my head, too, my back, my shoulders. But I couldn't feel anything. I barely understood what was happening. You leaned over me. You were smiling. You said, 'Are you okay? I was only trying to kill you.'"

Thunder.

"And I laughed. It was a joke, obviously. And I didn't know what you did. I couldn't feel anything. There was nothing in my head except this void. I couldn't touch it. It felt dangerous. I asked you about it again, later, when we were on the couch watching TV, in a kind of 'ha ha, wasn't that crazy?' way. 'No,' you said. 'It wasn't a joke. I was trying to kill you. And if you tell anyone about this, I actually will kill you.'"

Alex laughs. "I still thought you were fucking joking. In my head, I guess. In my body, I knew you weren't. Somewhere in there, I still remembered the moment of impact, even if my brain had blocked it out somehow. And I felt the aching for the next two weeks. The bruises. The pain in my skull. But I didn't say anything. I didn't do anything. Because I knew it wasn't a joke, even though I told myself it was.

"And time passed, and you still loved me, even though sometimes you hated me. It was the same every time. Nothing ever changed. It was understandable. My dad hated me. If my mom had gotten to know me — the real me, that is — I thought she would hate me, too. I ghosted people I dated. I talked about killing myself. We had that fight, and I didn't come see you in the hospital. And there was so much darkness, so much that I just couldn't remember. So it made sense when you told me that I'd said I wished you would kill yourself. I believed it. What else could have made you not want to see me anymore? What else could make you hate me that much? It was unforgivable. I thought I killed you. That's what I thought I was afraid of. Knowing the truth about myself.

"But that wasn't really it. I never told anyone, and then, that night, something snapped, and it seemed like I might. So you disappeared, and I tried to make myself not exist anymore. And now—"

"Now here we are," he says into his knees.

They watch the storm gather, the lightning not far off now. The thunder barely registers.

"Why?" Alex asks. The word drops out of their mouth like a lead weight.

He doesn't respond.

A tree cracks somewhere in the forest. The smoke grows thicker. The horizon is barely visible, the world cast in a haze.

"Adam," Alex says, "is this real?"

"What do you mean?"

"I know you're alive. I know you're on the island. But I thought I was seeing you because you weren't. I thought you were haunting me. Am I talking to you, or am I talking to myself?"

He shrugs. "Does it matter?"

"Yes. Of course it matters."

He doesn't respond.

"I want to remember," they say. "I want to remember how it felt."

Alex stands. They stare down at him, the small, vulnerable shape in this angry, massive world. They have an urge to pick him up and carry him with them, but they can't. They can't. And the longer they look at him, the more they don't want to.

They turn around, the waves of rot at their back. They fix their eyes on the trees, the cool spaces in between the tall trunks where the smoke is now curling. They don't look back.

———

Alex is on their knees, on the ground, the knives in their hands again. The rot is embedded in their lungs, the smoke in their eyes and ears and nose, and they vomit, retching over and over on the ground, the taste of the sleeping pills filling their mouth and the back of their throat. When they look up, the world is swimming in smoke around them. Adam is gone.

They pick up their bag, stumbling toward the bushes. When the thunder hits this time, they fall to the ground. The cliff is wobbling, seems about to crumble under their feet. Jutting out above the smoke, the silver fin looks like the peak of a mountain in hell.

I have to get into the trees, they think. They vomit again.

My mind. My mind is weaker than my body. My mind will tire before my body does. They crawl, dragging their bag on their ankle at first, then kicking it aside. Ahead of them, when they look up — where are their glasses? The world looks like nothing, they can barely see their own hands — and then a pair of eyes twinkles above a doggy snout, right above their face.

"Ella!" They cough. "Ella. We have to get the fuck out of here." The lightning and thunder are so close that they nearly overlap. The bushes are only a few metres away. The distance seems insurmountable.

Ella barks, then runs a few feet ahead to the bushes, then runs back.

"Just run, Ella!"

But she doesn't. She keeps going back and forth, back and forth.

"Ella—" Alex says, then they can't speak anymore. Ella won't leave. They have no choice. No, they do have a choice: they could lie here and let the smoke overtake them. They could finally become absorbed into nothing. This is their chance. Isn't this what they wanted, taking all those pills? To atone?

Smooth, they think. I am not my body. I am smooth and solid and small like a pebble. I am suspended in nothing. I am nothing. I am not my body.

They stagger to their feet.

There is nothing to do except run.

———

The pain flashes with the lightning. Alex will be nowhere, somewhere distant, and then it will double them over. Ella barks and barks and barks. *I am not my body.* Then they pick up the pace again.

They don't know where they're going. All the trees look the same in the near-darkness. They all light up, and then everything goes dark again.

I am not my body.

I want to be alive.

Ella barks, and Alex's foot catches on a tree root, and they slam, chin-first, into the hard ground.

They cry out. When they try to get up again, they can't. Their wrist is bent. They can't feel their ankle.

Someone is calling their name.

They scream. Ella barks. They scream again.

"ALEX!"

The light pours in through the cathedral windows. Like the holy spirit. Like a miracle. And then it is dark, because Amara, heaving, a kerchief over his mouth, is blocking out the light, and

Alex is coughing, or laughing, or crying, and when he grabs them by the wrist to pull them up, they scream.

"I'm sorry," he says. "I'm so sorry. I'm so sorry. We have to get out of here."

The light pours in through the cathedral windows.

Ella barks from somewhere up ahead.

Thunder. Branches breaking and trees cracking.

"I'm sorry."

"I'm sorry," they say. "I'm sorry."

On one leg they hop with Amara supporting their weight and they see Ella up ahead, the blue, lively eyes, and there, somehow, is the car, Amara's little silver Toyota. They look back and the fin is not there anymore. There is no mountain. There is no 709. Just flames above the trees. Flames and the world exploding.

*It's over.*

But now Amara has put them in the passenger seat, now Ella has jumped in the back of the car, and the windows are up, and the ground is crunching under the wheels and the air is not full of smoke anymore. They vomit at their feet, coughing and vomiting and coughing.

"Sorry."

"It's okay."

They are on the road. Ella is silent. Thunder. Out over the ocean, a thousand bolts of lightning, all hitting at the same time as they crest the hill.

"How did you—" They cough and cough.

"I heard you screaming."

"You don't know the path. Stupid city kid." Coughing, coughing, tears streaming down their face.

"I fucking dropped clothes on the ground behind me like Hansel and Gretel. So I could retrace my steps."

They laugh, even though it hurts.

He laughs too. The light from the fires illuminating his face.

"The house."

"Who gives a shit," he says. "It's not mine anyway. And I have renter's insurance."

"Where are we going?"

"Anywhere else. The other side of the island. The village. The ferry dock."

In the rearview mirror, Ella's eyes shine. Alex reaches back with their less-injured hand. They give her a scratch on the ear.

"I'm sorry," they say again.

"I'm sorry for calling you crazy. So we're even. It's all good." He looks at them, and they see that he's been crying.

"We're alive," they say.

"We're alive," he agrees. Behind them, the burning forest roars and hisses. Sirens wailing.

Quiet — so quiet at first that they don't notice, and then growing to a roar, hissing and pounding like the thunder — the rain begins to fall.

—

The car is stopping, and their seatbelt has been unclipped. Their eyelids are so heavy, their body so immobile. They put a hand to their face, finding nothing. Their glasses are gone, and everything is so blurry, a wash of hazy colour and motion. The motion is inside them, too, the nausea and consciousness coming in waves. There is someone under one of their arms and someone under another, big red shapes ahead — trucks? — and they are walking into a building, and a wall of light and noise surrounds them. People everywhere, the shapes of people, all around, all moving. Not horrible like it so often is, not a mass working to push Alex out, but a cocoon around them.

—

Alex is in a chair, wrapped in a blanket, and someone has put a plastic bottle of water in their hand. They squeeze it over and over, the heavy crinkling comforting.

"You should have a sip of water," Amara says: the biggest shape, the closest. "Do you want to find the bathroom?"

Alex nods. They stand, with help, but shake off the arm that comes around to support them. "No, no, no," they say. "Just show me."

They follow the shape of Amara through the small crowds of people. He holds the bathroom door open for them. It is so cold in here, all cold and smooth and white, and they can't resist pressing their cheek against the tile of the floor as they sit by the toilet.

They chug the water and vomit immediately, and almost as quickly they are a little clearer, a little more real. The shapes of their environment begin to resemble recognizable objects: mirror, toilet paper holder, trash can, sink. They wonder where they are.

They brace themselves against the toilet and stand. The water bottle is empty, and they fill it up from the tap. The chemical bitterness rising from the back of their throat burns, and they need to wash it away — and it feels like there's smoke in their lungs, smoke in their nose and their stomach and their brain. As they gulp the water, refill, then gulp the water again, they catch a glimpse of themself in the mirror. Even with the blurriness, they are a sight out of a horror movie: all cut up and dirty and bruised and bleeding, their hair snarled and tangled. But they're alive. They pull their face into a smile, and it's not a hard, fake smile, but a real one, one that echoes through their entire body.

———

"Are you feeling okay?" Amara asks worriedly as they emerge. He extends his arm again as they wobble out, and this time they take it. "You should see the emergency paramedic people they have here."

"Where are we?" Alex rasps.

"Fire station. Everyone in the area got emergency alert texts to meet here after the storm passed. There's some teen around who saw you and is really worried about you."

Alex hopes Leo and Anna's house hasn't burnt down. "What about Ella?" they remember. "Ella the dog."

"Oh, you won't believe it. I mean," Amara corrects himself, "I guess it's not any more unbelievable than you pulling a missing dog out of a burning forest. But it turns out the people that the dog belongs to live nearby. They're here now."

Alex sits down in the chair again, Amara crouching beside them. "See," he says, pointing over in a corner of the large room, "there's your teen friend. Should I wave them over?"

Alex nods, and Amara waves a couple of times, and out of the chatter appear Leo and Anna. Anna's arms are crossed over her chest. She is shivering, while Leo shifts anxiously from foot to foot.

"Are they okay?" he half-whispers to Amara.

"I can hear you," Alex says.

"Oh! Sorry! Are you okay?" Leo asks. "If there's anything you need, like, there's a tray of energy bars over there—"

"I'm fine." They cough again. "Did you see Ella?"

"I did. You'll have to say hi to Sarah at some point, when you feel better. We all can't believe you managed to save Ella from the killer."

"Hold up," Amara says, "the killer?"

"Sorry! Sorry!" Leo says again, frantically.

"Don't worry about it," Alex wants to say, but their words are muffled by a massive yawn.

"We're glad you're okay, Alex," Anna says shakily. "We'll leave you to rest now."

Alex begins to think about replying, but they are already nodding off.

—

Amara shakes them awake. "Hey," he says. "They're saying it's safe for us to leave now. It's over."

Alex yawns again, stretching their arms upward involuntarily. True enough, the noise in the big warm room has dimmed, and people are moving outward. "Great," they say. "Let's go."

"Are you sure you don't want to see the paramedic people?" Amara asks. "I got some bandages and stuff from them, but, you know. I don't know what happened to you. Do you remember?"

They do remember, even though the memory is in pieces, a pile of fragments that they can only touch delicately. Not so much what happened in the forest, not so much how they got here. But the crashing in the house, the darkness. The emptiness and the pills. The shape of Adam standing over them two years ago. The shape of him, small, on the edge of the burning cliff.

"Not really," they say. "It's all kind of blurry."

"We definitely need to check you for a head injury."

"I really just want to lie down."

But Amara is already hurrying them toward the paramedics, who give them a once-over so quickly and efficiently that they barely seem to have begun before they've finished: a splint for Alex's grotesquely swollen ankle, a folding wheelchair, alcohol rubbed on and wounds bandaged, their lungs listened to, a finger held up and moved in front of their eyes. Alex's eyes follow the finger as it moves back and forth, back and forth, like a strange metronome. "It doesn't seem like you're concussed," the paramedic says, putting down their finger. "But keep an eye out for any head pain, memory issues, anything like that. Or any persistent issues from the smoke inhalation. You might want to go back to the city and check in with your own doctor."

Alex nods, as if they have a doctor. Amara thanks them. Most of the people are gone, and as Amara rolls Alex out into the night, there is only one group left, standing outside near the fire trucks, trickling slowly onto a minibus. One of them is lurking near the back of the line. Alex and Amara roll closer, and even without glasses, Alex knows that it is Adam. Not a half-shadow, a figure in the corner of their eye or shadowed in a window, not a handprint left behind on a door handle. It is actually him, slouched, his hair messy. A person, a flesh-and-blood person, standing there right in front of them.

As he raises his gaze, they stare. He looks down again, straight into the ground. But Alex doesn't break until they reach Amara's car.

Look at me, they think, hoping he can somehow hear. There is no wavering anymore. It is not a rage made heavy with shame, not the way it was before, but a clear rage, clear and powerful. After all the time they spent doubting everything they saw, everything they felt, repeating over and over that they weren't in danger, they were never in danger, there was no one watching, nothing bad had happened — after all that time feeling the truth, knowing the truth, and trying to make themself forget. No wonder that they never seem to be standing on solid ground, that their perceptions distort and fade like shadows: how long had they been denied their own narrative? Not just with Adam, but their whole life. They weren't right about everything, but they were right about this. He had been here all along. And before that, almost the whole time they'd been together, everything they did was done with the knowledge that he could kill them: not because they were crazy and hateful and sick, but because he said so. Because he made sure they knew he would.

Well, look at me. Just try it. Try it and see what fucking happens. *I know who you are.*

Amara notices them staring. "Who's that?" he asks as they get into the passenger seat. Adam never looks back. He disappears into the minibus; the folding door closes. The bus, its tinted windows black and opaque, drives away.

Alex shrugs. "No idea. Let's go home."

# 6.

Alex is ready for it this time. They cover their ears just before the horn blasts, rocking the deck, and the ferry begins to move slowly out of the cove. They are leaning out over the chilled metal of the railing, the wind whipping their face with the contradictory dual sting of hot sun and cold ocean air. Their huge new prescription sunglasses at least provide some sort of buffer.

It is a blazingly bright day: bright blue sky, bright blue water, bright green trees on the fast-receding shore. When Alex takes their hands off their ears, they can hear the shrieking of seagulls as they circle around the cove. The tide is low, and they are feasting. Other than that, the shore is empty. No people clambering, no deer on the rocks, no matter how hard Alex squints. They had hoped a little bit that they would see that deer again. It would have been nice to know that they were okay.

The sun deck door slams closed behind them, and the slapping of sandals approaches. Amara appears beside them, and he leans out over the railing contemplatively before the wind nearly blows his hat off. He shrieks. Alex snatches it by the brim, catching the hat just in time.

"You really thought you could wear this hat up here and not have it blow into the ocean?" They hand it back to him.

"Well, what am I going to do, not wear a hat?" He places both hands on the top of his head, clamping the hat down. "In this hot sun?"

Alex kind of wishes they were wearing a hat. They had forgotten after all these years how vulnerable having short hair leaves you to the elements. Even though it's only chopped, not buzzed, their scalp still feels exposed. But they aren't going to tell Amara that. They just look at him, the brim of his hat blowing back up, his hands grasping to keep it in place, and they laugh.

"Oh, yeah, laugh it up," he says. "We'll see who's laughing in thirty years and who looks like they've lived a hard life on the salty seas."

It was only two weeks ago, but the storm seems so distant, like it happened to a different person. Alex's memories of it, already blurred from the drugs, grow ever hazier. Their days since then have been so full.

They went to the village and bought matching turkey vulture shirts with Amara. They returned to the galleries. They visited Leo at the café, sitting outside screaming and laughing and annoying his boss. Amara wheeled them around until they could start walking again; now they have a shiny black metal cane, purchased from the village pharmacy while they were waiting for their new glasses to get made. Mel and Tristan visited, and even though Alex disappointed their wishes for a rip-roaring tale of forest fire survival, they managed not to run away. They sat in their chair as everyone laughed, a cacophony of voices echoing through the forest, and they laughed, too.

The cottage, it turned out, was okay. But their plan to check on 709 never materialized. When they tried to venture down the path from the abandoned parking lot, they found a wall of barbed-wire fencing where the trailhead once was, the fading NO TRESPASSING sign replaced by new ones, their text bolder and more threatening. Nor could they take the pink-flagged route from Amara's cottage anymore; that, too, led only to a perimeter of wire and hostility. Leo's island gossip claimed that there was an armed security team there now, living in a trailer on the property, lying in wait for any would-be trespassers, setting up more and more fencing. Alex has made no attempt to get in; they assume the stuff that they didn't manage to take with them in their bag is lost forever. They do wonder, though, what became of 709 after the storm, what state it's in now, and whether they will, someday, have to account for their presence as the only witness of its demise. It was, as far as they know, one of only a few structures damaged in the storm: 709, a couple of houses on the east side of the island, and the Cathedral, whose residents were dispatched off-island weeks ago.

But they have heard nothing from Ella's parents, no inquiries after their safety, no reproaches, no threats. The only communication has been the silent disappearance of the deposits, and, from Amara's corporate landlord, a notice to vacate the cottage by the end of the month.

They are in the middle of the ocean, the island far receded into the distance, and what they do remember — what they remember more clearly than anything — is the rage. They remember Adam's stricken face, his downcast gaze. The surge of clear energy, the wave they couldn't hold back. They have held onto that, poured it into the deep pool in their mind, and whenever they are pulled away again, back into the old ways of knowing, the need to be alone, the belief in an evil that lies within them, they reach back into that pool, letting the wave wash over them: the anger at what had been done, what they had been made to believe, what they had lost in the process. It overwhelms them, sometimes, to let the pain in, and sometimes it feels like it would be easier to go back to the way things were before: not trusting anything they remembered, anything they saw, replacing the voice in their head with Adam's, with their dad's, with the version of themself who was poisoned to the point of immobility.

But they can't forget, now, that they were right to be angry. They were right to be frightened. The fear wasn't innate, a fundamental flaw in their being; it had been taught to them, warped into something all-consuming, big enough to conceal the truth that lay behind it, the instincts that screamed at them through every nerve in their body to run, hide, disappear. And when they remember, when they let themself feel the weight of the years spent under the threat of death, they return to this place they've found, the forest and the ocean, the little cottage and the large man beside them, all the plans they've made for tomorrow, and the wave recedes; they won't get washed away along with it.

They still see it sometimes, the darkness watching them, creeping in at the corners. It has different faces: a person looking at them strangely (had they met Adam? What had he told them?); a shadow in the forest; the sound of footsteps walking up behind them, or the revving of a car engine. But they recognize it now. They know its source, what it contains, why it wants what it wants. As blurry as it seems sometimes, they remember, as surely as they remember the feeling of smoke in their lungs when they cough, that they had known all along the reason they were really afraid.

Amara has taken off his hat, letting his arms dangle over the railing.

"You seem very contemplative," Alex says.

"I'm *feeling* very contemplative. I know this is the right time to go back to the city. I'm sure it is. I miss my friends, I miss seeing people, I miss going places. But at the same time . . . I don't know." He waves his hands around. "This sounds so stupid. I feel like I unlocked some kind of secret knowledge being on this island. As much as it was difficult being away from everyone, difficult in all kinds of different ways. We almost got fucking lightninged to death. But it was . . ." He is looking for a word, but he doesn't come up with it. He puts his hat back on his head. "I don't know."

"No," Alex says, "I get it."

"Right? Of course you do."

The shore is drawing closer. Alex starts to see the shapes of buildings, docks, cars, the rapid movement of real life.

"You know," Amara says, "once I get set up in the new place, you can absolutely stay with me. Like, I know I've said it before, but—"

"I know," Alex says. "Thank you. Seriously."

"Okay, good. As long as you know."

"But I think this will work. For now, anyway."

The old blue house is gone, just like Fen had always thought it would be: razed to the ground for luxury condos. But there is a new house, older and shittier but even bigger, with bizarrely shaped rooms of various sizes. Em sent them pictures of the tiny room that will be theirs for as long as they want it, so tiny that the bed barely fits in it, with a weird little window that faces an oak tree. Under the oak tree are the big wooden boxes where Em has planted their garden, herbs and edible flowers and tall stalks of kale and bitter greens. Fen, they said, has been making the best salads in the universe.

"I think so, too," Amara says. "As long as we're still going to hang out."

"Obviously we're still going to hang out."

"Good." He laughs. "Good, glad we have that settled."

They can hear the intercom turn on, the muffled voice speaking. The ferry is approaching the dock.

Amara sighs, picking himself off the railing. "Time to go back to the car, I guess."

"Can I actually meet you in the parking lot? I'm just going to stay up here for two more minutes. I'll get off on the foot passenger walkway."

"Alright. Don't get lost," Amara says, and disappears through the heavy door.

There is so much to worry about. They have no job. They have some money, but not that much. They don't know how they'd get back to school, or even if they want to get back to school. They are in pain that has no explanation. They are, really, in much the same position they were when they boarded the ferry going the opposite direction. No one saw the pickup truck guys again after the storm. Leo said their house might have been one of the damaged ones, that they might have moved back to the city.

Alex has avoided thinking about any of this. They have tried their best to exist only in the present. But it is hard to ignore with the shore in sight, knowing that as soon as they step off the boat, they will be back on the land mass where everything happened. Back in the city, where the past and its inhabitants can find them, where every corner holds the threat of memory returning embodied. Every hopeful point in their life has been followed by a steep decline, worse with every descent, and to feel hopeful now — why would it be any different than before? Knowing why they are afraid can't prevent all of it from happening again. It can't happen again. If it happens again. There is no time to linger, though. The boat is almost docked, and they can't keep Amara waiting.

Alex grabs the rubbery handle of their cane, leaning against the railing. The ferry creaks and groans as it starts to make contact with the dock, and behind them, Alex can hear other passengers beginning to congregate on the deck, ready to exit through the walkway.

In the glittering water beside the boat, an odd little shape bobs. It is shiny and grey, with soft, round contours: a whiskered face, eyes closed, mouth in the shape of a smile.

"Seal!" Alex calls. They wave, not caring what the other passengers might think. "Seal!"

The seal's gleaming eyes open. It looks at Alex for a long moment. Then, slowly, it fades into the water and disappears.

# ACKNOWLEDGEMENTS

Thanks to the entire team at ECW Press for their support and incredible work on this book, particularly Jen Sookfong Lee, Jen Albert, and Pia Singhal, whose edits and care made this story what it is.

There is no baseball in this particular story, but it wouldn't exist without everyone who read, published, and edited my baseball writing. Special thanks to Joshua Howsam, my first-ever editor at BP Toronto; Meg Rowley, for not being too mad when I abruptly disappeared to write this book; and Patrick Dubuque, without whom I might never have written any fiction or believed in any of my weird ideas. Short Relief forever.

Thanks to all the brilliant faculty and students I've worked with at the UBC School of Creative Writing — there is some part of me that will always haunt Buchanan E.

Thanks to Kirby and Rita for welcoming me into your home, where I finally figured out how to write, and into your family, too. Mom, Anthony, and Joe: I love you, and thanks for putting up with me. Eric, Naomi, Dante, EJ, Sofia, and everyone who's been part of my life from near or far: you're everything. And, most of all, Taja and the creatures: I love you forever!

RJ McDaniel is a writer, at least for now. Their essays on baseball and other topics have been featured in *Catapult*, *PRISM*, and VICE Sports, among others. They live in Vancouver. This is their debut novel.